CLUB 42

CLUB 42

A CHOOSE-YOUR-OWN EROTIC FANTASY

JOANNA ANGEL

CLEiS
PRESS

Published in the United States by Cleis Press, an imprint of Start Midnight, LLC, 221 River Street, 9th Floor, Hoboken, New Jersey 07030.

Printed in the United States.
Cover design: Jennifer Do
 Cover photograph: Shutterstock
Text design: Frank Wiedemann
First Edition.
10 9 8 7 6 5 4 3 2 1

Trade paper ISBN: 978-1-62778-306-4
E-book ISBN: 978-1-62778-519-8

Library of Congress Cataloging-in-Publication Data is available on file.

Dedicated to my sister, Sarah.
You fucking hipster.
I love you.

"Get on stage and show me what you can do. I have to put another girl up in two songs," said . . . a guy whose name I didn't know yet. I wasn't sure if he just didn't introduce himself to me, or if he did introduce himself and I didn't hear him over the blaring collection of Top 40 hits from three summers ago. It was 11:30 a.m. on a Tuesday in Midtown Manhattan, and I was surrounded by carrot juice and naked women.

Let me explain how I got here.

Approximately three hours ago, I was two hours deep into my shift at Fix, an incredibly average coffee shop in Hell's Kitchen, NYC. Despite the oddly adventurous name that sounds like a Halloween theme park, Hell's Kitchen is an incredibly unexciting neighborhood, which explains why I was able to easily find a job opening for a barista. I lived in Brooklyn—where the coffee is always amazing, the tip jars are always empty, and all the barista jobs are taken.

One year ago, I was living in Singapore, eating some of the world's freshest dumplings, and working on a documentary film about a film. I wasn't a Singapore local—I'd learned about three sentences of the language and thought I had respect from the locals, but everyone knew I was just one of the college kids on the NYU campus, very much part of the U without the NY. My graduation thesis was a documentary film about a lost film in Singapore. After researching all year . . . I never found that film. It was definitely fucking lost.

The result of my research led to an underwhelming C+ grade. At least if I had failed out of film school, I could have made up some anti-establishment reason, like I was just too avant-garde for even an avant-garde film school. But that wasn't the case. I was declared incredibly average by the world of academia, and that's not exactly something you can put on a resume.

While I never mastered the art of finding, or documenting, a lost film, I did learn that I had a strong passion for drinking coffee. Unfortunately, after a few weeks at Fix, I'd learned that I had very little passion for *making* coffee for other people, particularly people who insisted on ruining a perfectly fresh Ethiopian bean pour over with an entire cup of full fat milk. That was the order I accidentally spilled all over a woman in a crisp, white pantsuit. Fortunately for her (or me?), the cold cup of lactose swimming inside my cup of perfection stopped the coffee from third-degree burning her, but it certainly didn't stop the beverage from staining the suit. I didn't like this woman's taste in clothes, or her taste in coffee, but alas. I was fired . . . from a job I never really wanted, but needed . . . and rent was due in a few days.

I left the coffee shop and walked right past the train that would take me to another train that took me home. I was in no rush to go home, or anywhere for that matter. Walking through Manhattan with a determined expression on my face always felt productive. Everyone always looks like they have such a clear purpose in New York. I strutted the streets, not showing any of the guilt of someone who'd just spilled a cup of coffee on a customer and gotten fired from a minimum wage, under-the-table job. It felt like I'd just committed a murder and was comfortably walking the streets with blood on my hands.

Oh yeah. Let's get back to what got you excited in the first place—the naked women. See, I cleverly put that in the first paragraph to rope you in. I probably lost you somewhere along the way with the pantsuit and Singapore and whatnot, but don't worry. I'm getting closer to the part about the naked women, and I promise you that the rest of this book will have lots and lots of naked people in it.

My aimless walk led me out of Hell's Kitchen and into Times Square. It's very un-cool for a Brooklyn hipster to be in Times Square, passing things like Guy Fieri's restaurant and shops that sell very illegal not-endorsed-by-the-team-whatsoever Yankees hats. At least Times Square embraces the fact that it's completely douchey, and doesn't attempt to be a "neighborhood" like Hell's Kitchen. You have to respect that. Times Square never even tried to be hip. It doesn't care. It laughs at hipsters all the way to the bank.

Hopped up on caffeine and hypnotized by the oddly striking, bright blue Chase Bank advertisement above me, I tripped and fell on my own vintage kitten heels, and was helped up by the hand of a heavy-set guy with olive skin and a thick mustache who had been handing out flyers outside of a door that said "Club 42."

"Are you okay?" he asked.

"Yeah! I'm fine!" I answered. "Thanks, I'm sorry."

"All good!" He smiled. "Be careful out there." He handed me a Club 42 flyer, which seemed rather pointless considering I was standing in front of the club already. Wouldn't it have made more sense to go to a different part of town? Or literally stand anywhere except right here?

Oh. The flyer said "free admission" on it. That was the point of this flyer—to make sure the people passing by wouldn't just pass by. This trick worked, on me at least.

Club 42 was an unoriginal name, to say the least. This was literally a club, on 42nd Street. Well, a *strip* club, that is. I wondered if this was the place where Cardi B used to work? I knew she used to work at a strip club in Manhattan, and since this was the only strip club I had ever been to in Manhattan, there was a very good chance this was the same one. I walked in, without any entrance fee, and no one asked to see my flyer.

A girl with a greased-up high ponytail sat in the entrance of the club, furiously tapping away on her phone with long acrylic nails that sounded like raindrops on a rooftop. She was sitting in front of an empty coat room, which was lined with lonely wire hangers swinging back and forth in the short gust of wind that resulted from my swift opening of the door. It was eighty-five degrees with about 400 percent humidity. No one this time of year had a coat.

"Auditions are in the back," she said, barely looking at me. I tried to hand her my flyer, and she didn't care even in the slightest. I walked toward the back, because this ponytail lady had directed me to the back, and it felt like the right thing to do.

A tall, stocky man in a suit opened a heavy door for me and motioned me to come inside. I felt like I was being led to some kind of high-end drug deal. As he opened the door, the muffled sounds of outdated pop music became loud and clear. I tried to hand that same man my now crumpled flyer. He didn't want it either.

The room was filled with neon. Neon signs, neon

LEDs that lined the stage, neon lights around the bar, neon light-up floors, but different colors of neon that flashed intermittently between blue, pink, green, and yellow. Apart from that, it felt like an intimate dining room with lots of little tables and seats—and a stage with a pole in the center. A handful of women walked around in lingerie, drinking coffee, and shoving their breasts into men's faces.

I gravitated to the bar. The "bartender" took a freeze-dried egg sandwich and put it in a convection toaster oven. I was familiar with this device because they had the very same one at Fix.

"Are you new here?" the girl behind the bar asked. She was short and skinny with long, straight brown hair and short bangs, and she was wearing a blue corset (holding tiny, perky breasts that didn't quite seem like corset material), little black shorts, fishnets, and sparkly Ugg boots. It was one of the strangest outfits I'd ever seen.

"Yes," I said. I reached in my pocket to hand her my free admission flyer—perhaps she could redeem it for a free toaster sandwich? I was determined to use this for something.

"Auditions start in a few minutes—should be easy. I think you're the only one." She smiled.

Well that was very sweet. Now I felt bad that I'd internally made fun of her outfit.

But what audition was everyone talking about? I kept thinking it was a code word for something that happens in the afternoon at strip clubs, or perhaps it had something to do with the "free admission" flyer. Admission sounds a lot like audition.

"Can I get you a drink?" the bartender asked. It wasn't

like me to drink before 5:00 p.m., but since I was recently unemployed, I figured what the hell, why not?

"A um, a PBR?" I shrugged. I had no idea what they served here. I couldn't see any alcohol at all by the bar, but I assumed it was hidden somewhere. She laughed. Was she making fun of me for drinking PBR? I really needed to get back to Brooklyn. What the fuck did they drink in this part of town?

"It's full nude here—no liquor," she replied, and she pointed at the stage. A blonde, buxom woman crawled around the stage on all fours, and yes, her vagina was just inches away from a man in a suit, who I'd *thought* was drinking a beer, but looking more closely, I realized it was actually just a bottle of root beer.

"Have you worked full nude before?" the bartender asked me.

"No," I replied. I mean, I wasn't lying. I'd certainly never worked at anything in the nude.

"The girls all say it's easier—the guys got only one thing to spend their money on!"

Just then, a man in blue jeans and a blue button-down shirt came up to the bar and asked for a carrot juice. The bartender opened a minifridge and handed him a Naked brand carrot juice, which I found . . . fitting. In this establishment, "Naked" applied to juice without preservatives and to exposed vaginas.

A tall, fit, dark-haired man wearing a black suit, with a coiled earpiece behind his ear, came rushing over. He exchanged a few words with the bartender, and they both pointed at me. I couldn't hear what they were saying—the music had just been turned up several decibels. But I smiled and waved. Should I attempt to hand this guy the flyer?

"Get on stage and show me what you can do. I have to put another girl up in two songs."

"Huh?" I replied. *Wait. What? Get on . . . what? Me? Excuse me!*

In retrospect, maybe this should have been obvious: they thought I was here to audition to become a stripper. This was why I was granted free admission sans flyer. I was about to open my mouth and explain that this was a giant misunderstanding, and like, order a round of carrot juice for everyone and laugh or something.

But I held my breath. In this moment I thought to myself, well . . . maybe I should audition to become a stripper? I had nothing to lose. There were about twelve guys in here, and I didn't know any of them. There was something very comforting about that "bartender," and I felt like she wouldn't steer me wrong. She told me industry trade secrets like "girls say it's easier." Just the other day Cardi B came up on my Pandora playlist, and no other music I listen to sounds anything like Cardi B—that had to have been a sign.

I'd spent a year looking for a lost film that I never found—and I'd been unemployed for the past eighty plus minutes. Life had felt very much without a purpose lately. Maybe this was a purpose.

I took a big swig of root beer (in retrospect that was actually a bad idea) and looked at the man in the suit with determination on my face. "I'm ready."

"Okay. Go get changed, quickly." He pointed to the general back of the club and said, "Dressing room is back there."

But the truth was, I didn't need to use this dressing room, because I had nothing to change into. I mean, it was a strip club, did I really need clothes? I thankfully *did* have a matching bra and panties set on because I'd planned on getting laid later. That's a whole other story.

"No thanks," I replied. Maybe he'd appreciate how resourceful I was?

"What?" he said. He just looked confused.

"I don't need the dressing room!" I replied.

"You can't get changed on the floor," he said.

"That's fine! I'm fine," I yelled over the music.

"You're going on stage like THAT?" he said.

No one else here was in a polka dot summer dress and kitten heels. This could be part of my . . . brand. I'm sure Cardi B had her own signature thing—this could be mine! There was no law anywhere that strippers had to wear neon and sparkles and shiny stiletto heels, right? My dress was from Marc Jacobs (well I didn't buy it there, I found it at a thrift shop and I was rather proud of the find), and I was happy to flaunt it on stage.

"Where did you work before?" he asked.

"Fix!" I proudly answered.

"Never heard of it," he said. I mean, I wasn't going to lie about my previous employment, but I hoped they wouldn't call and ask for a reference.

The man in the suit shrugged and rushed me toward the stage—like, the same stage the other dancers were on. I'd imagined I'd be taken to some back room and a couple people would judge me, à la *American Idol*, but that was not at all what happened. This was technically not even an "audition"—I was just . . . working?

A slender girl walked off the stage, fully nude except for gold stiletto heels, holding a gold bikini in her hands. I looked at the way her calves tightened up when walking in the heels, and how that tightness continued up her body to her perky ass. Her heels magically made her long legs look longer, and they arched her feet in such an elegant way I instantly developed a foot fetish. I could now see how these stilettos made more sense than my one-and-a-half-inch heels from a thrift store, made of worn leather that I'd attempted to fill in with a black Sharpie. I pranced toward the stage and smiled at the girl walking off, and in exchange, she gave me a mean look and didn't smile back at all.

There was no turning back now. "Work It" by Missy Elliott came on. Apparently, it was time for me to work it!

The businessmen by the stage seemed intrigued. One of them put down his root beer. I could see them all looking at me—I mean, they were in chairs surrounding the stage, and I was on the stage, so they had to look at me. First and foremost, I swiftly unclasped my fanny pack, which was cinched onto my waist, and let it drop to the ground. It made a loud thump on the stage because of all the loose change in there. Oh well—I'd made my presence known. I lifted my dress up, and two guys walked away. At the start of the song there had been six guys watching. The chorus hadn't even kicked in yet, and now there were four. Ouch. I'd dealt with rejection before, but usually I was just ghosted in text messages—I'd never seen it happen so blatantly and so quickly.

The song kept going and the lights beamed. I put my hands against the pole and did whatever form of twerking I could do. It had always felt ridiculous when I'd attempted to do that at random bars (only when enough alcohol was in me and the right hip hop song came on), but something about holding onto a pole made my ass gyrate in just the right way. My dress only had a handful of small buttons in the back, and it was totally impractical for this situation. I was beginning to understand why bikinis were the preferred wardrobe, but I had to just keep shaking my ass. Hopefully no one would notice me painfully trying to wrap my elbow around my head to unbutton the dress that was stuck around my torso.

One of the guys near the stage laughed and motioned for me to come over. I got down on my hands and knees and crawled over, attempting to do so to the beat of the music. He smiled, motioned for me to turn around, and unbuttoned my dress as the other guys hooted and clapped. I pulled the dress over my head, so excited for it to be off that it took away any anxiety I had about undressing in front of strangers. Everyone seemed so happy for me— and by everyone, I mean the four people.

"Is it your first day?" one of the guys asked.

"Yes it is!" I replied. He slipped a twenty-dollar bill in the center of my bra. Holy shit! It took me several grueling hours to make that at Fix. I felt a rush. A guy in a paisley tie pointed at my bra with a circular motion. I held onto my tits, and he threw some dollar bills on the stage. Soon, all four of the men were showering me with money! If I had to estimate, there was a good thirty-four dollars surrounding me (with big help from that original twenty-dollar bill that had started everything off).

I'd heard this song many times before, but I was hearing it differently now. I got on all fours and arched my ass. I peeked my head over to the side of the stage and saw the boss man over there with his arms folded. I cracked a smile at him. I could grin and shake my ass and win anyone over right now—I just knew it. He glanced at his watch and yelled, "I need to see you naked before you get off the damn stage."

"What!" I yelled, still gyrating. I didn't want my precious new fans to know what was going on.

He came closer to the stage, and I stood up. If I'd been in a movie, there would have been a record scratch, and silence. I was upset because we were at the breakdown part of the song, and I had big plans for that part.

"I need to see you naked—take that off!" He pointed at my bra. My twenty-dollar bill guy clapped his hands, shouting, "Yeah take it off!" Like my bartender friend had told me—this was a full nude club, and there was only ONE thing to spend your money on. So I walked back to center stage, stripped out of my matching Amazon Prime lingerie, and . . . shook my money maker. I bounced my *B* cup breasts as best I could. I got back down on my hands and knees, but this time my pussy was completely exposed to the men nearby. It was inches away from them, and I felt . . . free.

They threw more money. I rejoiced. I was actually having fun. I wouldn't necessarily say that I was shy, but I'd never thought of myself as the type to throw their pussy centimeters in front of someone's nose with confidence. Right now, I felt confident enough to try just about anything.

The song ended. The crowd cheered—or, four people cheered. My twenty-dollar fan shouted, "You're gonna do great! Congrats!" I picked up my clothing and the money on stage, and I felt like Miss America, waving and smiling and blowing kisses, picking up crumpled dollar bills instead of bouquets of roses. I walked off the stage and back to the bar with my tits and ass and not very groomed pussy exposed. The bartender chuckled.

"Tony will kill you! You can't be on the floor naked— put something on!" Of course his name was Tony.

"What?" I replied, which seemed to be a recurring response of mine here. "So, I *have* to be naked on stage, but I *can't* be naked here?"

In the past five minutes, I had definitely become an exhibitionist, and I truly enjoyed being naked at a bar. One of the men who had watched me on stage now walked toward me. I smiled and waved at him, feeling like a celebrity kindly acknowledging one of my adoring fans. Tony intercepted him, his expression not nearly as excited as mine. I was fumbling to throw my dress back on, which, I realized, was just as inconvenient to put on as it was to take off. Marc Jacobs could have thought more of strippers when he created this dress.

"Well that was . . . something," said Tony. "I'm guessing you haven't done this before."

"Well, technically no," I said.

"Well, I'm short on girls . . . so I guess I can put you on the day shift. Any day Monday through Thursday. Shift starts at 10:00 a.m. and ends at four. Definitely can't use you on weekends. You can start—"

To see what happens if Naomi starts her shift today, turn to page 13.

To see what happens if Naomi starts her shift tomorrow, turn to page 119.

"Follow me downstairs and get me your ID, and I'll go through the rules," said Tony. Everything was happening so fast. I'd never known strip clubs even had day shifts. Perhaps this was when the more dignified customers came in, and Tony totally sensed how smart and sophisticated I was, and therefore wanted me to be with other people like myself.

I'll just keep telling myself that.

I followed Tony into his office with my dress still only half-buttoned. On stage I'd felt like an empowered naked woman, but here I felt disheveled, like I'd arrived at a job interview hungover. I reminded myself that this was not an interview—I already got the job—and I was also one of the only women in this building with clothing on.

The office was small, with exposed brick and pipes, an old PC that didn't look like it had been turned on in a long time, and a desk covered with random phone numbers written on yellow Post-it Notes. I'm not sure why these weren't just entered into a cell phone? There were stacks of cardboard boxes full of bottled waters and sodas, and a giant safe about half the size of one wall, with a state-of-the-art keypad on it. It was by far the most modern piece of equipment in here.

He took my ID and thoroughly inspected it with various lights and scanners and such. He then had me fill out some incredibly unofficial-looking paperwork, a stack of stuff that was photocopied (some pages even handwritten) and that required my signature, all of which more or less spelled out that I was over eighteen and I fully understood that I had to be nude.

"What's your name?" he asked. He talked the way people think everyone talks in New York, but barely anyone actually does.

"Naomi," I said. "It says it right here on my ID!" I pointed out, as if he couldn't read, or as if he wasn't aware that legal identification clearly did, in fact, state people's names.

"You want to use your real name on stage?" He looked at me, slightly puzzled, and slightly disgusted I think.

"OH!" I replied. "Sorry. Yes. No. I wouldn't do that. I understand now."

"Yeah, most girls pick the name of their favorite movie star or something. But do whatever you want. Just tell the DJ whenever you think of it," he said.

"Okay. Got it." I didn't really . . . but I assumed this would all be explained later.

"Well," he looked at his watch, "there's a few hours left of the day shift. You can stick around till it ends."

"Thank you." I smiled, as if this was an extreme act of kindness to allow me to expose my genitals to strangers drinking carrot juice and staring at pussy in lieu of eating lunch.

"House fee is forty-five dollars," he said.

"Excuse me?"

"Did you not hear me?" he asked.

"No, I heard you, I just don't know what a house fee

means. I'm sorry," I added, though in fact, I don't think not knowing that was worthy of an apology at all.

"Oh, oh yeah. Well, THE FEE TO WORK HERE IS FORTY-FIVE DOLLARS," he said, speaking loudly and slowly and using large, nonsensical hand gestures like he was playing charades—only nothing he pantomimed resembled what I would think of as "fee" or "work" or even "forty-five." He lowered his voice a bit and continued, "Some girls pay when they come in and some pay on their way out. But for your first month, you gotta pay at the beginning."

Okay, brain. Come back. I needed several moments to process this. I had to pay to work here? I'd never heard of such a thing. Was this like a resort fee at a hotel? Were Wi-Fi and snacks included with this cost? I looked at Tony inquisitively, and he just held his hand out. He was very confident in this fee. He was not going to explain it or justify it. I counted the money I had just made on stage and handed it to him—it tallied up to forty-three dollars. He nodded.

"You can give me the rest later," he said with a smile.

I was now officially two dollars in debt from being a stripper. Times were tough.

Suddenly, a girl came through the door. She was tall and thin, with hair dyed an unnatural platinum blonde, though a hint of black roots revealed its true color. Okay, maybe she wasn't so tall, but she had very high clear heels on, so she did *appear* tall. She had on a neon pink little slip with a long and loose cowl neck covered in rhinestones that dripped down her chest like an icicle. I could see her perfectly pointy, seemingly unnatural tits peeking through. They weren't huge, maybe a big C or a small D. I'd look like a bean pole wearing a neon body stocking had I put this dress on, but her breasts made this unflattering piece of fabric sit on her perfectly.

As she stormed in, the droopy pink rhinestones jiggled from side to side. She sat herself down in a chair and took a rubber-banded wad of bright purple monopoly-looking money out of a garter belt that was around her thigh. As she bent down, her right breast became completely exposed—not just a nip slip, the whole thing hung out loud and proud, and now I could confirm that they were enhanced, but very modest for a fake breast. I'd assumed everyone in the world with fake boobs had giant ones.

"Here you go!" she said, with a thick accent that sounded like a mix of Puerto Rican and Staten Islander. She smiled, winked, and folded and unfolded her arms indignantly. I wasn't sure if she was insulting him or flirting with him. She threw the wad of fake money on the table. Did someone pay her in Euros? Did Tony here have his own underground currency exchange program? If there was a forty-five dollar fee to be employed here, I could only imagine the exorbitant conversion rate he must charge.

"That's my girl, Brandi," Tony said. He counted out the purple money and then opened his safe. He had a swift method of covering his hand while he typed in the code. Brandi might be "his girl," but not his girl enough to know the code to that giant safe. He pulled out a wad of hundred-dollar bills, and that was such a small wad in such a large safe with so many other wads. What the hell was Tony doing in this rinky-dink club? There was seemingly enough money in there to retire on an island somewhere—and not, like, Long Island. Like, a nice one.

He doled out $600 and handed it over to her. She asked for a one-hundred-dollar bill to be broken up into twenties and then she gave him sixty.

"That's for you," she said.

"Aw thanks babe!" Did she really just give him a tip for handing her her own money? Was that normal? There were a whole lot of unexplained fees here, but right now, I had negative two dollars to my name so I needed to get to work.

I hadn't opened my mouth, but it must have been clear I was asking questions because Tony started answering them. For someone who didn't know me, and didn't even really like me (I think), he read me pretty well.

"If a customer doesn't have cash, they can get this money with their credit card and then pay you with it," Tony said, waving the purple bills in his hand.

"You new here?" said Brandi.

"Brand new," said Tony.

"What's your name?" she said.

"She doesn't have one yet," Tony laughed. I was having a hard time answering any questions here. I wasn't feeling very empowered. Apparently I needed to go back upstairs and shove my vagina in someone's face to the sound of seven-year-old hip hop to regain my confidence.

"Awww, you're like REALLY new," Brandi said.

"Yeah, I am," I admitted.

"Well, I've got a customer waiting for me up in VIP.

He likes doing doubles. I'm sure he'd LOVE a new girl. Wanna come with?"

To see Naomi go with Brandi to the VIP room, turn to page 19.

To see Naomi explore the club herself, turn to page 82.

"Ummm, yeah!" I said.

Brandi pulled me through the strip club, past the stage and the DJ and the bar. We arrived in a dark hallway lit with what looked like those constellation stickers I bought at Sharper Image and put all over my bedroom in high school. There were several spaces lined with dark velvet curtains. Brandi opened one of the curtains and revealed a scrawny man sitting on a decadent velvet bench, dressed in khakis and a patterned button-down top, with glasses and dark hair. His hands were in his lap, and he was looking at the floor. I felt like we were detectives walking into an interrogation room, and this khaki guy was definitely guilty of something.

Brandi sat on his lap and played with his hair. To say the least, her pink sparkly getup and his khaki garb did not complement each other well. There's no other scenario in the universe where these two people would be interacting like this.

"Scotty! Look! I brought a friend," she said. Scotty seemed excited.

"Oh- y-y-y-y-es. D-d-d-d-o you guys like to play together?" he asked.

"She's new here and I can't WAIT to play with her," Brandi said, while hamming up the hair playing a little more. It truly looked like a soothing massage—this girl knew how to rub a head.

"Come on Scotty, I want to play! You know what you have to do." Brandi pouted like a little girl on Santa's lap who wanted a pony. And then something incredible happened—Scotty reached into his pocket, opened his wallet, and "ponied" up five hundred-dollar bills. He handed all of it to Brandi, and she handed two of them to me. Just like that. Scotty was far superior to Santa. Santa charges people to take photos with him and rarely comes through with anything you ask for. Scotty pays for an electric bill in the blink of an eye.

Brandi folded up the money and rubber-banded it around her garter belt. I unzipped my fanny pack, which had now morphed into a very inconvenient clutch. I pulled out my wallet and placed my new crisp lap-sitting money next to my metro card and my long-expired student ID, which I still used to get discounts wherever I could. But if I could find myself a Scotty, I wouldn't need a 15 percent discount on anything ever again.

Brandi kissed him on the cheek. "Thank you!" she said. "You're the best—you're always the best. Love you!" She smiled at me and pulled me onto his lap, and while his knee was incredibly bony, I found a way to balance my also bony ass on him. Brandy removed her dress by untying one single tie in the back. I could see the convenience of this contraption. I must remind you, I was still in my red polka dot, polyester dress. Had anyone walked in here at this moment—with Brandi wearing nothing but clear heels, and me sitting properly with my legs crossed and my hands folded on Scotty's leg—it would have looked like Scotty took his daughter into the strip club after taking her on a tour of a local college campus.

Brandi gyrated her tight round ass against Scotty's crotch, while I remained perched on his lap. I could see her ass and pussy—everything was so smooth and perfect, not one ingrown hair or pimple in sight. Scotty smiled and kept his hands at his sides. I assumed that was a protocol here, and I commended him for sticking with it because I don't know how he didn't reach out and grab her.

"It's her first day, Scotty!" Brandi said, looking at me with her piercing brown eyes.

"Ooooh really?" he replied.

"Yeah! I wanna take good care of her," Brandi said.

She reached over and slid my dress up to my breasts, while continuing to rub her ass against Scotty's crotch. The multitasking was incredible. She smelled like lavender and vanilla and peaches all mixed together, and the scent was mesmerizing. My dress unfortunately came to a halt at my breasts. Brandi gave it a good head start, but I was aware that it was my job to continue to get this damn dress off. I had gotten paid generously by Scotty, after all.

I was done fussing with the buttons in the back. I pulled the dress over my head and heard it tear as it slid over my ears. I didn't care. Brandi giggled, and her adorable reaction made this entire interaction less awkward. She slid her smooth fingers up and down my body, and it felt like my matching bra and panty set just disappeared. She was some kind of magician, clearly. And now . . . I was naked.

Brandi lay back with her ass still on Scotty's crotch. She pulled me over and laid me on top of her, facing her, as if Scotty and I were creating a Brandi sandwich. I moved along with her, around and around. I was naked against

Brandi's naked body, but Scotty was completely clothed with his hands to his sides. It was bizarre, yet erotic.

I could feel her pussy lips against mine. Her fingers moved over my back, and our pelvises pressed together as we went around in a circle. Scotty got more and more excited. I understood where he was coming from, because I too was getting aroused. I inhaled all her pleasant stripper scents, and it was intoxicating.

She pushed me down until I was on my knees on the floor. And as she focused on this backward dry hump against Scotty's crotch, she took my head and pushed it into her pussy.

"I want you to lick me while I make Scotty cum," she said. I appreciated how direct she was, and I thought this was an excellent plan. She didn't even know my name . . . and come to think of it, I didn't know my name either, and that was fine. I stuck my tongue into her pussy lips as they moved around. I did my best to follow along. I'd never had a threesome before, and I still don't think this counts—I'm not sure what exactly the word for this was.

I stuck my tongue deep into her, and her pussy tasted just like the rest of her body smelled. I felt like I was licking a pussy while shopping at Bath & Body Works, and I liked it. I licked and licked and inhaled her pussy as best I could. She moaned, but I wasn't sure how much was real and how much was a performance paid for by Scotty. I wanted to be sure she actually enjoyed my tongue, so I licked her harder and stronger, searching for her clit. She could fake it for Scotty, but she couldn't fake it for me! I wanted to give her a real sensation. I wanted to feel her quiver.

"You're such a dirty girl," she told me in a high-pitched voice.

There was a train of pleasure going on. I licked Brandi and she rubbed on Scotty. The harder I licked, the faster she rubbed. I liked having this effect on her—I felt like I was a crucial part of contributing to Scotty's boner, even if I wasn't in direct contact with it. I couldn't relate this to anything I'd done in the past, so I just paid attention to what my body and my tongue told me to do, and that was to keep licking with as much gusto as I possibly could.

Brandi moaned beautifully. She was certainly an expert at turning people on. Scotty was now moaning too, and I had my mouth full doing my thing. He breathed heavily as he moved his hands to hold onto Brandi's hips—I could tell he was restraining himself from touching anywhere else with his invisible handcuffs. There was a musical medley of moans, and suddenly, Scotty quivered and shook uncontrollably. Then he stopped and lightly pushed Brandi off him, looking exhausted.

I saw a big wet stain around Scotty's crotch. Perhaps he should have worn darker pants—khakis were not the best choice of wardrobe for making a mess. I was embarrassed for him, but he didn't seem embarrassed at all. He was proud. I had to give him credit for that.

I wanted to keep licking Brandi, but it seemed like the paying customer got to decide how long things went on in here.

Brandi giggled. "You bad boy."

"Th-th-th-th-thank you," he said, looking drunk. He pulled out another hundred-dollar bill and handed it to her, and he walked out. She pulled two twenty-dollar bills out of the rubber-banded wad around her garter and handed them to me. I was perfectly fine with the sixty/forty percentage split. And honestly, a part of me wondered whether I could lick her again for a few more minutes if I gave the forty back.

"You're fun!" Brandi said. "You okay? Some of the girls here fake it when they do doubles, but I like doing the real thing." I still wasn't entirely sure of all the lingo here, but I thought I understood what she meant.

"Oh, yeah, that was amazing! And thank you for including me," I said.

"We need to think of a name for you," she said. I genuinely liked that she had decided she was a necessary part of this process. I naturally thought of Cardi B. She was my inspiration, even though we looked absolutely nothing alike and had virtually nothing in common.

"Naomi . . . G. My name is Naomi G!" This wasn't very creative. My real name was Naomi, and my real last name was Greenfeld . . . so Naomi G was just a shortened version of my actual name. But it just rolled out of my mouth, and it felt right, and it also kind of sounded like Cardi B—but not so much like Cardi B that if she ever checked in on her old strip club, she would get mad at me. I wouldn't want to get on her bad side.

"Alright! I like it!" Brandi said. From a distance I heard the DJ saying, "Calling Brandi to the stage . . . Brandi, come to the stage."

"Shit!" she said. "I gotta go on stage—I'll see you after!" She kissed me on the cheek. I put my slightly torn dress back on and smiled. It wasn't even 3:00 p.m., my internet bill was paid, I had been an integral part of someone else's orgasm, and I had a cool new name. I felt like an important contributing member of society . . . or, at least, of this society. I confidently walked out of the dark room, toward the music and the neon lights, excited to see whose pants I could mess up next.

To continue with Naomi in this fantasy, turn to page 26.

To go back and see Naomi explore the club herself, turn to page 82.

I entered the strip club part of the club. There were a few customers by the stage, and a few standing near the bar waiting for nonalcoholic beverages. It was early afternoon. Did these men have the day off? Being at a strip club in the afternoon on a weekday showed an impressive dedication to tits and ass. I've had men show up three hours late for 10:00 p.m. booty calls who lived four blocks away from me.

I wasn't sure what to do with myself at this point, so I just . . . found a wall and leaned against it, like I was the James Dean of the strip club. Brandi was now on stage, so I figured I would remain propped up against the wall, watching her.

She strutted around the stage, demonstrating some incredibly fine-tuned twerking skills. Her body stayed still while her ass moved like a separate living organism, shaking to the exact beat of the music. The eyes of the customers tried to keep up, as they blindly handed over all the money in their wallets. She kicked her legs up and landed in an upside-down position on the pole. Somehow, amidst this sexual acrobatic display, she managed to strip off her shiny pink dress midair. The dress slipped from her fingers and fell to the side of the stage, and she laughed and glanced over in my direction. From the "oopsie" look she was giving me, I deduced that this dress falling on the floor wasn't intentional. *I'm coming for you Brandi! I'm here to save your dress!*

I grabbed the dress and attempted to hand it to her from the side of the stage. But she said, while still upside-down, "You know what, keep it! I got another one just like it!" Then she spun around the pole. While I took great pride in my thrift shop stripper aesthetic, I was also honored to have been invited into this sisterhood of the traveling pink sparkly stripper dress. Perhaps one day I too would pass it on to another stripper in need. "Take this too," she added, as she slipped a pink garter off her left thigh and threw it at me, like I was a bridesmaid at her wedding. There was a matching pink garter on her right thigh with a stack of folded money under it, which she obviously kept for herself. She swung around the pole, wearing nothing but folded money, and I will admit, it was a good look for her.

I went to the bathroom and did a complete wardrobe change, like I was Cher, or something. I crumpled up my Marc Jacobs getup, which was once a prized posses-sion, but now felt like a nuisance. I slipped on the dress and slid the garter up my thigh, with the determina-tion to fill that thing up with rent, or at least half of it. I walked out of the bathroom feeling like a sparkly pink superhero.

I wandered around the club aimlessly, but also confi-dently. Brandi eventually found me, now in the same exact dress I was wearing, only hers was silver. Where the hell did one buy these outfits? Let alone multiple ones in different colors?

"Now, you gotta check in with the DJ—I'll introduce you!" Brandi said. I followed her blindly. I knew I had just been up on the stage not that long ago, but after seeing Brandi dance, the thought of going back myself was intimidating. This wasn't a funny experiment. This wasn't a weird accident or a whim. I was . . . actually at work?

If the strip club was an ocean, then the DJ booth was the lighthouse. It was elevated, and the DJ sat at the top in a circle of enclosed glass, watching over the sea of strippers—and more literally like a lighthouse, he actually did control the lights. There was some generic techno beat playing on a loop. It was repetitive and mundane, like a specific kind of elevator music designed for night clubs instead of office buildings.

Brandi pushed through a mini–barn door at the top of the fourth stair that led to the DJ booth. My friends in Brooklyn commonly think that "real" DJs spin vinyl, and all other forms of DJ are bullshit. While I have nodded and smiled and agreed on the issue for the sake of conversation, I never actually cared about who was a "real" DJ and who wasn't. But I will say that this set-up looked rather legitimate to me. It wasn't just a little booth to play music and do recreational drugs in, this was the command center for the entire strip club. A cluster of buttons and controls for smoke, a different one entirely for lights, and a feed showing security camera footage of the front door, the stage, and little rooms that must have been somewhere in this club but that I hadn't seen yet.

The DJ also had an impeccably well-organized desktop, with rows of folders named things like "Chevalle," "Kendra," "Angelina," and "Sabrina." While there was nothing vintage or rare about his music collection, and none of his three computers were designed by Steve Jobs (yes, I'm afraid they were–*gasp*–PCs), this looked very "real" to me. He was the man behind the curtain, and his random selection of Top 40 hits from different decades was the brain, heart, and courage the strippers needed. And to his credit, unlike the other DJs that I knew, this guy apparently got up in the morning. And there's something to be said for that.

The DJ was pale and skinny, with a leopard print shirt and long black hair. I wasn't sure if his hair was greasy or intentionally combed through with gel to give it a bit of a "wet" look, but either way it complemented his animal print. He had giant headphones on, and he was nodding his head to the beat, clicking away on a mouse, furiously dragging and dropping folders like he was preparing for a digital battle. Brandi tapped him on the shoulder and interrupted his trance.

"Hey TJ!" she said, yelling over the music.

"Sup Brandi!" he replied with a smile. I saw him pull out a mini-whiteboard from behind one of the computers and write Brandi's name down in red dry-erase marker. "Whatchu feeling like for your next set?"

"Enough of this techno shit," she said. "Play me some Lil Wayne, Jay-Z, maybe Travis Scott? Some old, some new! Mix it up!"

"Aww come on. You know Tony doesn't like too much hip hop on the weekdays." He shook his finger at her like a parent scolding a kid for eating too much ice cream.

"Well, tell him to suck my dick." She took a ten-dollar bill out of her cleavage and put it in his hands. TJ the DJ took the money, but, hesitantly.

"I'm telling him you said that if I get in trouble!" he said.

"I'll tell him right now," she said, and she grabbed a walkie-talkie tucked away behind his sea of laptops, clicked the side of it, and shouted into the speaker, "Tony, suck my dick." She and TJ giggled. And then the walkie-talkie beeped, and a fuzzy sounding voice replied, "Lick my nuts."

Brandi and TJ the DJ laughed hysterically at this response. What the hell was I doing here again? Should I chime in and tell someone to do something to part of my nonexistent penis?

Mid-laughter, TJ's expression suddenly changed. He threw his headphones back on and faded out of the looped techno and into a remix of a Katy Perry song from a few years ago. He grabbed the microphone and said, "Coming to the sage it's Kendra! Kendra coming to the stage!" This he said in a radio announcer voice—or should I say, strip club announcer voice.

"Alright, hip hop it is." He immediately snapped back into conversational mode and slipped his headphones off. That was impressive. I'd been standing silently in the dark, observing all this, but suddenly I was very much not in the dark . . . because in that whirlwind moment when TJ went full DJ, he hit some kind of switch that made the lights flash, and one of them was right above my head. He saw me and did a double take.

"Oh hey—this is Naomi G. She's new," Brandi said.

"Hey! What kind of music do you want to dance to?" he asked. More stressful decisions I was completely unprepared for. I had to come up with a fake name, and then also had to come up with some kind of soundtrack to complement that fake persona. The classic punk and modern discordant alt-rock that filled my iTunes probably weren't going to work here. I already knew from my eaves-dropping that I couldn't request any hip hop . . . Tony and

I were very far from any kind of jovial dick sucking or nut licking relationship. What should it be?

"You like rock? Techno? Top 40? R&B? What's gonna get you moving around up there?"

To see Naomi dance to rock, turn to page 32.

To see Naomi dance to R&B, turn to page 40.

"I'll um . . . I'll dance to rock!" I said. It seemed like the most vast and generic category, and it felt safe. Being a bit of a music nerd, I was suffering from second-hand embarrassment. No one used the term "rock" anymore. People said "classic rock," or "punk rock," or sometimes even "hard rock," but plain old "rock" isn't actually a genre of music anymore. Was he going to play Bob Dylan? Did rock mean Third Eye Blind? Did rock mean Marilyn Manson? Eighties hair metal? Elvis? It could technically mean any of these, and while none of these selections particularly inspired me, none of them offended me. So, rock it was.

He nodded, and I saw him spell out the name "Naomi G" on his mini-whiteboard. TJ the DJ put his headphones back on and disappeared back into the matrix of buttons and lights. Brandi exited the booth and I followed her out. We were now on the floor, and I felt like we were two wandering kittens out in the wild, if the wild consisted of about eight businessmen uncomfortably sitting around staring at an empty stage, waiting for a vagina to appear.

"There might not be a lot of people here now, but trust me, people here at this time are coming to spend money—and they're gonna spend it quick. You've gotta get them in VIP before the other girls get to them."

I was taking notes, listening to my stripper mentor, but

my mental note-taking was interrupted with an announcement from TJ.

"Calling . . . Naomi G to the stage! Coming up next . . . It's Naomi G!"

"Shit, I guess you gotta go!" Brandi pointed in the direction of the stage. I was on my own now.

I walked out onto the stage to the song "American Woman" by Lenny Kravitz. A song I forgot existed, but I somehow knew all the words to, without ever having owned a single Lenny Kravitz album. The men by the stage nodded their heads. One of them even mouthed the words to the chorus, and the chorus was basically the entire song.

Okay. Here I go. I attempted to look "Tyra Fierce," as Tyra Banks would say on *America's Next Top Model.* Tyra always said the look you gave the audience when you first walked out on the runway set the tone for your performance, so I gathered up all the fierceness inside me, took a dead stop in the middle of the stage, and stared at the four men gazing at me. Yes. I know I said eight before, but four of them were whisked away by other strippers, one of them being Brandi. That was okay, though. She'd left me the Lenny Kravitz enthusiast, who was now playing air drums in addition to mouthing the words.

I grabbed onto the pole in the middle of the stage. I had no idea what to do with the pole, of course, but my body just gravitated toward the phallic piece of metal. I leaned against it and shimmied back and forth. I turned around, used the pole to balance myself, and shook my ass slowly back and forth. As I arched my back, the dress perked up and showed off a peek of my pussy. I mean, I knew the thing was going to come out shortly, but I figured I should tease them until at least the, um . . . eighth time Lenny Kravitz said the song title.

I felt guilty about it, but I had to admit I was enjoying dancing to this song. It didn't fit with the genres embraced by my Brooklyn hipster culture—while listening to *some* modern pop songs would be considered acceptable, this hit from ten plus years ago was not ironic enough. But I couldn't help it—something about this repetitive guitar riff made me feel sexy. I didn't want any of these men to throw me against my bedroom wall and fuck me. I wanted them to *worship* me, and while I'd never considered myself a seductress, the combination of Lenny Kravitz and TJ the DJ's skills instilled the power in me to transform. Naomi G didn't have any doubts or weaknesses. She was confident and sexy, she existed to turn you on, whoever you were . . . and she listened to "rock."

I turned back around, and my back slid down the pole. My legs naturally spread open—they kinda just did that. My dress was technically still on, but with my knees facing straight up, my pussy was exposed. There was something very seductive about my breasts still being covered but my vagina being exposed. I can't quite explain it, but I liked it.

I spread my lips open . . . you know the ones. The guy playing air drums stopped playing air drums. He did, however, keep mouthing the words to the song, looking directly into my vagina, like he was singing to it. I wasn't exactly proud to identify as an American woman, especially in the country's current state, but my vagina was totally fine with it. I slid my fingers up and down my lips, so my pussy was now singing back to him. He put a stack of dollars in front of him.

I got down on all fours and crawled over to him, but I realized that with my face pointed at him, my vagina was facing the wrong direction. He picked up his fake drumsticks and began to play the god damn air drums again.

I moved into a yoga bridge position, where I grabbed onto my ankles and I thrust my hips up. The stem of my heels worked perfectly as something to grab onto, like two mini–stripper poles on the bottom of my feet. My pussy was now propped up and fully exposed. He stopped his air drums again. Thankfully, this guy's passion for real vagina overrode his passion for fake drums.

I waved it around, up and down, hypnotizing him with my entire pelvic area. He threw dollars at me—I couldn't count how many, but it was definitely more than I would make in a tip jar in an entire shift at Fix. I clenched my fists tighter around my heels and swirled my vagina around in a circular motion. TJ changed the lighting configuration just slightly, and I could feel my vagina illuminated, as if it was going to be beamed up into strip club heaven as a reward for its good behavior. Mr. Air Drums continued to hand over his stack of money, throwing it bit by bit onto the stage. His stack became smaller as my pile of ones became larger. It was a live demonstration of redistribution of wealth, as if my pussy had the power to break up the capitalist monopoly.

Lenny Kravitz was starting to say goodbye. The song was going to end soon. Me and Mr. Air Drums had a good thing going here, and I wasn't sure if our relationship would last once a different song came on. Luckily, a few more men had walked over. How exciting! My exposed yoga-bridge pussy was doing alright for itself, but it needed to get out to different parts of the stage and entice other people.

TJ the DJ chimed back in on the microphone in his official sounding announcer voice. "Alright guys, we've got Naomi G . . . Naomi G on the stage. Don't be mean, show her that green if you wanna see her take her dress off. She's got one more song—put your hands together and show some love for . . . Naomi G!" I was embarrassed. Was this normal? Or was I just doing a really bad job, to the point that TJ felt like he had to step in and force people to give me money? I had my own little thing going, I was fierce and untouchable here, and I didn't want to appear desperate or greedy. I really needed to have a conversation with this TJ guy and explain to him my brand.

But then, people *did* put their hands together, did clap, and did in fact throw a bunch of dollar bills on the stage. Or, um . . . "green" as he called it. I couldn't believe it. His extortion haiku yielded some impressive results.

I stood back up and leaned against the pole again as a new song came on. What was this? Oh. I was pretty sure this was Nickelback. There are a whole bunch of bands that blend together in my mind, and they all kind of sound like Nickelback to me, but I think this actually was Nickelback. It had a faster tempo, so it was time to pick up the pace, but before I decided what my new dance moves should be, I had to take this dress off. I slid the spaghetti straps off my shoulders and it fell to the ground quite perfectly. I stepped out of the dress and pushed it to the side. I moved my hands up and down my body to the tempo of the music . . . and, please don't tell anyone I said this but, it was the perfect tempo.

I got back down on all fours and did an over-dramatic hair flip that actually turned out much better than I expected it to. I saw my long strands of brown hair fly up in the air and then land back in place, looking so much sexier than they had before. I was moving around a bit faster, now, and I broke a bit of a sweat. I could feel the droplets of moisture running through my hair, and it helped style it perfectly with that messy, sex-hair look.

I didn't have large breasts—they were perky Bs—so it felt a bit silly to shake them . . . but it did feel appropriate to smack them. Something about the sweat and the sweet sounds of Nickelback just made me want to smack my own tits. With more of an audience and a faster song playing, I had to spread the attention around. I couldn't just use my pussy-hypnotizing powers on one person.

I got on my back and positioned my legs in a perfect *V* shape, and from my point of view I could see one man's head as if it was coming directly out of my pussy. Then I touched myself. Not like a full-on masturbate-to-completion type of touch, just a little rub, and as I rubbed, I looked directly into the eyes of the stranger in between my legs. He was handsome in a slightly older, silver fox way—like if George Clooney had a less attractive brother or something. He was handsome enough to get a four-and-a-half-second vagina rub, and I was genuinely excited by him watching me. I spread my pussy for him to see. He gave it a little half-smile, and then threw some dollar bills at me. The whole interaction felt quite polite.

I shimmied my bare ass over toward the next guy. This

guy was younger—he looked close to my age, but he'd clearly taken a very different path in life. He had neatly trimmed short hair, a clean-shaven face, and a multi-piece suit. He took a sip of a green Naked juice, and it left a green residue on his lips. I licked my lips, hoping to Jedi mind trick him into licking his lips, because the green residue was kind of bothering me, and I wanted it to go away. He did not pick up what I was throwing down, but now he seemed excited that I was licking my lips, so it still worked out to my advantage.

He loosened his tie—I liked that my naked body gave off the kind of energy that made you want to sit back and get comfortable. He handed me a five-dollar bill, and I licked my lips even more, but now slower, trying to mentally communicate that I was capable of giving good and enthusiastic blow jobs.

While I didn't exactly know this song, I could feel that it had hit its climax and was starting to wind down. I got on all fours, flipped my hair again, and combined all my moves into some kind of stripper finale that ended with my pussy facing the audience. The song began to fade out, so I stood up and went back to the pole—it just seemed to make sense to end where I started. TJ chimed back in over the last few beats of the song.

"Alright everyone, give it up for Naomi G! She's available for private dances and VIP rooms. Coming up next, it's Sabrina, Sabrina now coming to the stage."

I collected my pile of money and my dress. *Should I take a bow? Should I curtsey?* I felt like I needed a definitive exit here, but as I stood there awkwardly figuring out what to do, another stripper walked onto the stage in pigtails, a short red plaid skirt, and white knee-highs. She gave me a threatening look—well, as threatening as a girl in pigtails could possibly look—and I took the hint and scurried off the stage.

To go back and see Naomi dance to R&B, turn to page 40.

To continue with Naomi in this fantasy, turn to page 48.

"Um . . . R&B! Sure!" I said. I picked my absolute least favorite genre of music. I honestly couldn't even name five R&B songs, but from what I understood, this genre was specifically invented with the intent to turn people on, so I felt like it was appropriate for the task at hand.

TJ nodded and put his headphones back on, scribbling "Naomi G" on his whiteboard. Brandi turned around to exit the DJ booth, and I followed. I was officially a stripper in training. On my training day at Fix, I'd been forced to stand behind a scrawny metrosexual man who was supposed to teach me how to use the cash register for less than minimum wage, but mostly just taught me the reasons how and why everyone drank coffee incorrectly. Shadowing a fellow stripper with perfect breasts and a superhuman ability to make money juggling said breasts was a far better training situation.

I followed her onto the floor. She studied the clientele intently and put her hand on my shoulder.

"Alright well, I know it looks empty, but all it takes is one black card to get you through the day here—and I can smell one in the vicinity." She continued to scan the room, as if she had some kind of military grade X-ray vision device hidden in her fishnets that sensed how much money each person had in their wallet . . . or to their name, for that matter. I nodded and took mental notes. But my concentration was interrupted by the sound of TJ's omnipotent voice.

"Coming up now to the stage, it's . . . Naomi G! Naomi G, coming up to the stage." It felt so official hearing him announce me. I was an integral part of the strip club ecosystem, and I liked it. Sorry Brandi, we would have to finish this lesson later. I had places to go and things to do.

As I walked onto the stage, a woman with an incredibly large ass was gathering up a pile of dollar bills. She glared at me as if I was somehow imposing on her turf, which put me in quite the conundrum, since I was just following the orders of the disembodied voice that had clearly stated I should be "Coming up to the stage." I stood in the corner and waited for her to finish collecting her clothes.

A song by Post Malone started playing. I had heard this song many times before, but I didn't know the name of it, or the words, and I also had no idea that this was considered R&B. I'm still not sure if it is. The woman was taking her time collecting her bills, and one of the customers even handed her a few more dollars while she was bent over cleaning up her cash.

"NAOMI G TO THE STAGE," I heard TJ say again, with much less finesse than he had before. The woman rolled her eyes and walked off the stage, swaying her ass, leaving me three-fourths of a Post Malone song and my own very flat ass to arouse people with. I was off to a rough start.

There were five men sitting by the stage. Wait, no, there were four. One got up as soon as he saw my unfriendly, large-bottomed coworker on the floor. He followed her giant ass in a hypnotic daze with a large stack of bills in his hand. It's safe to say I wasn't his type anyways.

I walked right past the pole and steered clear of it. I was far too flustered to even think about dealing with that pole right now. Instead, I got on my hands and knees and kinda just crawled around. This song had an incredibly slow tempo, and it was difficult for me to move slowly enough to stay on beat. I propped myself up on my knees and ran my own fingers through my hair. I had rather long hair, so it ate up a decent amount of time.

Searching for something else to do, I spread my legs open and did what was basically a reverse cowgirl dry hump of the stage. I transitioned onto all fours and pushed my ass back and forth—now I was dry humping the air, apparently. I was making this all up as I went along, so I decided my quick strategy here was to just keep re-enacting sexual positions and riding fictitious cocks.

Surprisingly, I was getting aroused cycling through my spank bank while looking into the eyes of strangers wearing suits. No one wore suits anywhere in Brooklyn. It felt like I was in a different country. Dollar bills were being thrown at me. I mean, no one was "making it rain," but I could confidently say they were making it drizzle.

My doggy-style dry hump seamlessly transitioned into a slow motion twerk. I was now teasing the fake cock, taking a break from getting fucked by it, and just making it beg for more. As I shook my little ass, my sparkly dress rose up to my hips, exposing my pussy. It was remarkable to experience the convenience of the stripper dress. I mean, people really underestimate the brilliance of these cheap pieces of fabric. This dress knew what to do. It cooperated so well with my body, and it was miraculous how a piece of clothing could highlight how you look naked.

Now that my pussy was already exposed, I wondered if I should take the damn thing off? I got back up on my knees, with my torso facing the crowd. I slid the spaghetti

straps down my shoulders, and the dress delicately
dripped down and exposed my breasts. The lighting on
the stage illuminated my nipples, and the reflection of the
pink sparkles gave them a bit of a glow. The music gave
them their own soundtrack. It was literally my boobs'
time to shine. I pushed my *B* cups together, slowly, to the
beat of the "R&B," and I bounced up and down. At this
point, I was summoning an air cock to titty fuck me. It
was the realest fake cock I'd ever had between my tits. I
looked every audience member in the eyes, hoping that
with the power of all of our imaginations, they could feel
their cocks in-between my tits, and I could jerk them all
off and get showered in a pool of imaginary jizz. The
dress remained on my torso, reminding me of the times I'd
used a hand towel as a bath towel, and shamefully walked
from my bathroom to my bedroom attempting to cover up
what I possibly could, only here I was proud of my nudity
and the lack of coverage was very much intentional.

I looked straight into the eyes of a man in a khaki-
colored suit who had short, spiky hair—but not, like,
punk rock spiky hair, like a blatant-product-of-hair-plugs
spiky hair. He had a clean-shaven face, a gold watch, a tie
patterned with that signature Burberry plaid. He sipped
on a nonalcoholic beer, and as my titty fuck move got
more intense, he drank his beverage slower. This song was
making the entire club move in slow motion. He sipped
the last drop of the fake alcohol, sat back in his chair,
threw a few bills on the stage, and I could see him starting
to sweat a little. The song wasn't even over! I was so proud
of myself for turning this man on in such a short amount
of time. I mean . . . he was incredibly uncomfortable, but
that's to be expected when you're in the beginning stages

of a boner, and you're also in public, and you're also in a suit, and you're also being deprived of any alcohol.

I enjoyed the effect I had on him. It was like a big shot of self-esteem had been injected into my veins, and I felt powerful, sexy. I moved closer to him, and I pulled on his tie. While I wasn't a fan of hair plugs, I was a fan of Burberry plaid. I loosened his tie, and I felt like this was both sexual and practical, because the man definitely was sweaty. I used the tie to pull him toward me, simultaneously pulling me toward him. I had to make sure not to pull too hard—I knew how expensive Burberry ties were. I unbuttoned his top two buttons, all while maintaining eye contact with him. I swear, something about this "R&B" music gave me the power to unbutton shirts without looking, or asking, for that matter. Now he was transformed into a super ultra-relaxed businessman, and I hoped that made him want to stay a while.

The song ended, and TJ seamlessly transitioned into another song by The Weeknd. This song came out a few summers ago. I remember finding it buried inside of a mix Spotify hand-picked for me, and I thought I had discovered the next big thing, until I realized it was already a radio hit. I didn't appreciate Spotify sneaking parts of pop culture into my sophisticated indie music playlists without my consent. But, I'll admit . . . it was a good fucking song. It was also perfect to get naked to, even though I believe the lyrics were about doing narcotics and cheating on people . . . but that's beside the point. It was time to actually take my dress off.

I stood up as gracefully as I possibly could. I felt like the reveal of my naked body should occur while I was standing up, even though everyone already saw my tits, ass, and pussy. This was still a climactic moment, I mean, there had to be someone out there wondering what my belly button looked like. Hair plug guy followed my body with his eyes as I slid the dress off. It fell to the ground immediately. I was now standing inside of a perfect pink shimmery puddle, naked. I stepped out of it and managed to swiftly kick my dress to the side of the stage. Then I crouched back down into a squatting position so I could get back to eye level with the hair plugs.

After a few slow beats, I realized I was giving this guy a little too much attention and unfortunately his stack of bills was running low, so I moved over to the next guy. But before I shimmied over, I tried my best to mentally relay, "Don't worry hair plugs, when I'm dancing for these other guys, I'll be thinking about you the whole time!"

I had long legs, and they were kind of getting in the way at the moment. I was trying to get up close and personal with this small group of suited and booted men, but my five feet of leg kept getting in the way. *How do I get my ass and pussy closer to their faces without falling off the stage?* I had to think on the fly while still swaying to the beat of the music, but luckily inspiration hit. I got on my back, lifted my legs in the air, and strategically had them land on the shoulder pads of the guy in front of me. My body was like a diagonal plank, with my head on the ground and my legs elevated.

The guy whose shoulders I randomly chose seemed pleased with this development. The placement of my legs gave him a perfect view of my pussy, and he was a gentleman. He admired it, he studied it, and he didn't touch it. He smiled and threw some bills on the stage, following the journey of my pussy without taking his eyes off it for an instant. I was so consumed with moving to the beat of the music that I forgot I was naked. I know that sounds oxymoronic, to forget that you're naked because you're concentrating so hard on showing your pussy to people, but I was dedicated to the task at hand, and any ounce of self-consciousness I'd ever had about my body disappeared. It didn't matter how big my breasts were, it mattered how I used them. It didn't matter if stray unshaven hairs were lining my pussy lips, all that mattered was that the man paying to see the pussy got a good view of the pussy.

I felt like I was losing balance, and the song was about to change tempo anyway. I got up and put my hand on the pole. I sort of did my own "Ring Around the Rosie" type thing, which just felt right for this part of the song. After one quick circle, I leaned my back against the pole and slowly slid down it. I spread my legs open and looked down—I never actually got this clear a view of myself. I mean, I'd never had the opportunity to sit in a room with professional lighting and just hang out there with my lips spread open. I mostly had sex in the dark, and masturbated under the covers. I never spent much time in the shower out of respect for roommates and the water bill. This was some nice, necessary time for me to get to know all the little nooks and crannies and folds of my vagina.

It was a little on the meatier side. If it was a belly button, it would be an outie. I could feel the cool, circulated strip club air coming through a vent in the wall and blowing against my clit. It tingled, like it was winking to everyone, letting the whole room know that it was the spot to push on if, in some alternate universe, they had been permitted to make me cum. The thought of these suited strangers reaching their foreign arms out and rubbing my clit and fingering my exposed holes while TJ the DJ continued to spin R&B really got me excited. Such a filthy little secret fantasy I was having here on this stage, and I could tell that everyone could smell my horny scent because the light drizzle of dollars was almost turning to rain.

The song came to an end. A slightly less disgruntled stripper than the one before was on the side of the stage now, waiting to make her entrance. She stood there with her arms folded in a long, dark purple gown, with slits on the sides going all the way up her legs. It was like a bridesmaid's dress gone wrong. Or right. However you want to look at it.

"Alright everyone, give it up for Naomi G! She's available for private dances and VIP rooms. Coming up next, it's Layla! Layla now coming to the stage."

I quickly collected my dollar bills and crunched them all together haphazardly in my fists. I slid my little dress back on and I exited the stage.

To go back and see Naomi dance to rock, turn to page 32.

To continue with Naomi in this fantasy, turn to page 48.

I walked off the stage and felt accomplished. I'd figured out how to be a stripper. I didn't know what I looked like out there, really, but I *felt* like I looked awesome. I was holding on to a wad of cash, I had no idea how much. I was sweaty, halfnaked, clutching a dress and dollars at the same time. The sweat from my fingers caused them to shift, and the movement caused several crumpled dollars to fall from my grip. I reached down to gather them, and then even more fell. There had to be a better system for this. I sat backstage, causing an inconvenient fire hazard, attempting to gather up my money and quickly put myself back together.

My face was moist from sweat. If I wiped the sweat off, my meager makeup would come right off with it. But if I slathered on more powder, that would be terrible for my acne-prone skin. I had a whole list of people I was on the fence about in terms of telling them I was a stripper, and my dermatologist was a very low priority on that list. Hopefully she'd prescribe me twice the retinol without asking any questions.

My brief moment of contemplation about skin routines was interrupted by Brandi.

"Good job on stage! You made a couple bucks up there!" She sounded very much like a proud parent, and since I didn't plan on telling my actual parents about this profession, I appreciated the validation.

"You better get back down there—right when you get

off stage is the best time to get dances from these guys," she said.

"What do you mean?" I replied. I had just danced for them, after all, and I felt like I deserved at least a five minute break, and maybe a coconut water.

"As soon as you get off stage, you gotta ask these guys for dances. They have short attention spans. Once a new girl goes on, they'll forget about you," she said. "That's how you make money here, you run off the stage, find a lap, and grind on their crotch for twenty dollars a song. Multiply that by a lot of songs, and you've got your rent paid."

I had never calculated my rent in songs. This was a very artistic way of budgeting finances.

"Come on!" she said. I followed her back to the main floor of the club. There were a handful more customers now. Some were by the stage, some by the "bar," and some just sitting in the red padded seats by the wall. There were multiple signs on the wall explaining that cell phone use was prohibited in the club. Brandi told me this was to prevent any kind of filming or photographing of the dancers or customers. Between the dancers who hid their job from their friends, parents, and lovers, and the customers who hid this outing from their friends, parents, and lovers, it was like . . . none of us were supposed to be here. The strippers and the customers in strip clubs enter into a secret hand-shake. If a tree falls in a forest and nobody hears it, did it make a sound? And if a person goes into a strip club and doesn't text, tweet, or take a selfie in it . . . did it actually happen?

"So, look around the room and see if you think

anyone's feeling you. See, all those guys who were by the stage when you danced are gone now. They either got snatched up by someone else in VIP, or they left! That's why you gotta get 'em fast," Brandi said.

She was right. *Where did all my admirers go?* I thought we had something special up there. I also didn't know how Brandi could have such a meticulous mental log of who came in, who left, and who was by the stage when I was dancing, but I supposed it was some kind of stripper sense that gets developed over time. Or perhaps her close pal TJ the DJ had another mini-whiteboard keeping track of it all.

"So what do I do, just walk up to them?" I asked.

"Yeah! Sit down next to them, talk to them, you gotta feel it out. Sometimes I just get straight to the point and ask if they want a dance right away. Sometimes I sit down and bullshit for a bit before I ask."

"But what if they say no? Then what?" I said.

She laughed. "Sometimes they're gonna say no. Some days, they all say no. Some days, they all say yes." This felt like some kind of strange team-building exercise they'd have you do at a corporate office to make everyone get along with each other. And really, what better way to get along with someone than to rub on their crotch?

"That guy over there, see? He's looking at you!" Brandi pointed to a younger gentleman in the corner of the club. He looked like he was in his early thirties, with freshly cut short blond hair, a short-sleeve plaid polo, and dark pants.

"I don't think he's looking at me," I said. "He's looking at you!"

"Nah, that's all you. I can tell. The younger guys never

like me!" She laughed. It was impressive that she knew her demographic. I had a lot to learn.

To see Naomi give a lap dance, turn to page 52.

To see Brandi give a lap dance, turn to page 58.

It was apparently my actual job here to make the first move. This was something I had very little experience with, even when I had full confirmation from friends that a certain person was into me. Here I had nothing but a glance to go by, and I'm still 99 percent sure the guy wasn't even looking at me.

He didn't have quite the same confidence in his strip club etiquette as the other men in the club. He kept folding and unfolding his arms, and crossing and uncrossing his legs, like he wasn't entirely sure what to do here. This entire set-up was designed that way, though. If you weren't sitting by the stage, and you weren't purchasing a carrot juice, and you weren't getting a lap dance, well then you were in some kind of strip club purgatory, waiting for someone to whisk you away into stripper heaven, or hell. Whichever you preferred, and whichever you could afford.

I sat down next to him in a dark corner of the strip club where TJ's lighting didn't reach. It was as if he was trying to hide, though if he really wanted to hide then he wouldn't have come to a public strip club in the first place.

"Hi!" I said, with a cheerful inflection to my voice, trying to counteract his awkwardness. The pink sparkles helped with the peppiness. I automatically appeared at least 30 percent happier just by wearing the dress.

"Well, hello there," he replied. "I saw you on stage. You . . . looked really sexy up there."

"Aww, thanks!" I grinned. I wasn't sure what the

proper segue into a crotch riding request was. *Do I talk about the weather? Do I talk about what I watched on Netflix last night? Or do I go in a different direction and tell him how horny I am . . . or something?* All three seemed like the wrong choice.

"What's your name?" I blurted. That seemed like a safe place to go.

"Charlie. Or Charles, or Charlie . . . my friends call me Charlie. So, call me Charlie!" This was a smart move on my part after all. Asking him his name opened up an easy lane for conversation, where I could investigate the groundbreaking story of how Charles became Charlie. Plus, somehow just saying his name instantly made him seem more comfortable. He had a clean-shaven face, hazel eyes, and he smelled like a fresh scent of Old Spice.

There was something soothing and familiar about his face. Wait. It was very familiar.

"Well Charlie, where are you from?" I asked.

"I'm from Westchester, but I live in Manhattan. I mean, no one here is really from here, right?" He chuckled.

Well shit. He certainly was familiar. I'm from West-chester, and this was Charlie Silversteen. He went to my high school. He was a junior when I was a freshman, and he was known throughout the school as pretty much the greatest person to ever grace the planet. Captain of the football team, and the debate team, and he scored the role of Sweeny Todd in the high school musical. He dated my childhood best friend, Jill, who officially graduated to way-too-cool-to-be-my-best-friend after she started dating him, which led to an unexpectedly lonely freshman year. Charlie and Jill got married shortly after high school, he went to Yale, and . . . I guess the rest is history.

And now, here we were, sitting in the dark corner of a strip club, making small talk that could potentially lead to a dry humping.

"Well I'm . . . Naomi G. Nice to meet you!" I said. I said it with as much confidence as I possibly could, cursing myself for using my actual first name. He didn't question it. He had no idea that I was an abandoned friend of his wife's. And since I hadn't spoken to Jill in over ten years, our statute of limitations for friendship was definitely over. As far as I was concerned, I had every right to solicit crotch rubbing money from her husband (if they were even still married).

I felt a unique chemistry with him. His clean scent was infectious, and his nervousness was endearing. If current-day Naomi G could go back in time and tell freshman year Naomi with cystic acne and thick glasses (sitting alone at the lunch table, longing for her lost friend Jill) that this would be happening in her future, she wouldn't believe it. She would also be curious as to why someone in a short, sparkly dress and no underwear was wandering around the cafeteria.

"Would you like a private dance?" I asked.

"I'd like that," he said.

I knew he was going to say yes. I could just feel it. I could smell his attraction to me, stronger than his Old Spice. And I mean, of course I was attracted to him. THIS WAS CHARLIE SILVERSTEEN. Hell, if my mother knew that I was giving Charlie a lap dance, she'd forgive me being a stripper instantly.

Brandi was close by—I could see her a few feet down from me on the same red cushion bench that Charlie and I were on. She was dry humping away on a significantly older guy. I took a quick glance around and saw several of the other dancers grinding on different customers, so I quickly took note of what was going on and adapted to my situation.

"Well okay! Let's do it!" I said. I mean, why waste any time? I saw that the other girls were engaging in this act naked. So I stood up, while Charlie remained sitting. I held his eyes and slid my dress off. I licked my lips, and he slid his pelvis down just a little, and I found my own way to straddle him and press up against his pants. This was interesting!

I bent my knees and lunged my exposed pussy onto his fully covered and fully clothed dick. I could see the importance now of wearing clean pants in here. (I actually noticed that the other girls had some kind of cloth in between their vaginas and the guys' pants. I had a mental list of "stripper things to get" and I added this to the list.) I touched his face and I breathed into his ear. I could feel his chest rising and hear him breathing too. Were we supposed to just dry hump in silence? Well, I know it wasn't silent, there was loud music playing, but were we supposed to speak? Or just breathe? I asked a generic question to put a feeler out there.

"How does that feel—do you like that?" I could feel the small poke in his pants slowly growing to a large poke in his pants. I was victorious. That had to be a surefire sign that I was dry humping appropriately.

"That feels so fucking good," he said. *Yeah duh. I knew it did!*

I pushed up against him and put my lips right next to his. We were both breathing in each other's faces. I could feel his cock getting harder and harder, and I pressed my pussy up against it. It felt so strong, like it might just burst through his pants . . . and quite honestly, I wouldn't mind if it did. *Ooops. Sorry Jill!* Fortunately, Charlie's Ivy League education afforded him some expensive pants, and his penis was not going to break this quality fabric.

"Am I . . . bad?" he asked. I wasn't entirely sure where this was going. Was this a rhetorical question?

"No? I don't think so," I said. His boner toned down like two decibels. So apparently this was the wrong answer. I had to get the boner back to full force, so I backtracked.

"Yes, Charlie, you're bad!" I said. I felt his cock throbbing its way back to full boner mode.

"I'm married. She'd kill me if she knew I was here," he said. It took all of my might not to say, "Oh yeah, she definitely would."

"You're a bad boy, Charlie," I said instead.

"What are you gonna do to punish me?" he asked. I was still furiously dry humping away. His pants felt like a cloth condom on top of his fully erect cock. I continued to ride him, and then . . . well, I smacked him across the face. He did say he wanted to be punished! He looked shocked, but happy. He smiled a giant smile, and he grabbed onto the side of my ass and jackhammered his cock into me as much as he possibly could. I smacked him again, and I can't believe I'm saying this, but he dry humped the shit out of me. I was bouncing up and down in the air, and it was amazing and beautiful that this kind of behavior was actually acceptable in public. Or, well . . . here.

He stopped for a moment and collected his breath. I smacked him harder across the face.

"Don't stop. Or . . . I'll tell your wife!" Ohhh. Now

this was a blackmail dry hump. This was getting exciting. He started again, and I wasn't sure if I regretted egging him on like this. He was going full force, and he had quite the stamina. He had been captain of the football team, after all.

I have to admit, his boner was hitting the exact right spot on my clit, and I was getting turned on. "That's right, Charlie, just like that." I could feel him tensing up, and I gave him one extra hard smack for good measure. He shook, he got an adorable and scared look in his eyes, and . . . I felt a warm puddle explode inside of his pants. I got off of him and sat next to him, breathing heavily. I felt like we needed a cigarette or something.

"Are you okay?" I meant this with sincerity, because I was smacking him pretty hard, and now he was sitting inside of a puddle of his own jizz.

"Oh yeah, that was great. You're great. Thank you." He handed me sixty dollars. I remembered Brandi telling me this was a twenty-dollar operation, so I guessed this was some kind of tip for the bells and whistles. He got up and headed toward the bathroom. I folded the three twenty-dollar bills around my garter, and I felt a true sense of pride. The crumpled dollar bills stuffed inside my fanny pack felt so elementary right now. I had moved on to bigger bills, and I displayed them proudly on my thigh.

To go back and see Brandi give a lap dance, turn to page 58.

To continue with Naomi in this fantasy, turn to page 67.

"I swear, he IS NOT looking at me." A few moments ago, it was a sixty/forty toss-up of who he was looking at (favoring Brandi, regardless of this guy's age), but at this moment, he wasn't looking at anyone. He was staring down at the floor. If tits and ass weren't your thing, this establishment had a plethora of colorful shiny lights, and a large legitimate disco ball hanging from the ceiling. However, one thing this place did *not* have was a nice floor. It was a faded retro '70s paisley pattern, interrupted with decades of dried chewed up gum and . . . who knows what else. With all the tits and ass and shiny objects, why was this guy looking at the floor?

"Alright, suit yourself. He looks young, confused, AND he's got a Tom Ford jacket on. For future reference, that's like a fucking unicorn in here. You should never pass that up!" She strutted away, with her ass perfectly swaying side to side. Was she doing that intentionally? Or did her ass just do that? I was behind her, so if this was intentional, then I suppose it was a treat just for me, and I was appreciative of this gift of ass I was being given.

I followed the ass. Not just because I was mesmerized by its juiciness and enamored with the little dimples on each cheek. I was also a stripper in training, trying to learn the best way to give a proper lap dance.

Brandi approached the young man, who was still staring at the floor. I found a close corner that TJ the DJ's lights couldn't reach and sat there, observing. The guy was blond and looked like he was in his early thirties. Close to my age, but a completely different species. I doubt this guy ever drank PBR out of a can, or lived in a railroad apartment. In fact, I doubt he even knew what a railroad apartment was.

He was sitting on a long, red-cushioned bench that lined the perimeter of the club. I barely had time to blink, and Brandi was already towering over him, standing in between his legs (which had definitely been closed a moment ago), with her chest up against his face. How did she get in between his closed legs so quickly? And HOW THE HELL WAS HE STILL LOOKING AT THE FLOOR!

"Hey babe. What's going on?" she said to the top of his head. Finally, he looked up, right into her breasts.

"Oh, hey. Sorry. Hi. I'm good. I don't want a dance," he fumbled. Wow. I was shocked. *Is that legal? All she did was say hello! Could he at least thank her for putting breasts on his head? Did a jacket from Tom Ford give you the right to reject someone while staring directly into their nipples?*

She smiled, combed her fingers through his hair, and kissed him on the cheek. She didn't seem phased by the rejection. I could see in her body language that she took this as a challenge, instead of a failure.

"Well sweetie, you came here for something. If you don't want a dance . . . what DO you want?" He froze like a deer in headlights. Side note, I don't know why I ever say that because I don't own a car and I've never seen a deer, but you get the point. His "deer in headlights" expression was similar to my response to TJ the DJ when he asked what kind of music I wanted to dance to. Both this guy and I came to the strip club very unprepared to answer obvious questions we should really have known . . . and we both needed Brandi to guide us to the answers with her breasts in our faces.

She softened her approach by sitting next to him and putting her hand on his leg. Her original stance was one that said "I'm going to eat you alive," but now it kinda seemed like they were going steady. His leg had been twitching uncomfortably, and her touch seemed to calm his nerves. TJ's lighting scheme changed, and what looked like a spinning rainbow-bright soccer ball on the ceiling illuminated his face. Now that his head was up, the breasts were out of the way, and the party lights were on, I could see that he was pretty handsome, with piercing blue eyes and a clean-shaven face, not to mention a chiseled jawline. He had a charming and familiar face. Actually, it was very familiar. Wait a second.

"Where are you from?" Brandi asked.

"I'm from Westchester." I was worried he would say that. I was also from Westchester. Well, that's where I grew up. I had no connection to that city anymore, other than it being a place I brought my laundry to when I was guilted into visiting my parents. Being from Westchester is even less cool than working in Times Square. And that's saying a lot.

"Well, my name is Brandi! What's your name?" She transitioned from her slightly more formal sitting-next-to-him pose into a more loungey position and draped her thick legs over his. They were basically snuggling.

"I'm Charlie. Hello!" he replied.

I definitely knew who this was. Charlie Silversteen. He went to my high school (well, I guess it was more like *our* high school), and he was a junior when I was a freshman. He dated my friend Jill, who wasn't really much of a friend of mine after she started dating him. Charlie had led an exciting life as a junior on the football team, with parties and proms and a driver's license to entertain Jill with. My mediocre stash of comics, and the occasional handful of cigarettes I could steal from my dad's drawer, could not hold a candle to the world of excitement Charlie had to offer, and Jill and I had drifted apart. Charlie and Jill eventually got married. My mother insisted on filling me in on their lives whenever I spoke to her, and I always had to remind her that Jill and I hadn't spoken in over a decade, and Charlie and I were never friends.

"That's a cute name," Brandi said. I always thought so myself. It was a fucking adorable name. But it's doubtful she had the same genuine passion about his name that I did. I have a feeling she would have loved the name even if it was, like, Clarence or something.

"Well Charlie, what are you in the mood for? You didn't come all the way from Westchester just to sit here . . . you came to have some fun! So let's have some fun!" She giggled and moved her hands up his body until she was rubbing his shoulders. He instantly seemed more calm. Charlie was able to throw touchdowns on the field in front of everyone in Westchester and then dump a cooler of Gatorade on his teammates' heads, so why couldn't he utter a sentence or even look up from the ground in a strip club? I wasn't sure what kind of statement this made about society, or Charlie, but there was an underlying message there.

And then, well . . . things got a lot more interesting.

"Look," he said, "I'm . . . there's something that turns

me on, and I told my wife once and she got mad at me. She told me to never talk about it again. But I can't keep it in. I can't stop thinking about it."

"What is it? You can tell me ANYTHING," Brandi purred.

"You sure?" he asked.

"Yes, of course, sweetie," she said. I could sense her maternal instincts. Knowing how to calm down a pent-up horny man is a lot like knowing how to calm down a crying baby.

"Okay, so . . . once . . . a long time ago . . . years ago . . . I was, you know, going down on my wife. She was actually my girlfriend at the time. And you know, I was really going crazy down there, and she lost control, and I don't know what happened. She, you know—"

"She . . . had an orgasm? That's the goal, right?" Brandi laughed.

"Well, yeah, that but . . . she, um . . . she peed. We were a little drunk, you know. I don't know . . . she started peeing, or maybe it was squirting? But it went in my mouth, and I really liked it. When she figured out what was going on, she stopped. She got really embarrassed even though I told her it was okay! And she got mad at me. And now she won't let me go down on her anymore. I just want to taste it again."

Now that I thought about it, Jill always did have a weird thing about going in public bathrooms. She got through all of freshman year without ever using the bathrooms in school, ever, because she was deathly afraid of them. But regardless, Charlie was the lead in the high school play, he allegedly scored a perfect score on his SATs, and he was the captain of both the football team and soccer team. He was not a public restroom. His mouth had been very NOT public, and had remained only open to Jill for many, many years now, and she should really, out of the goodness of her heart, have peed in it.

I sat in the dark corner listening intently to every word. I was figuratively on the edge of my seat, but not literally, because then I would not be in the dark anymore.

"Tell me more about it, while I grind on your cock," Brandi said, and she gently put her hand on his crotch. He reached into the pocket of his pants and handed her two twenty-dollar bills. She stuck them in the garter belt wrapped around her thigh, and she put both her knees on the couch, put her breasts back in his face, and slid onto him like a Tetris puzzle piece. It was a dance, but also a business transaction. But also, all done in the name of urinating in Charlie Silversteen's mouth, which was kind of beautiful.

I was taking copious mental notes. All that talk was the foreplay, or therapy maybe? I wasn't sure. Maybe a bit of both. She slid her silver bikini top triangles to the side, and she smothered him with her breasts while grinding up and down on him. She had her mouth right next to his ear—I couldn't hear what she was saying to him, and he was mumbling a bunch of things to her that I couldn't hear either. She gracefully moved up and down while they stared intently into each other's eyes. He had his hands on her ass, and he was leaning himself into her as she pushed against him. They were having as much sex as they could possibly have with clothes on, without kissing.

He put his hands all over her ass and her breasts, without touching the nipples. She grabbed onto the collar of what I assumed was a designer shirt that came from actual Nordstrom—not Nordstrom Rack—and used it as leverage to grind up against his cock harder. I was aroused watching them. It felt like my ex-boyfriend and my current girlfriend were having sex in front of my eyes as a special kinky show just for me, only I never dated him . . . or her . . . and they weren't having sex. He started to smile, and she started grinding harder and harder. As she reached some kind of climax, she moaned heavily into his ear and then began to come down, going slower and slower, ending her dry humping as the song that was playing also ended. It was a good catchy beat to have in the background while talking about wanting pee in your mouth. She kissed him on the cheek and said, "I'll be right back."

Charlie had an almost empty bottle of Naked juice next to him on the couch. Brandi grabbed it. Was she offering to recycle his trash for him as a complimentary thank you for getting a lap dance? She walked away and grabbed my hand, pulling me off the couch as she walked past. I wasn't sure where we were going with this 70 percent backwash and 30 percent juice mix, but wherever it was, I was ready.

She pulled me into the bathroom, emptied out the remainder of green healthy drink into the sink, and gave the bottle a quick rinse. She handed it to me. Was I getting into the stripping industry at the wrong time? Were we going to go exchange this somewhere for five cents?

"How much did you hear?" she asked.

"Most of it!" I said.

"Good! I'm glad you were paying attention. Well . . . can you pee in this bottle for me? I'm pretty dehydrated right now."

"What!" I laughed. "Are you serious?"

"Yes! Come on! I know you can do it!" She pointed at the bottle of water in my hands, which I'd been nursing while taking notes on their lap dance. She locked the door to the bathroom. This seemed to be the women's bathroom for customers, but there were no actual women customers, so this bathroom was whatever we needed it to be.

She pushed me against the door and kissed me, and I was completely caught off guard. Wasting no time, she got down on the ground and went for my pussy. She licked me fiercely. It took her .00025 seconds to get to the same spot it took my last date a good twenty minutes to get to. Don't tell him I said that. This woman knew her way around a vagina. She curled her fingers and slid them inside me, and I was shocked that (a) this was happening and (b) her acrylic nails slid right in and didn't hurt at all. I felt my pussy clench up, so tight around her fingers, like it was going to snap them off.

She was fucking the shit out of me with her curled fingers. My legs trembled, I was so confused. I felt like the teacher I had a crush on was fucking me in some secret teachers' lounge. She licked my clit and moved her fingers in and out of me at record speed. In and out, and then . . . gush. I started squirting, or peeing, or whatever I was doing. I lost control of my own body, clear liquid spouted out of me, and Brandi continued to finger me as the liquid spilled. With her other hand she simultaneously got the bottle undeath me. Some of the liquid leaked all over Brandi's hands, and some went directly into the bottle.

I was quivering and shaking, moaning softly, and I wasn't sure if we were sneaking around—could you "sneak" sexual activity in a place where it was our jobs to be naked? But we were in a public bathroom with the door locked. I looked down and basked in the beauty of Brandi on the floor of the strip club bathroom. Her blonde hair, her slim hand that was half inside of my pussy, her *D* cup breasts, her tan smooth skin, and her curvy round ass . . . I was so turned on. I forgave Jill for ditching me for the juniors because she made this moment happen.

Brandi licked her fingers and grinned. "You taste good," she said. She got up and kissed me—I wanted to keep kissing her, but she clearly had places to go and bottles of my fluids to deliver. She screwed the top onto the bottle, kissed me on the cheek, and said, "Whatever he pays me for this, I'll give you half."

She unlocked the door and walked out. I stood there with a smile on my face and a dripping wet pussy. Just this morning I was fired for spilling fluids on someone, and now it was like I'd been promoted for that very same action. This was karma coming back to me in a very filthy way, and I liked it.

To go back and see Naomi give a lap dance, turn to page 52.

To continue with Naomi in this fantasy, turn to page 67.

Over the next couple of months, Brandi and I became quite the dynamic duo at Club 42. She was like my stripper sensei, and Club 42 was our dojo. I was typecast as her "shy nerdy friend," and I found it quite humorous. To my friends who knew about my new profession, I was by far the most bold and daring person they knew. But somehow, to her, I was "shy" even though I was spreading my legs open on the same stage that she did. One day she brought me a pair of thick black glasses with tape in the middle of them. She said they made her think of me. They became part of my wardrobe here, and I paired them with short plaid skirts and suspenders. I was Club 42's resident Steve Urkel.

On some days, we'd divide and conquer. We'd pick and choose sections of the club, designate one section to each of us, and lap dance our way through everyone. Then she'd attempt to work backward, and go back to everyone we'd already danced for, convincing them to get "doubles" with the two of us. I'd report to her if I knew someone was into busty blondes, and she would report back to me if someone was into "nerds." She had an uncanny ability to know the limit on anyone's credit card just by looking at it, and she also knew how to get them to spend to that limit, with a twinkle in her eye and a smile on their face.

She'd been dancing for over ten years, and she'd been at Club 42 for seven of them. Under her wing, I got some special privileges. Tony would let her run her own credit cards, so anytime a customer wanted a VIP room, she could process it herself—all the other girls had to track down Tony to do it for them, which was problematic when he was nowhere to be found. Sometimes he'd wave both of our house fees, just because.

She played a good ditsy blonde, but she was incredibly smart. I didn't know if she knew how smart she really was. She'd dropped out of high school and had no real formal education. If she applied her stripper sensei skills and used them to major in business somewhere, there was no doubt in my mind she'd be at the top of her class. On the other hand, I knew several people who did graduate at the top of their class in business school, and they worked at coffee shops, so . . . better she continued to channel her intelligence into the VIP room.

"The guy over there just asked me for a double VIP room—let's do it!" I said, running over to Brandi. I was proud of myself because this would be the first time in our stripper relationship that I would initiate a double VIP. She seemed a little confused, and I was moderately insulted.

"Which guy?" she said suspiciously.

"That one! Over there!" I said, pointing to an unassuming medium-build man in gray pleated pants and a white button-down shirt. She scanned him with her X-ray stripper vision.

"He's been here for over an hour and he hasn't tipped anyone," she said.

"Yeah, I know, well maybe he was saving it for someone special," I said. "Like us!" I was so excited, and she was so not excited—she kept staring him up and down and scanning the room. Perhaps the time had come when the student had surpassed the teacher! Or at least, gotten somewhere close. She still wasn't convinced, but she walked in his direction anyways.

"So, baby, you wanna take us to VIP?" she said. I stood next to her, pushing my glasses up and down my nose like a proper nerdy sidekick.

"Yes. Yes I do. I would like to purchase a private VIP room," he said in a completely monotone voice.

"Alright! Let's do it!" I said. I mean, sure, the guy seemed kind of weird, but it's normal for people to come in here and not know how to interact with us. I was a shy nerd after all, so I knew just how to fix it. I could read him *Harry Potter* or, like, talk to him about chess or something while Brandi and I took turns riding his cock outside of his pants.

"That's $400 for a half hour, and that doesn't include tip. We take cash or cards," she said matter-of-factly. She was usually much more flirtatious with the customers. Perhaps I should have just danced for this unenthusiastic man myself. This was not the same Brandi I was used to.

I noticed her glancing over at Tony in the corner of the club. They were communicating something to each other, but I wasn't sure what. They exchanged several meaningful stares, and then Tony ran in the direction of his office. The customer took out four hundred-dollar bills and held them in his hands.

"If I pay you this cash, would you perform oral sex on me in the VIP room?" he asked. Jeez. I'd had customers hint at doing "extras" before, but they were never so straightforward about it. What a polite way to ask such an impolite question.

"Nope. We don't do that here," Brandi replied.

"But don't worry baby! We will still have a lot of fun!" I added, trying to lighten the mood. Brandi had her arms folded and didn't seem at all amused. What the hell was going on? Why was she not taking this guy's money and trying to get everything else in his savings account along with it?

"Is there anyone I could talk to here about purchasing crack/cocaine in this establishment?" he asked. Okay, so he wasn't going to be interested in me reading any *Harry Potter* passages. Apparently this guy was into blow jobs, and crack.

"Nope! No one here, at all, has any of that," Brandi said. "You should take your money and go somewhere else, this is a licensed gentlemen's club that runs 100 percent legally," Brandi added. And then, we all sat there in silence. I didn't think this interaction could get any more awkward than it already was, but I was wrong.

A group of a dozen or so armed policemen, a few in actual riot gear, and a giant, unfriendly dog with a K9 vest on it burst through the double doors. As you might assume, it wasn't here as an emotional support animal for any of the strippers.

"Usually the undercover agents come in a week or two before a raid. Did you not sync up your calendars or something?" Brandi put her hands on her hips and frowned at the guy who clearly was not going to be getting a lap dance.

TJ immediately stopped playing music. I'd say there was a record scratch, but there were no records to scratch here. It was definitely just a series of mouse clicks, and all the colorful epileptic blinking lights and fake smoke came to a complete halt. The girls in the club screamed, and the customers all got up and made a beeline for the door. The way that so many horny men ran in the opposite direction of so many naked women defied the basic laws of human nature.

Brandi grabbed my arm and dragged me toward the middle of the pandemonium with the screaming topless women in heels and sparkly thongs. They all attempted to re-dress themselves, while still panicking.

"What the hell is going on?" I whispered to Brandi.

"Just try to blend in and stay quiet," she replied. I didn't want to ask any more questions, but I did have a whole lot of them. This was an operation right in the middle of Times Square, with a sign out front, and a flyer guy forcing people to come in. If this was some kind of illegal operation, then they were sure doing a bad job of hiding themselves.

"Everybody, calm down, I need you all to follow my instructions and we'll be out of here as soon as possible," said a large, stocky officer with a tag on his uniform that read "JOHNSON." "I need everyone to get out your IDs and hand them to me," he added.

"Officer, can't you see we're naked? We don't exactly have our wallets on us," Brandi retorted. The other girls laughed, and so did I. I'm not entirely sure if laughing at armed policemen was the smartest thing to do, but it certainly lightened the mood. The K9 dog sniffed around the carpet of the club. This carpet had to have been there since the '70s, and it simply wouldn't be fair to blame any of us for any remnants of narcotics that might be inter-woven into the fibers. Someone needed to explain to the dog that this was just a case of a long-overdue recarpeting.

"Where's the locker room in here?" Officer Johnson

turned to TJ to ask this question, which was ridiculous since he was one of the only people in here at the moment that never used the locker room. But naturally, the officer was looking at the only man in the room as the person of authority, even though the only authority TJ had was over what songs got played and what color the lights were.

"It's upstairs," TJ replied, and he pointed toward the stairs.

"Officer, why do you need our IDs? Is this a drug raid, or a sex trafficking raid? I'm guessing you didn't bring the dog here to sniff out underage strippers. Most of us don't feel comfortable sharing our personal information with you. I know a lot of you officers come in here asking for weird shit on your off hours." I saw some of the officers smirk. I scanned the room to see if any of their crotches came into memory, but none of them were ringing a bell. Brandi continued. "If this is a drug search, focus on what you came here to do, and don't compromise our fuckin' safety." I had never seen this side of Brandi before, and I was seriously impressed. She didn't even flinch as she flexed her knowledge to the pack of officers in her micro bikini, while all the other girls stood around trembling. This apparently was not her first stripper raid rodeo.

Suddenly Tony walked out of the bathroom. As soon as the door opened, the drug dog started barking and sniffing like crazy. It even let out a few dribbles of pee on the carpet as it lost control of itself, which would just be one added reason to get a new fucking carpet here.

"Officers! Good seeing you back here. How can I help you?" Tony said, trying to speak as loudly as possible over the barking dog.

"Everyone stay fucking still!" said a cop in riot gear,

raising his gun. I mean, were we getting our IDs or were we standing still? What the hell was going on here? And what was with the gun? Did they plan to shoot at a brick of cocaine if they found it? We didn't exactly have anywhere on us we could possibly conceal a weapon. We could barely find a way to conceal our own nipples.

Several of the cops ran into the bathroom, while the other cops kept an eye on the group of petrified strippers. I heard Brandi mumble underneath her breath, "Tony, you fucking idiot."

Moments later, the leader of this raid came out of the bathroom with several dripping wet extra-large Ziploc bags. Some were filled with an assortment of colorful pills, and some were full of what appeared to be cocaine. Brandi put her head in her hand.

Apparently when Tony was trained as a drug dealer, he'd skipped the lesson on how to flush drugs down the toilet properly and efficiently.

"Well," Officer Johnson chuckled. "Looks like each and every one of you are accomplices here in a drug ring— how many bags of cocaine did your manager get you to sell with every lap dance?" He looked directly at Brandi. If there was some stripper drug ring going on here, I was actually offended no one asked me to be part of it, and I certainly didn't deserve to go to jail for something I was so inconsiderately left out of.

Several girls started crying. I knew a few of them were mothers, and some were battling to get citizenship. I mean, being an accomplice in a drug ring doesn't look good on your record in any circumstance, but I imagined it would be a lot worse if you were waiting for a work visa to be processed.

While I was still incredibly offended that Brandi, someone I really considered a friend here, didn't invite me to her secret drug ring with Tony, I put my ego aside and focused on the problem at hand. Was there anything I could do to smooth this over? Maybe I could try to flirt with the officers . . . or maybe that would make everything even worse.

To see Naomi try to flirt with Officer Johnson, turn to page 75.

To see what happens if Naomi keeps her mouth shut, turn to page 77.

"**O**fficer Johnson!" I said, squishing my *B* cups together and batting my eyelashes behind my taped, thick-rimmed, lens-free glasses. "Is there ANYTHING else I could do to make this better?"

This sentence had seemed to work fabulously in a cop-themed film I'd watched on Pornhub just the other night. And Officer Johnson did, in fact, have the bulging muscles and industrial-strength handcuffs needed to satisfy this plotline.

"Excuse me?" he replied, frowning. "You seem like a nice girl, don't make me write you up for solicitation of an officer."

"I can be nice, or . . . I can be REALLY bad," I suggested. I mean, clearly, he was flirting back. Right? He really left that one open. Also, why was it that even when I was almost getting arrested for being an accomplice to an underground drug ring at a strip club, in a short skirt that showed off my actual asshole, somehow I was still typecast as a "nice girl?" Humph.

Brandi grabbed my arm and hissed, "What are you doing? Just be quiet!"

I faced Brandi, my fake glasses slipping down my nose, and turned around, lifted up my skirt, and showed Officer Johnson my ass. "The officer here is going to punish me," I said.

"No. No he's not. Just stop it!" she said, and she stepped in front of me, ruining any chance of this heroic fantasy playing out. "None of us are accomplices in a drug ring, because *Tony* here is just an asshole customer in *my* club."

Officer Johnson's mouth opened, and then snapped shut. He turned to Tony, whose smirk was impressive for someone in the middle of being handcuffed.

"What is she talking about?" Officer Johnson asked Tony.

Brandi cleared her throat. "What *she* is talking about is that *she* is the manager here. And *she* would like you to get this drug-dealing asshole out of her club!"

To go *back and see what happens if Naomi keeps her mouth shut, turn to page 77.*

To *continue with Naomi in this fantasy, turn to page 79.*

I opened my mouth, took a deep breath, and attempted to speak—but I looked straight at the gun being pointed toward my face, and I froze. Perhaps today was not the day to be some kind of martyr who dies on the stiletto cross to save the strippers.

"Alright guys," Tony said. "You caught me. Took you long enough, assholes. But guess what? I resigned as the manager a couple of weeks ago. I'm just here hanging out! You know, just a customer, looking for some new customers for my drug business. Too bad none of my old friends here wanted to buy any drugs. I guess I'll have to hit up Pumps in Queens instead. The ladies there are a little more rough around the edges."

"What the fuck are you talking about, Tony?" the officer said. Apparently, they were old pals.

"I said, I'm not the manager here anymore, so none of the girls are an accomplice to anything." His tone was firm. "Take me down to the station, I've still got a cell with my name on it."

"If you're not the manager, then who is?" the officer asked. Tony turned to Brandi.

"I am, officer," Brandi said.

"What?" The officer seemed genuinely confused by this turn of events.

"Yes. I'm the manager here. And I'd like this drug-dealing piece of shit out of my club," Brandi said.

To go back and see Naomi try to flirt with Officer Johnson, turn to page 75.

To continue with Naomi in this fantasy, turn to page 79.

"Aww—it's always good seeing you again, Christina!" Tony said. I knew this was Brandi's legal name. I guess calling her that . . . sounded more managerial?

All the girls were dead silent, though the dog could not stop barking at the large supply of drugs right in front of it. It must be really exciting to be a drug dog who's just found so many drugs.

"I have my license and all my paperwork downstairs. I'd be happy to go get it for you if you take the gun out of my fucking face," Brandi said.

"That's what you wear to work as a manager?" Officer Johnson said, scoffing at her.

"I'm the manager at a strip club. Not a Sunday school. Are you gonna write me up on a violation of dress code? What is this?"

The officers all shifted, confused. Tony and Brandi kept exchanging looks, having a full-length discussion with their eyes. I had no idea what plans they were secretly scheming, but I did know that Brandi had everything completely under control.

The cops escorted Tony and all the drugs out of the building. The girls turned to Brandi, unsure of what to do next.

"Alright everyone . . . let's get back to work! Come on TJ, put the music back on! Joey, get out there and hand out some flyers. Let's get some life back in here and make some money! If anyone's got any questions, come find me. I'll be in my office," she said. Everyone cheered, moments later the music came back on, and all of the strippers breathed an enormous sigh of relief. We conversed with one another, hugged each other, and a few cursed Tony's name for getting us into that mess.

Brandi turned the other direction and walked toward the office. I followed her in there and sat down in the very same place that I'd met her, only this time, she was on the other side of the desk.

"So, do you want to fill me in on . . . anything?" I nervously asked.

"No, not really. There are some things that are just better if you don't know," she laughed.

"So are you really the manager?" I said.

"Well for now . . . technically, yes. And technically, I guess I have been for a while. I just haven't really showed up for work."

"What?" I said.

"Doesn't matter," she replied. "Anyways, I want you to go home—"

"You're firing me!" I gasped.

"No! I want you to go home, and report back tomorrow at 5:00 p.m. I'm promoting you to the night shift." She winked at me. I didn't know if the wink was a code for something else, like perhaps an invitation to the secret drug ring, or if I was actually being promoted to the night shift with a flirtatious invitation.

"Really?!" I said.

"Oh yeah, really. And you better be ready. It's a whole other game here at night. It's fucking packed. Go get some new clothes, get some rest, and bring your *A* game tomorrow. We've got a huge bachelor party coming tomorrow night, and I'm gonna put you on stage when they first get here." She smiled, her bikini still just barely covering her nipples.

"You got it boss!" I said.

I was about to walk out, but I hesitated. I wasn't entirely sure how appropriate it would be to say what I wanted to say, but I'd just had a gun pointed in my face ten minutes ago, and I was pretty sure she was partly responsible for it happening, so all rules about what was "appropriate" had gone out the window.

"I'm gonna miss doing doubles with you," I said.

"Well," she replied, her mouth quirking up. "You don't have to. I have a really great private VIP room right here that you're welcome to any time." She winked at me and said, "Come here, Harry Potter."

I climbed over the desk and jumped into her managerial chair, and I kissed her for several minutes. Then I got down on my knees and ate her pussy as she shuffled papers around and picked up the phone to yell at soda suppliers and such.

Let me tell you, it was a whole lot sexier when she did it.

THE END

To go back and find a different fantasy, turn to page 119.

"Um, that actually sounds a little too advanced for me! Thanks for the invite though, I'll catch up with you later."

She shrugged her shoulders, kissed Tony on the cheek, and left the office. I sat in complete silence, unsure of what to do next. The phone on his desk starting ringing, which was impressive because it was such an old phone I'd thought it was like, a prop, a set piece to make the room more office-like. He picked it up and immediately started cursing at the person on the other end about a missing shipment of coconut water. I saw this as my cue to leave, but I hoped that his yelling would resolve the problem, because I did love coconut water.

I wandered back upstairs and found myself back on the strip club's main floor. It took my eyes a moment to re-adjust to the frantic club lighting. I wandered around aimlessly, and I didn't seem to be the only one who was unsure of what to do—there were about a dozen customers sitting around an empty stage, staring blankly at nothing but revolving disco lights and a pole. Were they all imagining someone up there? What was going on?

A moment later, I saw a stressed guy in a Hawaiian shirt and baggy black pants with headphones around his neck running through the floor toward me. He stopped me in my tracks. The sight was jarring, perhaps because Hawaiian shirts and headphones were normally synonymous with fun times, vacation, and tiki drinks . . . anything but stress.

"Hey! New girl, what's your name?"

"Oh um . . . Naomi but . . . I don't really—" I started.

"All my dancers are in VIP, and I need someone on stage, stat. Can you hop on there?"

"Um, sure! Yeah, sure! No problem," I replied. Look at me. My first day on the job, and I was saving the strip club already. What would they even have done had I not stumbled in here today? How would they function? There were horny men staring at an empty stage, and I was the only one who could fix it.

"Thanks." And he disappeared into the darkness of the DJ booth, looking less stressed as he walked away, slightly closer to the energy of someone on a beach in Hawaii.

I got back on the stage. A completely different crowd of people surrounded it now. When I was on stage before, the "crowd" had been disconnected—individual men ignoring each other. Now, there were about a dozen people surrounding the stage, and they were all interacting with one another. Their ties were loosened, and some of their jackets were on the backs of their chairs. If I had to guess, they were younger professionals between the ages of twenty-five and thirty-five. It was early afternoon, and apparently this was when the more rowdy suited men came in. A loose tie and an unbuttoned collar is about as rowdy as you can get in a club with no alcohol.

I walked out to the tune of "You Shook Me All Night Long" by AC/DC. Everyone knows this song, but mostly the chorus. The group of suits all collectively sang different versions of the song, all shouting what they thought the words were, until the chorus kicked in and they finally sang in unison.

I slowly unbuttoned my polka-dot dress. I made this seem intentional and seductive, but I'd learned today that it was virtually impossible to unbutton this dress at a fast pace. The tempo of this song worked nicely with a slow unbutton. Thankfully, I was able to slide it off just as the first chorus kicked in and the united sing-along started. The hipster inside of me was silently judging all of them— that's just what we do when we see groups of people who are financially stable enjoying themselves. However, the naked side of me on stage appreciated all the excitement, even though most of it was for AC/DC.

I threw my legs up in the air and had them land on one of the guys' shoulders. The entire crowd got a kick out of this, so I decided to think of ways to interact with each person by the stage. I pulled someone's tie, I took a fedora off someone's head and put it on mine, I grabbed some-one's root beer and sucked on the bottle like it was a tasty glass penis, and I pulled my panties slightly away from my pelvis, as if I was opening a wallet, motioning for the guys in the crowd to slide a dollar bill in there.

I felt like a naked circus clown, or a silent stand-up comedian. Neither of which exactly sounds all that empowering, but the truth was, this was a large group of men, and it was my job to control their chaos. And I was doing it! It turned out it took a lot less mental energy to entertain the perverts earlier. These people wanted nudity *and* some kind of vaudeville, and that's not an easy feat, even when your stripper career hasn't just started an hour ago.

I noticed that a shorter, stocky guy in a gray suit with

curly brown hair left the group, and from the corner of my eye I saw him walk to the DJ booth. He seemed to be the most vocal Angus Young enthusiast, and whatever he was doing, I hoped he came back before the chorus kicked in because it wouldn't be the same without him. He kinda led the sing-along, and his leadership encouraged the group to throw more dollars on stage.

But before we could hit another chorus, the song suddenly switched. I wasn't at all prepared for this. I had just gotten into a good rhythm here, incorporating some hair flips and perfectly timed boob and butt shaking when, instead of a rock and roll sing-along, the 50 Cent birthday song came on, and quite frankly . . . I had no idea what to do.

"Attention everyone! We have a birthday in the house! Josh! Where you at?" the DJ shouted, and the crowd clapped and hooted, all pointing at a skinny blond guy with large glasses and bright blue pants. Not a distinguished navy blue, a bright blue similar to the color of an iPhone text message. His expression was bashful, and his friends were pulling on his arm. He was so skinny, I feared if they kept going, they might actually pull his limbs apart. A big bald man wearing all black and an earpiece put a chair up on the stage.

"Come on! Josh! Get up there!" the DJ insisted. I mean, Josh very clearly didn't want to come up on stage, and didn't my input matter here? Shouldn't Josh and I get a say in this?

I've always hated it when people go behind your back and tell the waitress at Applebee's that it's your birthday, and then, BAM, everyone in the restaurant is clapping and singing, and there are balloons at your table, when all you're trying to do is eat some onion rings with your friends. I had experience as both the waitress at Applebee's who sang too many "Happy Birthdays," and a customer at Applebee's who has had "Happy Birthday" sung to them, and I knew full well that it was humiliating for both parties involved.

Poor Josh. Or, no wait, poor me. I had barely learned how to properly take my dress off—how could anyone possibly put me in charge of whatever this birthday chair ceremony was? What on earth was I supposed to do here? I looked up at the DJ for help, but couldn't catch his eye. I was on my own. Josh reluctantly walked onto the stage, assisted by the same guy who'd placed the chair there. The 50 Cent song continued to play, and ... then I was standing there in nothing but small heels and my underwear with a "Josh" to entertain. I had to think of something fast.

I presented the chair like I was Vanna White. Josh's inconsiderate friends clapped their hands and shouted for him to sit in the chair. Peer-pressured, Josh sat down. I stood behind him, and I loosened his tie. Of all the guys in the group, this one had the most tightly tied tie, which was fortunate for me because it gave me something to work with. I loosened it until it completely became unraveled, and then, on the spur of the moment, I decided to take this tie and use it as a blindfold. Because that was ... kinky I guess? And also, that way, much like me, Josh would have no idea what was coming next.

I tied the blindfold around his eyes. *Now what?* I theatrically unbuttoned his shirt, and his friends applauded and shouted stuff like "OH SHIT!" because, I guess, it was humiliating for a man to *gasp* remove clothing in here, even though the entire purpose of this establishment was to celebrate nudity. After his shirt was unbuttoned, I reached down and pinched his nipples. He winced in pain. I'm not going to lie, I kind of liked it.

"Awww Josh, does that hurt?!" the DJ said over the speakers, patronizing him. His friends threw tens and twenties on the stage. I had no idea my nipple pinching could be so valuable. I pinched them harder, pulling his skin until they looked like little tents on his chest. He yelled "Ouch!" and his friends continued to scream and cheer. I suddenly felt a little sorry for Josh, and I let go of the nipples, patting them softly.

What else could I do to the blindfolded Josh over there? Hmmmm. I saw he had a skinny leather navy belt on. It clasped together with some kind of gold, manly belt logo, a brand I definitely wasn't familiar with. I swiftly managed to pull the belt off, and as I did, I arched my ass toward the crowd. I took Josh's hand, pulled him off the chair, and placed him on all fours. It was kind of incredible that he just went along with everything so easily. All twelve of his big manly friends could barely get him on this stage, but I got him blindfolded and on his hands and knees without him even flinching. What a good boy Josh was!

I glanced down and noticed how loose Josh's pants were. I smiled a devious smile, and took it upon myself to pull his pants down, revealing his thin white Hanes boxers. I found this set-up to be completely fair, since now we were both on stage in just our underwear.

But really, why was I still in my underwear? I was so busy undressing him and finding creative ways to use his own clothing as weapons that I sort of forgot to take my own panties off. I bent over and removed my panties, and then . . . I went over to little Joshy's mouth, forced it open, and shoved my panties into his mouth. The DJ chimed in, delighted.

"Josh is that lunch? Or is that dessert?!" The crowd roared with laughter.

"You want a side of fries with those panties?" the DJ said, and everyone got a real kick out of this, too. Of course, he could have washed my panties down with some carrot juice if he'd liked, but for fries he'd need a different establishment.

Now that I had him on all fours with my panties in his mouth and his almost-bare ass sticking out, I whipped him with his own belt.

"How old are you turning Josh?" the DJ said.

Josh attempted to answer, but all he could do was mumble since my panties were in his mouth, and as we have seen, Josh was a very well-behaved guy. He was not gonna drop those panties until I let him. Even though we hadn't really communicated at all, I could feel his body language. Josh would not disobey me.

His friends shouted numbers, and from the chaos in the crowd I gathered that he was turning twenty-five. I made the crowd do a count of twenty-five lashes, my strokes getting progressively harder each time. I was enjoying myself and quite frankly, I could tell . . . so was Josh.

I could sense that the 50 Cent birthday song was coming to an end, and I wanted to close on a high note. I climbed on top of Josh, as if he were my pony. I used his belt/my whip as like a "giddy-up" mechanism and forced him to give me a ride around the stage. He came to a stop at some point, and the DJ taunted him, telling him he had to go fully around the stage. I whipped his ass again and forced him into motion. As I rode on his back, I saw his buddies throwing their last remaining bills at me.

The song came to an end. I got off of Josh, took the blindfold off him, and put my hand underneath his mouth, motioning for him to please return my panties. I gave him back his belt, and then I raised his arm up like he had just won a UFC match, and everyone clapped for him. I gave him a hug and a kiss on the cheek. "Happy Birthday Josh," I whispered in his ear.

He gave me the most bashful smile. He looked humiliated yet lustful, with puppy dog eyes and mussed hair, and while I couldn't hear him, I saw his lips mouth back, "Thank you."

After I collected all the cash on the stage, I went straight to the "bar" and asked for a bottle of water. The girl with the blue corset was still there. I felt like I hadn't seen her in years, so much had changed since the last time I saw her. In actuality, I'd only just met her a few hours ago.

"That was awesome!" she said as she handed me a bottle of water.

"Oh! Really? I had . . . no idea what to do up there. Was that what I was supposed to do?" I replied.

"Well, most girls just kinda sit on their laps and wiggle around for a few seconds," she laughed.

"Oh! That was . . . the last thing I thought to do," I said honestly.

"My name is Rachel, by the way."

"Oh! Yes, sorry, I'm . . . Naomi," I replied. I hadn't had the opportunity to come up with a nom de plume yet, but I felt a kinship with this girl, like we went way back, and I felt comfortable with her knowing my true identity.

"Well Naomi," she leaned in. "I work at a dungeon a few nights a week. You should come to one our play parties sometime! From how you acted up there . . . I think you'd really like it." She winked at me.

How interesting. The cute girl serving water and juice, who also happened to be the only clothed female in here, had a side that I certainly wasn't expecting. But I also wasn't expecting myself to be a stripper when I woke up this morning, so I guess you really can't assume anything.

To take the information on the dungeon, turn to page 91.

To turn down the invitation to the dungeon, turn to page 117.

Two months had passed, and Club 42 had somehow gone from being an ironic, accidental experiment to an actual career. I'd paid off a credit card whose debt had haunted me for years. I'd never paid anything above a minimum payment on any credit card before, so the thrill of logging into my account and paying off the whole damn thing made me feel like I was a Rockefeller or something. Granted, it was a card with a $700 limit on it, but it had accumulated about $500 in interest, and I basically thought I'd be paying it off until I was ninety.

I told a few of my friends about the job, and those friends told all of their friends, and then through the very few degrees of separation in Brooklyn, everyone in the borough knew. I could feel people whisper about it as I went to the same local spots I used to, and dating became quite complicated. I felt desired and diseased at the same time. I'd spend the day being worshipped by people I had nothing in common with and no real attraction to, and then I'd get ignored by men after sleeping with them once, men who listened to the same music I did, lived in the same neighborhood I did, and even sometimes went to the same college I went to.

I enjoyed the job, though. I enjoyed making small talk with other naked women from so many different walks of life, in between us exposing our private areas to pop music on stage and dry-humping customers. It was a unique comradery with a group of women I'd certainly never felt before. However, even though I had the folds of each of my co-workers' labias memorized, they were aquaintances at best. We were, after all, in competition for the same lap so things stayed both cordial and competitve. The only girl I'd actually become quite friendly with was Rachel, the nonalcoholic bartender.

So, on a random Saturday evening, after being ghosted by a musician named Rob that I had tentative plans to play Skee-Ball with, I texted Rachel and asked her about the parties she'd always tell me about. It seemed like an event happened in this underworld just about every weekend, and this weekend was as good as any to start. I was sick of constantly putting myself out for these . . . what do you call them . . . "fuckboys," and also, don't tell anyone, but I was getting sick of Skee-Ball. After you've gotten the ball in the top hole like four times in your life, there's very little to strive for. I deserved to be treated with respect, and I also deserved more exciting weekend entertainment than an ironic arcade game from the '70s.

Rachel replied to me with an address and a code word to say at the door. She also told me to wear all black. I slipped on a pair of tight black jeans, a black blazer, black heels, and a black camisole top. I looked more like someone ready to go work at Lord & Taylor than I did a dominatrix, but, as I'd learned from whipping a birthday boy with his own belt and blindfolding him with his own tie, the dominatrix comes from within you. If your twisted heart is in the right place, you can make anything work.

I arrived at an unmarked warehouse in the meatpacking district. It was in-between two other warehouses that were marked, which was how I knew that this was the correct one. One guy sat in a tall chair outside the door. He had a septum piercing and an eyebrow piercing, and two sleeves of completely filled-in black tattoo. He waited for me to speak.

"Um . . . pineapple?" I said. This was the password I was given via text.

He slid open a heavy metal door and pointed me toward a steep narrow staircase. I walked up the stairs, and as I got higher with each step, I began to hear heavy bass from some dark-sounding industrial music, bits and pieces of people's conversations, and hard, echoing "thwacks" and sex moans. From the sound of it, it was going to be a good night.

I got to the top of the stairs and entered a universe that made Club 42 look like an afternoon at my grandmother's house. In the middle of the room was a big black leather X with a buff man strapped to it, wearing nothing but latex tighty-whities. He was being flogged all over his chest by a tall blonde in a shiny latex catsuit and ten-inch platform stiletto heels. These were the same heels I always *wanted* to purchase when I went to the stripper store on 8th Avenue where I now got my clothes for work, but I never got them because it would be impossible to dance in them. The five- to six-inch heels were the most practical working stripper shoes—they were tall enough to separate you from the general non-stripper heel-wearing public, but not so tall that you'd trip and fall on yourself while seductively dancing in them. These ten-inch heels were not made for dancing. They were made for beating.

Another woman came over and assisted the catsuit blonde with her beating, using what appeared to be some kind of electrical rod to shock the buff man on his balls. The man winced in pain, and the women gave each other sinister looks as they continued their torture. After multiple whacks and zaps, he was patted on the head, and on the balls, and called a good boy.

I was on sensory overload in this black and red loft, which was filled with smoke and blasting electronic music. Standing to my right was what appeared to be a sophisticated couple. The man was in a three-piece black suit, and the woman next to him wore a long, black, sparkly flapper dress, with her hair in pin curls, and a feather hat. However, instead of a clutch as an accessory, she held a leash in her hand, with a human in a full latex suit and mask attached to it. The human was kneeling on the floor, sitting there patiently like a well-behaved dog while its owner had whatever conversation she was having.

Trying not to ogle too much, I made my way over to the leather couch in the corner. A woman approached, wearing a gag in her mouth that was attached to an entire contraption on her head, which itself was attached to a silver tray with cocktails and cigarettes on it. She couldn't exactly speak, but I could see by her expression that she was offering me whatever was on the tray. I grabbed a cocktail and a cigarette. I didn't normally smoke, but I also didn't normally go to dungeons that required passwords to get in, so . . . *c'est la vie*.

I lit up the cigarette, and a thin man scurried over to me on his hands and knees, with a black gag around his mouth that had an ashtray connected to it. I ashed my cigarette into his mouth receptacle, as if this was something completely ordinary to me, as if all my ashtrays were humans. I nodded at him, fully expecting him to scurry away, but he just sat there, obediently. So I continued to smoke my cigarette and ash into his tray, thinking . . . I may have found a friend here.

"Naomi! Hey!" said a stunning girl in a long black mermaid latex dress, who was now standing right in front of me.

"Um, hi?" I said, trying to think of how this girl knew me. But after a few brief moments it registered that this mermaid was Rachel. I did a double take.

"Oh, my god, hi! Rachel, wow . . . holy shit!" I replied. I was used to seeing her in Uggs and a corset—normally her hair was up and she wore very minimal makeup. Tonight, she had a perfectly eyelined cat eye, bright red lips, and long glamorous lashes. She stood tall, taller than me, and I could see high open-toe stiletto heels with red bottoms on her feet. These were *not* from the stripper store. These could not be purchased for $80–$120. These were Louboutins, and even my most lucrative day shift would barely pay for the heel of this shoe. I was taken aback. I was the one who spent the day opening the inside of my labia to strangers, while she opened bottles of water, fully clothed.

"This place is really neat!" I said, as I ashed into my human ashtray.

"I'm so glad you like it! You finally came," she said, noticing my ashtray. "Good boy, Ashey." She crouched down, and he looked grateful with his eyes. Ashey the Ashtray. I liked it. It sounded like the name of some kind of underdog superhero, with an underwhelming super-power.

"Well, this is just the surface. You have to experience what happens in one of the back rooms to really see what goes on here. Those rooms are for members only, but I know someone who works here who can hook you up!" She winked, making it obvious that she was the girl who worked here who was now going to hook me up. "What type of kinky play are you in the mood for?" she asked. This was a very good question—what did I want to do?

To see Naomi dominate someone, turn to page 97.

To see Naomi get dominated, turn to page 106.

Rachel brought me to a back room. I felt bad leaving Ashey behind—he seemed a little bereft as I walked away. Hopefully another smoker would come along and fill the void, or, more accurately, the ashtray. The room was home to some kind of long, leather, rectangular bondage ottoman with hooks on the side. There was a cage with a leather mattress on top of it, and a wall with a grate on it that was covered with whips and paddles and cuffs and strap-ons galore. So many different torture devices—some were self-explanatory (like a paddle or a flogger) and some, well some weren't. For instance, there was a giant 2,000-watt lithium battery connected to nipple clamps. I suppose if there was a power outage someone's nipples could be used as a generator, or something.

"I'll be right back with your own personal assigned slave," she said excitedly.

"Well, alright!" I said.

"I've got one you'll have a lot of fun with. He's here to serve you. He's interested in corporal punishment, and some dildo training, and of course whatever might please you!"

"You know I have no real experience with this, right? I don't want to hurt anyone," I said.

"Oh, he's a pain slut! He wants to get hurt!" She laughed and pulled down a thick paddle that looked like it had some extra padding on it, along with a giant flogger and a harness with a decently sized cock on it. Like, a nine-incher, or something in that range.

"Here's some good beginner toys to play with. They look like they hurt a lot more than they actually do—see?" She grabbed the flogger and swiftly snapped it against me. It was an exciting little shock to my system, and I giggled.

"You can go as hard as you want with it and it won't break the skin. Don't worry." Her explanation was so matter-of-fact, for a sex toy demonstration. "The safe-word we use here is 'mercy,' so STOP IMMEDIATELY if he says that. And since you're not using any hoods or gags, we don't need an alternate," she added. "Oh, and use one of these condoms for the strap-on." She pointed to a red leather box full of condoms. I loved how everything here was made of leather. Seriously, even the trash cans.

It took me a moment to process all this, but it made sense. The anticipation of this controlled torture play date was already exciting me far more than any "real" date I'd been on in a while. "Got it!" I said. It was incredible to see how fierce and dominant Rachel's personality was here. At Club 42 she was so demure, and so polite, and so soft-spoken. Here, she was assertive. I'd have agreed to just about anything she asked me to do. I suppose ... that's what a dominatrix specializes in, after all.

"I'll go get him. In the meantime, get changed!" She handed me a leather corset that zipped down the middle, along with the harness.

I removed my sophisticated suburban department store clothing and put on the corset. I was thankful that it zipped down the middle—it felt like a cheater, intro-to-corset garment, and I was okay with that. I pulled up the harness, and chuckled to myself that my pants were a penis. The penis itself was rather sturdy and covered a good amount of the surface area around my crotch. A whole bunch of thigh-high boots in various sizes were lined up in the corner of the room. I grabbed a pair and put them on. Zipping up my entire thigh in tight PVC was like giving my skin a shiny makeover. I stood tall, holding the flogger, with my boots and my large erect cock, and I felt powerful, and also horny, but this was a very different kind of horny for me. It was like my ego was horny. I wanted to fill my sexual senses with power. I didn't just want to get off, I wanted someone to work for it.

Rachel opened the door and brought in a guy in his mid-thirties. He wore a black T-shirt and a black button-down, and he had a latex mask on his face with the eyes, mouth, and nose holes cut out. He also had unhooked leather cuffs around his hands and his ankles. I liked this aesthetic. It was like business professional and kinky at the same time. I couldn't tell what his face looked like, but it also didn't matter. He was there to do whatever I said!

"Now, BEHAVE!" Rachel said to the slave. She caught my eye and smiled as she walked out.

"How can I serve you, Mistress?" he said. Wow. What a polite and exciting way to address me. I'd never been anyone's Mistress before, and I didn't want to get too ahead of myself, but I did have an appointment at the DMV next week to get a new license, and I was already wondering if "Mistress" could be my legal prefix. I thought I'd feel awesome all the time.

I peered down at my big cock, and I looked at the slave.

"You can start by getting down on your knees and sucking my cock," I said.

He immediately did exactly as I said, attempting to get

as much of my cock down his throat as he could. I knew what he was going through. I'd done the same thing when I'd had post-breakup sex with one of my ex-boyfriends, thinking one good blow job could reel him back in. That type of blow-for-your-life job was what I was getting right now. He stopped and gasped for air, and I smacked him on the cheek.

"Did I tell you to stop?" I said.

"I'm sorry, Mistress!" he replied, and seriously, he sounded so genuinely sorry. I wanted to accept his apology, but I knew I couldn't.

"Sorry? I don't think you're sorry. I think you just can't handle my cock." I was full of zingers, I just don't know where they came from.

"No, Mistress! Let me prove myself to you. Please." I could see genuine remorse and fear in his big brown eyes.

"If you can't suck my cock like a real man, then what good are you?" I said. He opened his mouth and tried to suck my cock again, and I pulled away.

"Lay down," I said. I pointed at the leather ottoman. He already had cuffs on his hands and legs, so it was simple to hook him onto the furniture.

My strap-on covered the front of my pussy, but I was able to lift it up just a little, and the opening between the two leather straps was just enough room for my lips to be exposed. I sat down on my slave's face, and he knew exactly what to do.

"You need to earn my cock back. Let's see how good a sex toy you can be," I commanded.

The latex on his face created such a smooth sensation against my pussy. Also, I won't lie, the thrill of having no idea who this man was made me horny. He was a faceless thing, whose purpose was to serve me. He was nothing but a skinny rod with a tongue. He stuck that talented tongue out, and I rode up and down his face, sliding back and forth on his smooth mask, suffocating him with my pussy. His strong tongue was flat against my clit, providing the perfect pressure for me to grind back and forth. I pushed myself deeper into his mouth, so he could swallow and taste my sweet moisture. I had a little bit of goofy fun for a moment and improvised, rubbing my clit right on his nose. I have a very sensitive clit, and just about anything feels good up against it, okay?

I got back to his tongue. Then, I parked my pussy on him and sat still.

"Alright, well, I'm tired of moving myself around. You need to make me cum already," I said. The slave started furiously moving his tongue in little flickers, at a speed faster than some of my vibrators. It's amazing how much effort a man can put into pussy eating when he's frightened. He started sucking on my clit, and I felt the heat of his breath flowing through my insides. It all felt amazing, but I couldn't let him know how well he was doing. I kept my moans to myself. He continued to lick me ferociously, his tongue muscles put to the test. I didn't know how often he did this, but he must have practiced at home. The man had stamina.

"You have ten seconds!" He licked and licked, and I knew . . . I was most definitely going to cum in ten seconds. I was holding it together pretty well, but my pussy felt incredible. I could feel everything tensing up inside of me, my legs shaking.

"Ten, nine, eight, seven..." I said. With each notch down, he sucked on my clit harder. I started pushing my pelvis into him, grinding into him again for even more pressure. By the time I got to one, my pussy juices were going down his throat. I felt such a release. Quite frankly, after such a long stint of shitty one-night stands, combined with never having any privacy in my own apartment, I hadn't had a good orgasm in a while. I'd get turned on at work while I touched my pussy on stage, and sometimes I'd get wet during my lap dances, but it was all a tease. It felt so good to cum inside this guy's mouth, this stranger's mouth, and he appreciated it like no other.

"You're a good boy."

He gulped down my moisture and replied, "Thank you, Mistress" in a deep voice, sounding not unlike a young Morgan Freeman, who . . . had just swallowed a tablespoon of my cum.

I uncuffed him and positioned him on all fours, much like I'd done to birthday Josh on stage. I unhooked his belt and pulled his pants and boxers down to his ankles. Lo and behold, he had a huge boner. He really got off on getting me off, and I found this to be quite beautiful.

"What do we have here?" I said, looking at his fully erect cock, which was partly hiding underneath him since he was on all fours. "Did I give you permission for that?"

"I'm sorry, Mistress. I couldn't help myself!" he replied.

I saw a tiny bit of shiny moisture at the tip of his cock, a drop of pre-cum. I grabbed his dick and looked him in the eyes, faux-furious.

"You understand me, you are not allowed to cum until I give you permission."

"Yes Mistress," he replied. I mean, I knew that's what he was going to say, I just wanted to hear him say it. I scooped up the droplet of pre-cum with my finger and shoved it in his mouth.

Then I grabbed a condom and put it over my dildo. I covered it in lube, which was readily available near all the toys.

"Now, let's see if you can handle my cock," I said.

I slid my cock into his asshole, and I must say, it went in with no effort at all. He had a nicely shaved, smooth ass. This was definitely a guy who left the house hoping to get ass-fucked. I loved the way my cock looked sliding into his asshole. I know there wasn't technically any sensation in my cock, but I could truly feel my own erection. I continued to plow into him, and he thanked me with every stroke. It was my first time doing this, but I felt like a natural. I'd had a cock inside my ass before, so I just followed the commandments and did unto others as I would have them do unto me.

He looked back at me, moaning with pleasure. I slid deeper inside of him, he arched his back and threw his neck back, breathing heavily. I could see pearls of sweat drip from his mask.

I grabbed a latex glove and put it on my right hand. It was like the hottest medical procedure ever done—I began to stroke his cock as I fucked his ass. He started to squirm.

"Stop!" he yelled. Now . . . was I supposed to stop? My instinct was to stop, but I remembered his safeword was "mercy." Not "stop."

"How dare you tell me what to do!" I said. I took my hand off of his cock and I smacked his ass hard, to the point where it turned pink. It turned out my own hand could do more damage than the flogger.

"I'm gonna cum! I don't know if I can stop!" he said. Man, I felt bad for the guy. I could see he really wanted to follow instructions . . . but he also really wanted to take my amazing ass-pounding. The way he worshipped me, and the way he followed instructions, and the way he took my cock so well, these were what made him such a good slave—but these good qualities worked against him right now that his infatuation with me and his cooperative asshole were making him want to explode.

I know I wasn't any kind of expert in this field, but I decided this guy was doing a damn good job, and I was going to go easy on him without letting him know it.

"Why don't you ask me for permission?" I said. "You never know, if you were a good boy today, maybe, I just might say yes," I whispered.

I returned to stroking his cock and pounding his ass.

"Mistress, can I please cum?!" He repeated it again and again and again, until it sounded like he was crying. I stroked his cock a few more times, and I could feel it throbbing in my hand, just aching to cum. The amount of power I had over him was incredible.

"Yes, yes you may."

I plunged deep into his asshole and grabbed his cock, milking his prostate and stroking him to completion. So much semen spilled out of him. I let it spill into my gloved hand. When he was done, I removed the glove and disposed of it in the upscale leather trash can.

He pulled up his pants and collected himself. He got down on his knees as I sat on the leather bondage ottoman. I patted his head—nice and smooth and wrapped in latex.

"Good boy," I said, and I smiled kindly at him. I truly meant it.

"Thank you," he replied, and I knew he meant that too.

I sat there in my post-play moment, patting his head, coming down off my mental and physical high, listening to the reverb of the electronic music outside the door. Enjoying this special Saturday night with a masked stranger whose name I didn't know, feeling a sense of connection I never knew I was looking for, but was glad I found.

To go back and see Naomi get dominated, turn to page 106.

To continue with Naomi in this fantasy, turn to page 115.

"I don't know what it is about me, but I seem to get a lot of requests in the VIP room at work to dominate my customers," I said. It was true. Customers who desired a run-of-the-mill, plain ole naked grinding dance from the other girls would specifically ask me to spit in their face or whip their ass, or call them a pathetic scum of the earth. I was never sure if I was supposed to take it as a compliment or not.

"Well you're a natural!" Rachel said. "I knew that right away—why do you think I invited you here?" She laughed a tinkling laugh.

"Well, I think I just need to really go there to understand what feels so good about being degraded," I suggested.

"You know, the best Doms are often also the best subs!" Rachel said.

"I didn't know that, but it makes sense. Well Rachel . . . I guess . . . I'd like you to . . ." I wasn't sure what the politically correct way was to ask someone to beat you up. But I didn't have to complete my sentence. Rachel grabbed me by the hair and looked into my eyes.

"From this point forward, you do exactly as I say." I obediently nodded. I couldn't believe this was the same girl who served carrot juice in sparkly Uggs.

I followed her into a private room, where I saw a few pieces of bondage furniture and a shelf from floor to ceiling that was full of whips, paddles, chains, ropes, floggers, dildos, clamps, and more. I mean, there were things I couldn't name because I had no idea what they were. This was like a high-end torture boutique.

"Sit!" Rachel said, pointing at me like I was a dog. I sat down on what appeared to be some kind of bondage bed.

"The safe word here is 'mercy,'" she said. "That's what you say if you'd like me to stop, and I will stop immediately."

"Alright!" I replied.

"Do you have any injuries, or any sensitive areas, or trigger words or hard no's I should know about?" she asked.

Already, this was exciting. I'd never been involved in any kind of sexual situation where my medical history came into question. Normally I was just concerned about a guy lasting longer than five minutes, and *not* passing out drunk in the middle of going down on me (which had unfortunately happened . . . more than once).

"No!" I said. I mean, I don't think I had enough sexual experience to even know what my limits were, but I was excited to explore them and figure them out with the same girl who served me coconut water when I needed it.

"Very well then. Now, remove your clothes," she demanded, and I obliged.

She grabbed a bundle of brown rope from the shelf. It looked like a supersized version of the twine I would use to truss a Thanksgiving turkey. She also grabbed a riding crop, a flogger, a few dildos, and a Hitachi Wand. We were standing in silence, and I was both petrified and horny. I was already beginning to understand the appeal of being submissive, and I had barely begun.

Before I knew it, she had started tying me up in the

rope. The bondage bed I was on had various hooks on the sides, which we used to attach the rope. She worked on me methodically, making me stretch my arms and legs out so she could measure how far some of my limbs were from the hooks. This was a kinky math equation, and I was the undetermined variable.

She spread my legs open as far as they could go and tied each ankle to a post on the bed. The rope was surprisingly smooth. It was the same beige color of twine, but it wasn't rough, which was a relief. While I did sign up to be dominated, and I did indeed want to feel like a personal fuck-toy and a slut, I did not want to feel like I was a stack of cardboard on the sidewalk ready to be recycled.

She took my arms and raised them above my head and did the same. I remembered the time my ex-boyfriend and I ordered some kind of bondage tape on Amazon and attempted to use it. He'd bound my hands behind my back, and I'd pretended for as long as I could that it was impossible for me to break out of it, trying to keep up with the sloppy role-play, but eventually, the tape just came apart and we gave up. However, right now, I legitimately could not move. It was a natural reaction to attempt to resist the ropes, to try my best to see how easily I could weasel out of them, and there was absolutely no way at all. If she left the room, I'd be trapped. I was literally at her mercy. There were devices in here that could potentially kill me, if she felt like it . . . and . . . well . . . that was pretty fucking hot.

She grabbed a riding crop and circled around the bed, staring at me with disgust. I could hear each step as her stiletto heels hit the concrete ground. I would have been trembling, if I could have moved.

"You think just because you're a stripper you can handle this?" she said. I wasn't sure what to reply, so I just sort of shook my head. It was somewhere between a no and a yes.

"You think you're so powerful up on that stage. You think you can just bat your eyelashes and shake your pathetic little ass and get anything you want, don't you?" I shook my head again, but she had a point. I genuinely did believe all of the things she was accusing me of right now.

"ANSWER ME WHEN I SPEAK!" she said, and WHACK. She smacked her riding crop hard on my left nipple. I screamed. I wasn't expecting that at all. I could feel a sharp pain in my breast, like I'd just gotten stung by a bee, but, like, a bee that made me horny.

"YES!" I said, getting back to her question of how cool I thought I was.

"YES, WHAT?" she demanded.

"YES, RACHEL!" She whacked my right nipple, which I actually appreciated because my nipples were feeling incredibly uneven, and something about only one of them stinging made everything more painful. Not that I was going to let her know that this second whacking made me feel better.

"YOU HAVE NOT EARNED THE PRIVILEGE TO ADDRESS ME BY MY FIRST NAME. YOU SAY 'YES' OR 'NO MISTRESS' WHEN I ADDRESS YOU. DO YOU UNDERSTAND?"

"Yes . . . Mistress," I replied. I did understand, and I seriously regretted taking for granted all the times I'd called her Rachel. She continued to whack me all over my body with the crop. My nipples, my thighs—she even went down to the other side of the bed and whacked the bottoms of my feet, which hurt more than any other place I was whacked. I yelled and winced in pain … but also, felt compelled to thank her in between the yelling and wincing. I was both thanking her for making me feel good, and thanking her for not murdering me. Thanking her for continuing, and thanking her for stopping. There was so much pain and pleasure and uncertainty, and I had no idea what she was going to do next—no idea what my body could even handle. My lack of power was turning me on so much, at the same time that it was scaring the shit out of me. This was a very intense emotional roller coaster the carrot juice girl and I were having here.

By the time she stopped whacking me, my body was covered in goose bumps. I wasn't sure if I wanted her to whack me again, or if I was relieved that she had stopped. She circled the bed, and I attempted to follow her with my eyes, to try to predict her next move, but I couldn't really see much from this angle.

WHACK! She hit me right on my pussy lips. I screamed. This had to have been the most terrible and incredible feeling I'd ever felt. I wanted an ice pack and an orgasm at the same time. The blood rushed through my body, and this time when I yelled, it was a combination of a sex moan and a scared-for-my-life cry. She shot me a sinister smile and put a latex glove on her hand. With her covered hand, she caressed the goose bumps on my body, and then moved down to my beaten pussy. She jammed two fingers inside.

"Well, what do we have here? It looks like . . . your pussy is wet," my Mistress said. She took her fingers out of my pussy and shoved them in my mouth, I suppose to prove her point that, yes, my pussy was in fact wet. I sucked my own juices off her latex glove.

"Yes Mistress," I said.

"What a little slut you are. Getting wet from your beating!" she said.

"Yes Mistress . . . I am." Not to get too politically incorrect here, but I do enjoy being called a slut. I like the word. I know we're not supposed to use that word anymore, but truthfully I like it. I was glad Rachel, I mean, Mistress, and I were on the same page about this. Perhaps we could get a special sex worker pass to continue to use the word.

She aggressively stuck her fingers back in my pussy, interrupting my thoughts. The lubricated glove was cold at first, but growing warmer. She curled her fingers inside of me and circled my clit with her thumb. Her fingers felt more intense than all the hipster cocks I'd sampled in Brooklyn, combined. The spot she was hitting was creating an ache deep in my abdomen, while the sensation of being totally open to her heightened every pull and push. I wanted to buck against her, and the fact that I couldn't use my legs just made the "wanting" even more intense.

From my angle, I could see her arm moving rapidly and forcefully as her fingers dove in and out, again and again and again. With my body stinging and my pussy dripping, this all felt incredible. I could feel the blood circulation in my hands getting thinner, and my body began to get cold, but my pussy felt so warm. My legs were starting to squirm around, but she used the arm that wasn't inside of me to hold me in place. She was such a small, dainty girl, but she had so much mental and physical force over me.

My pussy was pulsating. I started pushing my pelvis up in the air, and she kept pushing it down and calling me a slut. Eventually I just lost control over everything in my body (not that I had much control to begin with). She pulled away, and . . . gush. A giant puddle of ejaculate poured out of me. Now I understood why these beds were made of leather.

I felt like I was in a complete daze. What the hell had just happened?

"YOU MADE A MESS!" she said. I genuinely felt bad about that, because I did live with a messy roommate, and I absolutely hated when she didn't clean up after herself. Even if her mess wasn't pussy juice, I thought it was incredibly rude. But I had also never tied her up and stopped her from cleaning up her mess. Had I not been tied up right now, I'd have been looking for paper towels immediately.

Instead, I just laid in a puddle of my own squirt, coming down from the orgasm high.

"I'm sorry, Mistress!" I said.

She ignored my apology and dug her fingers into me again. I tried so hard to resist but she kept going, jamming her fingers into my beaten and swollen pussy. I was yelling and screaming, and then . . . she stopped. I was breathing heavily, shaking, my legs twitching on the bed.

"Please Mistress! Please! Help me cum again. Please!" This may sound like an exaggeration, but I was sure I was going to die if I couldn't release myself again. This must have been what it felt like to have blue balls? It was painful with her hands in me, but it was more painful with her hands out of me. My pussy needed simultaneous pain and pleasure right now—it was screaming for attention like a wild beast.

She grabbed some clothespins that were strung together with twine. I figured this ancient contraption was there in case . . . you know . . . any of the dominatrixes needed to do their laundry or something. I mean, there was so much stuff on the shelf that looked kinky and sophisticated—between the rope and these clothespins, why was she using the stuff that looked like it came from Home Depot, instead of a high-end BDSM shop? Was there something about me that inspired her to get so . . . rustic?

I'm sure you won't be surprised when I tell you that she did *not* use the clothespins to hang dry any of her delicate dominatrix garments. She clipped the pins on my already-stinging nipples.

"AHHHHHHHHH!" I cried. A gust of warmth circled around my upper body. She jammed her fingers back into me, and I started gushing again. I screamed more loudly than I think I ever had before. I worried I was making too much noise, but I suppose this type of noise was normal, and even encouraged in a dungeon.

"WHAT A GOOD SLUT!" she said. Phew. I was glad to be doing a good job here. Really, I was.

As a grand finale, she took the Hitachi Wand and put it right between my legs. It felt so soft and sensual compared to the other pussy torture I'd gotten. I started cumming again, but a whole other kind of cumming than the squirting. The tension in my insides completely released. I was cumming so hard I was crying, and I couldn't stop thanking the Mistress for what she had done. My nipples were burning and my pussy was in ecstasy. Just as my orgasm began to wind down, she reached up and pulled the twine between the clothes pins, yanking them off my nipples. I couldn't believe that an entire layer of skin didn't come off with them. How did she do that?

I felt so much release. She took the Hitachi off my clit and just sat there for a minute, laughing and grinning. I was covered in tears and squirt. She untied my wrists and then my ankles. I'd forgotten what it was like to have control over my own limbs, and it took a few moments to process that I could actually move my arms again. I sat up.

"Thank you, Mistress," I said. She smiled.

"You did fucking amazing," she replied.

"No, YOU DID, Mistress," I insisted.

"You can go back to calling me Rachel," she laughed.

"Well, I'm not sure if I want to!" I said. She grabbed the back of my hair and looked me deep in the eyes, and then kissed me. As we kissed, we listened to the reverb of the electronic music blasting from the other room. I felt truly connected to her. Sometimes a slut just needs some good old-fashioned romance. I never thought I'd be getting that in the back room of a dungeon, but I most certainly was.

To go back and see Naomi dominate someone, turn to page 97.

To continue with Naomi in this fantasy, turn to page 115.

O NE YEAR LATER . . .

Ashey the Ashtray is kneeling on the shiny hardwood floor of my high-rise penthouse apartment in Manhattan. Ashey pays me a generous wage to sit at the foot of my couch and well . . . be my ashtray. He also pays for this apartment. I never thought that picking up a smoking habit could be so profitable.

There's another slave in the bathroom scrubbing my Japanese toilet with a toilet scrubber gag attached to his mouth. Another slave is folding the laundry, and another is just underneath my calves, serving as my coffee table in the center of my open floor plan living room. I like to rest my legs on him after a long, hard day of torturing everyone here. I work a few nights a week at "Ananas," (that's the name of the dungeon—it's "pineapple" in French, get it?). I also do some sessions out of my apart-ment. I mean . . . I know I'm just lounging around in my living room right now, but technically I'm working, and while my ashtray, my coffee table, and my toilet scrubber may all look distressed, trust me, they're happy right now. In fact . . . WHACK!

"TOMMY, YOU KNOW THE RULES HERE."

"Sorry Mistress."

Sorry about that. My coffee table was clearly getting a boner, and he knows that's not allowed without asking.

I still work a few days a week at Club 42. It's a good

playground to meet some new clients, and well, it turns out I also happen to like dancing. Oh yeah, and my wife works there.

"Good boy, Rucifer! Good boy!" Rachel just walked through the door with our pet Rucifer on a leash. She was taking him on his afternoon walk through Central Park. He's part pet, part stockbroker. A mixed breed, he's very loyal, but not so well behaved. We're working on it. Rachel puts Rucifer back in his cage, and sits next to me on the couch, stretching her legs right next to mine across Tommy, the human coffee table. A slave rushes over and hands us both a bottle of carrot juice.

We sip on our healthy doses of beta-carotene, holding each other's hands, both of our palms covered in fingerless latex gloves. I look out the vast windows surrounding us, staring at the city underneath me. It's a perfectly clear day, and I can see the NYU campus where my city life began. I can see the multitude of coffee shops who never hired me, and the one that fired me. I see the strip club that saved me, and then the dungeon where I found myself. There were times in this city when I wanted to give up, when I didn't think I could make it, when I was one coffee spill away from moving back in with my parents. Now, this city submits to me.

THE END

To find another fantasy, turn to page 119.

"Thanks, but I think I'll pass for now. If I change my mind, I'll let you know!" I replied. I was hoping my cheerful tone would offset my complete lack of desire to visit a dungeon, but she still looked kind of offended.

"By the way, you can't be naked on the floor, remember?" I had my polka dot dress draped on me like a robe and my lingerie scrunched in my hand like it was some kind of lacy dishrag. I was sweaty and chugging a bottle of water. I looked like a hungover hipster who'd made a pit stop at a strip club on their walk of shame home. Which, come to think of it, was not actually that far off from how I got here.

Just then, Brandi walked past me, and stopped in her tracks when she saw me attempting to button up my dress, chug water, and *not* drop what I think was about half my rent on the ground.

"Oh hey!" she said. She seemed so happy to see me, and I had no idea why, but her smile was so heartwarming, I found myself happy to see her right back.

"Hey!" I replied. I mean, that seemed like the appropriate reply.

"Here, I grabbed this from the dressing room for you. I swear to god I'm gonna have a panic attack if I see you try to put that on one more time," she laughed, handing me a little pink sparkly dress. I felt honored. This was a hell of a lot more exciting than the day I was handed a coffee-stained apron at Fix. I slipped it on, and I felt free.

"Thank you!" I said.

She pointed toward a relatively dark corner of the floor. "There's a customer over there who's staring at you," she said, smirking. "Go give him a dance!"

"Oh. I don't—"

"You have to grab them right after you get off stage, before another girl does," she urged. She nudged me toward him. "Anyway, should be easy after that birthday boy."

At this point, I'd done everything I could possibly do on that stage. And she was right—a lap dance didn't seem so "advanced" after I'd whipped a man with his own belt. Although, I wasn't entirely sure it was me the guy was looking at. "I think he's staring at you," I suggested.

Brandi shook her head. "Seriously, does it matter? You want the dance, or not?"

I balled my dress up and stashed it at the edge of the bar. The bartender glared at me and kicked it out of view of the customers. Apparently, we were not friends anymore.

"Come on!" Brandi said. "Are you coming?"

To see Naomi give a lap dance, turn to page 52.

To see Brandi give a lap dance, turn to page 58.

I had so many questions, and Tony wasn't going to answer them. He was already out of my eyesight by the time I'd formulated a reply. *He said the shift starts at 10:00 a.m., right?* Was that official? Did that mean I needed to be there at 9:30? Did I need to fill out a W-2? Or . . . anything? This seemed too unofficial for a job in Times Square. But even so, I was excited to begin.

"Congrats!" the bartender said. "The girls all really like working here—it's a good club!" she added as she threw an Ellio's pizza into the toaster oven. I didn't know it was legal for anyone in New York City to ever eat frozen pizza under any circumstances. I suppose when vaginas are exposed, anything is possible.

Later that evening, I was finally back in my comfort zone—a bar with alcohol in it, surrounded by people in clothes. Real clothing, you know, like unwashed T-shirts with the names of cities on them, ripped jeans that were purchased purposefully torn, and cowboy boots, even though we were nowhere near a ranch or any cattle that needed tending. Brooklyn was my home un-sweet home, and while lots of unique things here were "cool"—like having a diner booth as apartment furniture, or drinking wine from a can, or playing professional Skee-Ball—being a stripper, especially a stripper in Times Square, was certainly not cool. But none of us cared about being cool, that was the point of our deliberate alternative lifestyle, so the fact that I was being so blatantly uncool was actually . . . cool, right?

I was on my third date with a guy named Rob. I'd met him a few months ago at a party that happened in my living room. When strangers started meandering into my apartment at 1:00 a.m., I was understandably pissed at my roommate Jessie, who, as a side note, I referred to behind her back as "Messy Jessie." What? The dishes were always hers, and she never cleaned them. Anyway, I had recently gotten my job at Fix, which forced me to wake up at 5:00 a.m., an ungodly hour in New York City, where it might be excusable to be out from the night before, but it's definitely not okay to be waking up to *start* a day. Unfortunately, it turned out a coffee shop job in Hell's Kitchen wasn't sophisticated enough of an excuse to call off a party in your living room that you couldn't call off anyways.

But back to Rob. Yes. He showed up on my couch with a pocket full of pre-rolled joints on a random Sunday. He had been dragged there by one of his friends, a person who was kind of friends with Messy Jessie. Rob had shoulder-length black hair, a lot of unfinished tattoos that were so far from being complete I'm not entirely sure what they were trying to be, a muscular build, slightly tanned skin, piercing brown eyes, and, I assumed, a closet full of torn flannel shirts that could just as easily have been from a gas station as from John Varvatos. Either way, it was wonderful.

We exchanged eye contact multiple times throughout the night. He didn't say much, but whenever he spoke, it felt like it was directed at me, like we were the only two people in the room. He was a musician. I consistently made efforts in life to *not* be attracted to musicians, but it never really worked out. There's something about their arms, their hair, and . . . their inability to get their lives together that is just so . . . satisfying.

He was in some band that was on tour, but not on tour at the moment. So in between one tour and the next, he was crashing on a friend's couch, the friend that was sort of friends with Messy Jessie. A few hours after I met him, his large, curvy, unexpectedly beautiful penis was in my mouth. While he didn't return the favor in any way at all during this particular encounter, I was so turned on by the sight of his cock that it somehow didn't matter. I swallowed every last drop of his semen, and what seemed like moments later, I was telling hoity-toity suit-wearing young professionals about the new brand of oat milk we had available in our lattes.

Since that first encounter, Rob and I had exchanged somewhere close to twenty thousand text messages. Those texts led to meeting up for incredibly cost-effective dinners and drinks, since after all, I did work at a coffee shop, and he was . . . in a band. We hadn't had sex yet, mostly for logistical reasons. Somehow we kept meeting and eating and drinking near "his place," and as previously mentioned, he didn't exactly have a bedroom. But on this night, we'd planned to play a round of Skee-Ball at the bar near *my* place (and then fuck each other's brains out in my bedroom, which wasn't anything fancy, but it was an actual room with an actual door). Since yesterday, the plan had been for me to go to work and then meet Rob at this very bar . . . but somewhere between going to work and going to this bar, I kind of became a stripper, and that wasn't part of the plan.

Now, Rob was definitely *not* my boyfriend. But he was the only person I was sending thousands of texts messages to, the only person whose dick had been in my mouth in the past month or so, and the only person I was smitten with. I assumed he felt the same way about me, and that our lust didn't require a pragmatic conversation about relationships and such. Should I tell him about my new job? Was that too much for the third date?

Technically, I wasn't going to be a stripper until tomorrow . . . or was I a stripper today? If I had been filling out some kind of form right now and it said "occupation: _____," would I write in "stripper"? Was I still technically a barista because sometime in the next fourteen days, I'd get a last check?

I walked up to the counter and ordered two PBRs and a pizza to share as I waited for him to arrive. I paid with the crumpled singles I'd earned earlier that day, and something about it felt so victorious. *Rob better get here fast*, I thought. I was hungry and horny and had about forty unexpected dollars to my name. Anything could happen.

When Rob showed up and saw the pre-ordered pizza and beer sitting on the table like magic, he was duly impressed. Oh yeah, Rob—we don't have to go dutch on this one, and you don't have to pull out your credit card that's almost always declined anyway. He gave me a kiss. He smelled like body odor disguised in cologne, and not disguised very well. I don't know why the term BO gets such a bad reputation. When you break it down, it's just the odor from someone's body . . . and that's incredibly intimate isn't it? I wondered if that was how the four people felt near the stage today when my pussy was inches from their face. Could they smell it? Did they like it? I mean, I knew my pussy didn't smell like a dirty band guy, but it was a hot day outside, and I'm sure it had its own special, intimate charm.

"How was your day?" I said. I rushed to say this first so I could avoid talking about my day. Thankfully, Rob had dedicated his entire afternoon to binge watching a season of *American Pickers*. If you've never heard of it (which you probably haven't), it's a show about these people who roam the country in search of antiques. So many people dream of growing up to be a rock star, but Rob anxiously awaited the days that his tour would end so he could watch twenty-plus episodes in a row of a television show about people who search through the trash. He had so many episodes to excitedly walk me through, I had no time at all to admit to him that this pizza was paid for with pussy gyrating money.

"And then, they find this naval artifact just sitting in this dude's basement that's been missing for half a century!" he said. It's amazing the things you can find interesting when you really want to fuck someone. I genuinely at this moment cared about naval artifacts recovered by people on a reality TV show. I hung on to every last word.

"Wow! That's crazy!" I said, shoveling down pizza so fast that I burned the roof of my mouth. "Try to hold off on the next season so I can watch it with you," I giggled.

"Alright." He paused. "I'll try." This meant we were getting somewhere in our relationship. He was already showing that he would make sacrifices for me.

The antique trash gave us enough excitement to just focus on his day and not mine. Our thin metal tray of pizza turned to nothing but pieces of crust and crinkled up napkins, our pint glasses of PBR became empty. I gave him a kiss, and he gave me a filthy stare, and we both knew what this meant—we were going to skip Skee-Ball.

Back at my apartment, he threw me against the wall, which . . . may or may not have been a great idea, because the walls were awfully thin here, and there was a strong chance we could simply fall through it and land in the middle of a group of hipsters. He reached his hands inside of my panties. Unfortunately, the lights were off and he didn't even get to acknowledge that they matched my bra. *It's okay. Enough people saw my panties today. Shhhhh.*

He played with my soaking wet pussy and fingered my clit up against the wall. Why does everything sexual feel so much filthier when up against a wall? There was a bed right there. My bedroom wasn't big at all, it was definitely about 80 precent bed, and with all the shelves and piles of random things on top of each other, there was only 20 precent of cleared wall, so of course we chose *that* space.

He REALLY wanted to make me cum. I could tell. He kissed me and moved his fingers around—in some magical way, he knew exactly where to go and what to do. Musicians never know what to do with their lives, but they always know what to do with their hands.

My legs shook, and I was kind of angry at him that he made me cum so hard. I laughed and threw him on the bed. It was time to get down to business . . . and to get away from the one foot of available wall. I slid his pants down to reveal his very large boner. I climbed on top of him, and my pussy was so wet that I slid right onto him. The first time I'd seen his cock, I was actually intimidated—there truthfully aren't a lot of well-endowed hipsters over here in Brooklyn. Lots of people with wit, charm, and home breweries . . . but not large penises. I had purchased a bottle of lube shortly after I saw his cock. But my dripping wet pussy certainly didn't need it now. I could have fit two more of them in there if I needed to.

Oh. Now that was a thought. I wondered what the rest of his band looked like. . . . Okay, never mind.

I rode him, sliding my pussy up and down his cock. I wasn't used to riding this much cock, so those extra seconds that it took to get from the top to the bottom were unlike anything I'd felt before. We laughed, we were always laughing. I was never quite sure if I was laughing at him or with him, but I knew for sure that *he* was laughing with me. His cock stretched me open, filled me, completed me. The feeling of us joining together on my IKEA bed was incredible. I didn't want it to end.

But it did.

He pushed me off of him mid-grind and came all over his own hairy stomach. I lay on his chest and wrapped my legs around him, kissing him, and watching the jizz disintegrate into his body hair. For a while, we simply lay there and listened to the sweet sounds of car alarms and stalling trucks through the window.

"What time do you have to get up for work?" he said.

"Oh! Not till like . . . nine," I replied.

"Oh, sweet. I thought you had to go at like 5:00 a.m.," he said.

"No . . . not . . . anymore," I answered.

Rob wasn't technically my boyfriend, and I wasn't sure I was technically a stripper at this moment, so technically I wasn't a liar, and in the court of relationship law I figured I would be declared innocent. Should I explain to him what I was really doing tomorrow morning? He would never guess. Mostly because I look nothing like a stripper, and also because nobody ever assumes anybody is stripping in the morning.

Should I tell him?

To see what happens if Naomi keeps this a secret, turn to page 127.

To see what happens if Naomi tells Rob, turn to page 242.

"Cool," he said. And then he shut his eyes. I was shocked and a little offended that he wasn't the least bit curious as to why my schedule had changed. But since his entire schedule consisted of nothing but watching Netflix until whenever his next tour started, I suppose I could understand why this concept of needing to be anywhere at all at a certain time was beyond his powers of comprehension.

I lay on his chest, wide awake as he snored. I felt like this was our first and last night together, like something was going to change as soon as the sun rose, and there would be no going back. As if tomorrow I was going off to join the Secret Service, only it wasn't so secret considering I'd be naked in a room full of people.

I had been so obsessed with this little bubble of pizza, beer, and orgasms that I'd forgotten about my life outside of Rob. I had friends. I had parents. I had . . . an elderly lady who worked at the bagel shop around the corner from me who always knew my bagel order. I had an occasional drug dealer who let me buy bags of weed on credit . . . because we were cool like that.

Was I supposed to tell all of these people that I was a stripper? Would any of them find out if I didn't tell them? My parents never went to strip clubs . . . did they? Wait. WHAT IF THEY DID? My friends were mostly broke and, also, extremely anti anything that went on in Manhattan. My friends would only go to Manhattan if they were making money, and even that was a stretch. None of them would go to Manhattan to *spend* money. Would they?

I tossed and turned and stressed over who might accidentally show up and see me naked. But then I thought to myself—*even* if any of my friends, my parents, my drug dealer, or the elderly lady that always knew to lightly toast my poppy seed bagel decided to go to a strip club in Manhattan, it would never be during the day. It would be at night.

And with that peace of mind, I fell asleep to the sounds of Rob's incredibly loud snores. They didn't sound healthy. He should really get that checked out.

I woke the next morning at 8:00 a.m. It felt disgusting.

When I got up at 4:30 a.m. to go to the coffee shop, it almost didn't feel real. It was sort of like I was playing a big joke on myself. When you're on the subway at 5:00 a.m., no one expects anything out of you. Makeup is optional at that hour, and if you have on two different colored socks, no one is reporting you to the MTA fashion police. Not that they would in Brooklyn anyway, since different colored socks were just ironic enough to be acceptable.

However, at 9:00 a.m., the subway is completely different. Life is happening. People are in a rush, with important places to go, with perfectly tweezed eyebrows and carefully styled hair. People who contributed to the news we read, the laws that passed, the movies we watched, and the technology we used were all awake at this time, ready to be a contributing part of the world . . . and I was there just in case any of them needed to get a boner on their lunch break.

I wasn't exactly sure as to how to prepare for today. I tried to be secretive around Rob in the morning, even though he was fast asleep as I was getting ready. I was worried he'd wake up and see me packing a bag full of things that no one would ever wear at a coffee shop. I grabbed a handful of necessities and threw them into a reuseable Trader Joe's grocery bag. I never thought the same bag I used weekly to transport discounted produce would be used for this purpose, but it truly was the perfect size bag, and it was quite durable. I threw in some makeup, my highest pair of heels, which weren't very high at all, and an American flag bikini that I'd bought ironically for a 4th of July rooftop BBQ last year. It seemed just as ironic now but . . . for different reasons.

Rob had no intention of waking up. He had no shame in making himself comfortable in a place he didn't live in. Wasn't he going to feel awkward waking up and seeing my roommate? More importantly . . . was my roommate going to feel awkward?

I arrived at Club 42 at 9:45 a.m. Fifteen minutes early seemed to be appropriate. No one was standing in front of the door. I guess the flyer guy didn't begin aggressively handing out unnecessary free admission flyers until after the club officially opened. I walked through the door. The girl with the greased-up ponytail was in the same exact position she'd been in yesterday, tapping away on her phone as if she never left. There was no music on. It felt empty and strange.

Two girls entered in matching tracksuit-type things. They didn't match each other, but the tops and the bottoms of their tracksuits matched. Both girls were short with large breasts—one was blonde and one had jet-black hair, but both had styled it in perfectly messy bun-ponytail hybrids. I mean, the perfect messy bun-ponytail that I was convinced only superheroes could effortlessly do. The perfect amount of hair falling down their faces, the perfect amount so delicately secured above their necks. One of the tracksuits was camo, and one was white with the word PINK spelled out in large letters. They were the same but different, with heavy Staten Island accents, speaking loudly over each other, but to each other, about construction on the Verrazzano Bridge.

My no-effort clothing consisted of mystery T-shirts that ended up in my drawers somehow, and quite frankly I don't know how a lot of them got there. And of course, the quintessential "D.A.R.E. to keep kids off drugs" T-shirt that had been in my possession since middle school. Were these girls' stripper outfits underneath the tracksuits, like UFC fighters who enter the arena in their branded sweatpants and then strip them off when it's time to fight? Regardless, I followed the track-suits through the unopened club because they seemed comfortable here, and I assumed they knew where they were going.

A DJ was speaking into the microphone, saying "test one two three" as he turned all the different colored lights on and off. I respected the professionalism—the day simply could not begin without the assurance that the green, purple, yellow, and red lights all worked. The two girls didn't notice I was following them. They actually didn't seem to notice anything but each other. Perhaps anyone who wasn't in a tracksuit was just . . . invisible to them.

They unintentionally led me to what appeared to be the locker room. The wall was lined with red lockers, with various types of combination locks and master locks securing them, and half-peeled stickers signifying a high user-turnover rate. The room was L-shaped, with a vanity mirror across one wall sporting half broken bulbs, and a long table beneath it. Now there were over a dozen girls, in so many different types of tracksuits. The room was filled with Louis Vuitton duffel bags, various oversized clear makeup bags, and lotions and sprays and eyeshadow pallets and foundations galore. I stood in the entrance taking it all in, with my stonewashed jeans and H&M oversized V-neck, my Trader Joe's grocery bag on my shoulder, looking like I was dropping off a Postmates order for one of the strippers. Until yesterday, I would have thought that was the more likely option, myself.

I found an empty chair and placed my things in it. The girls in the room were all undressing and talking and texting at once, with so many varying types of shaved and un-shaved vaginas. Some had a perfect landing strip, some were completely bald, some had a little tuft on top of the vagina. Mine was a disorganized mess that was all of these and none of these. At some point, my pubic hair would have to commit to whatever it was trying to be. It'd been having its own identity crisis for several years, and this job would force it to make a decision.

I felt invisible. Everyone was engrossed in their own routine—slathering powders and foundations on their faces with sponges or brushes, making small talk with each other with their breasts out. One girl somehow managed to put eyeliner and lashes on, eat an Egg McMuffin, and Facetime with someone who appeared to be her partner . . . all at the same time. I wasn't sure what she was saying because it was all in Spanish, but it was certain that she dominated the phone conversation, because the guy on the other end didn't get many words in.

I took out my American flag bikini and studied it, as if it was just one option of my many amazing outfits, and not, in fact, the only option. While this bikini had managed to be the star of a Bushwick rooftop BBQ, it wasn't even worthy of a third-rate act here. I slid off my stonewashed jeans, but kept my oversized V-neck T-shirt on. I attempted to squeeze into a small slice of mirror to fix my makeup, but I was elbowed in the face by a girl clipping in pieces of hair.

"I'm sorry," I said, as if I'd bumped into her, when she had clearly, and possibly intentionally, bumped into me. She had pale skin covered in colorful tattoos. She could have worked at one of the coffee shops in Bushwick that I couldn't get a job at. However, as she clipped hair extensions onto her head one by one, she transformed from a snobby barista into a friendly stripper. It was astonishing.

"It's cool!" she replied. That was generous of her, to forgive me for her own elbow hitting the side of my head.

She brushed bronzer onto her freckled cheeks and a clear iridescent lip gloss onto her lips. She was a redhead, with some extra red on her head from the clip-ins. The fake hair mismatched her real hair by a few shades, but it blended together into a unique highlighted ombre, like a modern-day little mermaid, in the sparkling ocean of a strip club. Her eyes were big and blue, her breasts were large and soft, like comfy pillows. She had a big toolbox of makeup—her own mini-Sephora at her fingertips. She slid her belongings over a few centimeters and gave me a half-smile. I now had about an inch of space to spread out my makeup collection, which luckily consisted of exactly six items.

I shyly slid on my American flag bikini bottoms without taking off my V-neck. I wasn't sure why I was being so awkward in this dressing room, after how I'd performed on stage yesterday. Maybe it was the bikini. I'd only worn this thing once, and it was purchased for a few dollars online from one of those no-name manufacturers. I tied the strings on the left side of my hip together. Then I tied the strings on my right . . . and the string just . . . ripped off. Just like that. Shit. The strings on the side of this thing were the structural integrity of the bikini. I slid the torn flag off me and held it in my hands, sighing. Ten minutes into my life as a stripper, and this bikini had failed me.

The redhead was now fully dressed in a neon green bikini with a complementing mesh dress on top of it. Her blue eyes, red hair, tattoos, and neon green outfit made her such a colorful and beautiful character. It was hard to stop looking at her. I'm sure this aesthetic worked to her advantage in this establishment. I, on the other hand, just sat with my bare ass on a plastic chair in my V-neck T-shirt, holding my broken American thong, unsure of what to do.

"I'm guessing you're new?" the redhead said.

"Yeah. . . . Is it that obvious?" I replied, complete with nervous laugh.

"Yeah!" she giggled. "I've only been doing this for a

year, and I feel like I've been here forever. You'll get the hang of it quick," she said. "Where are you from?"

"I live in Brooklyn," I answered, still dejectedly staring at the bikini strings.

"Me too!" she said. "Where at?"

"Bushwick!"

"No way! Me too!" She laughed again. I immediately felt more comfortable and forgot about the fact that my pussy was just hanging out on a chair, with nothing to cover it. I un-clenched the flag panties from my fist and threw them onto my one inch of designated table space, on top of my small but efficient makeup collection. The redhead looked at this pathetic little pile and chuckled. She dug into her bag and took out a neon pink minidress, with glitter interwoven into the fabric.

"Here you go. Take this. I ordered this online and it doesn't fit over my giant tits." She threw the dress on the table. Now my own little stripper-centimeter of space was starting to look more legitimate.

"Really? You sure?" I said.

"Yeah! I'm sure Tony didn't tell you anything. You must have no idea what to do," she laughed.

"Pretty much," I replied.

"I'm Melody by the way!" she said. "Well, my 'real' name is Elizabeth, but I go by Melody."

"I'm . . ." I paused. What was my name here? I hadn't given that any thought. I mean, should I just go by my actual name, Naomi? I thought quickly ... a montage of all the powerful women I have ever admired in literature and movies and television charged through my brain. Was there some kind of algorithm to this—my first pet's name and the name of the street I grew up on, or something like that? Damn it. Who was I?

I took a deep breath, intending to tell her the first thing that came to my brain, but just then, I saw my phone light up. It was a text message from Rob, with a photo of his beautiful, thick cock, comfortably hanging out in my bed. Melody clearly saw the giant penis on my phone—I had my texts and picture messages default to showing up on my home screen.

"Holy shit!" she laughed. I was embarrassed, as if it was my own penis that I'd accidentally flashed in front of her face.

"Sorry about that!" I said, flipping my phone over. My mind jumped to my date last night, and I remembered Rob's ramblings about *American Pickers*. While I'd only half listened to what he said, I remembered that the show took place in "LeClaire, Iowa." What a pretty name for a town in the middle of nowhere. I liked this name. Thank you, Rob. Your cock and your peculiar taste in television had inspired my stripper name.

"LeClaire is my name," I said confidently. It sounded French, and all things French were sexy.

"Claire?" Melody said. She didn't hear the first part, which was the part that made it exotic. The second part had zero sex appeal and made me think of the elderly lady with the hat and flowers in the game Guess Who.

"No, *Le*Claire!" I said, stressing the first syllable.

"Alright LeClaire. Nice to meet you!" She smiled and tightened up her bikini, which made her giant juicy breasts perk up even higher. I was still sitting there with a long T-shirt and no pants. It was time to get that sparkly pink dress on and bring this character to life.

But wait. Rob's penis.

I picked my phone back up, and Melody kept laughing.

"You get it girl! Fuckin'-A," she said. I blushed, secretly glad Rob's penis was getting me some credibility around here.

Followed by his penis, I saw a text message: "Miss U. What place do U work again? I'll come by and get coffee say hi!"

Shit. While I patted myself and my pussy on the back for getting a rock star with a giant cock to show interest in me so quickly, I certainly wasn't ready to have this conversation. I had to officially begin my career as a stripper before I told him I was a stripper.

"I'm working in the back today! Not a good day to come by . . . I'll text you when I'm done!" I replied. It was vague. I do remember when I worked at Fix, once a month I'd lose the privilege of serving coffee to unappreciative yuppies, and I'd be in a stuffy basement without much ventilation doing inventory. So . . . while this lie was based on *a* truth, it was not *the* truth.

I slid the pink dress on, and it felt tight against my skin. But it easily slid on, and it would also easily slide off.

"That looks WAY better on you," Melody gushed.

Suddenly, Tony, the guy from yesterday, opened the locker room door.

"If you're not on the floor in three minutes, I'm adding an extra twenty to your house fee," he growled. The girls in the room giggled and hooted, seeming to equally respect and disrespect his authority all at once. In a flurry, they all perked up their breasts, sprayed themselves with various perfumes, and re-applied lipstick. It was like the last ten seconds of a *Chopped* challenge, when the chefs took their final moments to plate their meals.

"Come on!" Melody said. "I'll show you around!"

To stay in the locker room, turn to page 138.

To go with Melody, turn to page 146.

"Thank you, but I need a few more minutes to get ready here. I'll see you out there!" I replied. I know what you're thinking, but no, it wasn't because I was nervous to start my life as a stripper. I felt guilty about Rob and I wanted to call him . . . and give his dick pic a proper response.

Melody walked away without really responding to me. She'd offered me her hand and I'd figuratively slapped it away. She'd also given me the clothes off her back, or, well, in her bag. I made myself feel better by reminding myself there was no way her tits were going to fit in this dress. I'd saved this sparkly thing from the trash.

I saw a small restroom in the corner of the dressing room and went in there with my phone. "Restroom" was a generous description—it was a toilet, a tiny sink, and an open pack of dried-up baby wipes on the floor. No paper towels. No scented candles. The amenities here were worse than a one-star Airbnb.

I called Rob. He answered immediately.

"Hey babe!" he said. I blushed. I had so many moral qualms with that word and how it even became a term of endearment in the first place. But none of that mattered right now. Rob had called me babe, and it made my pussy wet.

"Hi!" I said.

"What are you doing?" I giggled. What *was* I doing? I reread the text I'd sent him so I could continue this lie properly. Yes. I was doing coffee inventory. It was a shame I'd even started this lie, because telling him I was in a sparkly pink dress that barely covered my pussy and I was sitting on the toilet in the dressing room of a strip club in Times Square was so much more arousing than counting out quantities of coffee lids.

"I took a bathroom break, and . . . I was thinking of you," I said. This was technically true! Go me.

"Oh yeah?" he answered. "I'm sitting in your bed, thinking about you."

"Well," I replied, "you better be. You can't think about other people in my bed!" I laughed. He was quiet on the other end. Was that too . . . possessive? I mean, I thought it was a valid request. He would have to get his own bedroom if he wanted to have boners in other people's honor.

But it turned out, his silence wasn't because of my very first demand in our not-relationship. He was quiet because he was jerking off. I could hear his heavy breathing. The thought of him sitting in my bedroom in our puddle of sweat and sexual fluids from the night before and stroking his beautiful cock was so disgustingly hot. I reached down and touched my exposed pussy, finding it dripping wet. I wished he could bend me over this ceramic toilet and stick his giant cock inside me. I wasn't sure how he would even fit in here because there was physically only enough room for one stripper-sized human, but my hungry, wet pussy would have found a way.

"I want you," I said. Such a generic thing to say, but sometimes it's the only thing to say. People far more poetic than me have used the same phrase to express their carnal desires. The Beatles. Marvin Gaye. Bob Dylan, to name a few, and now me, in this strip club bathroom. It's the lyrical equivalent of, "I really really want to have sex with you, right fucking now."

"Aww fuck, babe. My cock is raging hard right now."

"Keep stroking it," I said. I was angry at his hands—I wanted my mouth and my pussy to be the only things that could make his cock raging hard. At least, in my own bedroom. I wanted to swallow his cock, I wanted him to fuck my face, and I'd never wanted anyone to do that to me until this very moment. It must have been something about the glitter and the dingy bathroom and the fact that I was lying that made me feel so dirty, and it was incredibly frustrating that I couldn't release this newfound sluttiness all over Rob's cock. All I could do instead was cling for dear life to the cell phone between my ear and my shoulder, with one hand on my gushing pussy.

"Are you touching yourself in the bathroom at work?" he laughed.

"Maybe," I replied.

"You should've had me come over there. I could've fucked your pussy in the back of that coffee shop."

Uggggh. The image of Rob fucking me over a bag of beans while a bunch of snooty Hell's Kitchen residents complained about the density of the foam in their lattes flashed through my mind. Then the image of Rob fucking me over this toilet in my heels and stripper dress—the two fantasies jumped back and forth in my brain like I was flipping between porn on two different channels and I couldn't decide which one was better. The innocent barista getting railed in the back? Or the slutty stripper getting pounded in the bathroom? Hmm. This was a tough decision that I actually didn't have to make, because this was phone sex, and anything could happen in my head.

"I'd fucking love that," I said.

"Don't toy with me. I'll come over there right now and do it—I don't give a shit. I'll walk right in with my boner and fuck you."

He would, probably. Guys in bands have some super-human ability to have sex anywhere, and not ever get in trouble for it. Now I was even more turned on, and while I was really enjoying this bad barista fantasy, I had to keep it in check seeing as how I wasn't actually at the coffee shop.

"Oh come on! Don't get me in trouble!" I giggled.

"But I want to," he said. I could hear his breathing progressively getting heavier, and then turning to grunting and groaning. That was good news, not only because he had the sexiest grunts and groans in the universe, but also because he was obviously not on his way out the door to head to a coffee shop with a boner.

I slid two fingers into my pussy.

"Rob, I want you to stay in my room and fuck the shit out of me as soon as I get home. I want to walk through the door, and I don't want you to say hi, I don't want a kiss, I don't want a hug, just bend me over and stick your cock inside me. Okay? I want it. I need it again."

He took a deep breath. It sounded a little different, like his grunts and groans were underwater.

"Hello?" I said. "You there?"

"Oh yeah, I'm here," he said. It still sounded a bit different.

"Did you put me on speaker?" I asked. It would make sense—he probably needed to use his other hand . . .

"Nope," he said. He breathed in heavily.

"What are you doing!" I was dying to know.

"I'm sniffing your panties," he said.

"OH MY GOD!" I replied. "Which panties?" I asked, as if I had sniffable and non-sniffable panties and I wanted to be sure he sniffed the right ones.

"The one's you wore last night. They were in the bed," he laughed. Those panties had had a very productive day. They'd walked from Hell's Kitchen to Times Square, they'd been taken off and put back on at the strip club, then taken off again by Rob. They'd gotten more action than any of my other panties, and now they were getting sniffed by Rob. The thought of him inhaling the scent of my sweat and juices, mixed with a twist of crisp dollar bills, was so gross and sexy and wonderful that it made me finger myself harder in this tiny bathroom. No one had ever sniffed my panties before. What a kinky bastard. I appreciated his honesty, and even pride, in sniffing my panties. The fact that he told me made it hot. Had someone sniffed my panties and NOT told me . . . they would have been a certifiable creep.

I fucked myself with my fingers as hard as I could while keeping the phone against my ear.

"Mmmmm, so fucking good," he said. "You were real fuckin' wet in these."

He knew it. I mean, he knew it before he sniffed my panties, but now there was physical proof of how attracted I was to him. There was no sense in trying to be coy or shy or in playing hard to get. *Just take my fucking pussy Rob, it's yours. You jerk.*

"Yeah, I was, and I am now," I replied. Not that I had any panties to get wet, right now—I just had moisture dripping down my thighs.

I imagined my arms pinned back and Rob bending me over the toilet, sliding his cock in and out of me, holding his hand over my mouth to muffle my voice so no one could hear us. More and more fingers slid inside my pussy as I imagined him fucking me harder.

"Put the phone near your pussy," he said.

"What? Really?" I replied.

"Yes. Really. I wanna really hear it."

I moved the phone down so he could hear the sounds of my fingers inside me. I knew it was turning him on, so I fucked myself even harder to make more noise, like I was turning the volume up on my pussy, or something. I kept going, harder and faster. The thought of him listening to me and sniffing my panties back in my bed was driving me crazy.

I kept going until I came. I put the phone back up to my ear so he could hear me moaning.

"Fuck, I'm coming!" I said. I shook, but balanced myself in my heels and still kept the phone against my shoulder. This was the most impressive multitasking I'd ever done, but this orgasm was worth it.

"I'm coming, I'm coming," I repeated. It felt like he was right there, but at the same time it was incredibly hot that he wasn't there—that he was somehow able to get me off without touching me. I mean, yes, my hand did the manual labor, but he did all the work. Like he had possessed my body to masturbate.

It was the kind of orgasm that didn't leave you satisfied, though. The *amuse-bouche* of orgasms. It needed to be followed by more orgasms.

I was just contemplating how to get myself off again when someone knocked on the door.

"The fuck is going on in there? If you're gonna turn tricks, do it in the fucking VIP room. Not here!"

It sounded like Melody, because . . . shit, it was Melody. I hung up the phone. I wiped my leg with the three remaining dried baby wipes on the ground. I collected myself and opened the door. She looked really confused when she saw I was alone.

"Well," I paused. "I was . . . talking to that dick on my phone," I said. "I'm sorry." She had clearly been impressed by that penis, perhaps she'd understand?

"I need to pee," she replied, pushing past me. "And," she added, "I'll take my dress back. I'd rather save it for a girl who actually wants to work." Then she slammed the door shut behind her.

Abashed, I took off the pink dress and put it next to Melody's things. I stood in the dressing room naked, listening to the thumps of the music from the club. I wasn't sure what to do. The irony of having nothing to wear at a strip club made me chuckle, but it was actually a problem.

What the hell was I doing here? I hated Times Square. I was the one at parties who sat in the corner and silently judged the other people dancing. I didn't like anything sparkly and pink, and even if I did, that didn't matter because that dress had been stricken from my wardrobe as quickly as it had been added.

Melody walked out of the bathroom. She stood right next to me, looked in the mirror, and sprayed herself with some strawberry-scented spray. She made no eye contact with me whatsoever, like I was a ghost. The ghost of LeClaire. The French stripper, who wasn't French. And wasn't a stripper, if we're being honest.

My phone rang. It was Rob. I turned the sound off,

but he continued to call. I looked at the screen, the missed calls. I stared at the dick pic. All I really wanted right now was another orgasm, and I didn't want it to be in that small bathroom. At this point, I wasn't even sure if I'd be allowed back in there. Melody may have blacklisted me from the bathroom.

I put my stonewashed jeans and oversized V-neck back on. I grabbed my makeup and my torn American flag bikini and threw them in my Trader Joe's bag. I walked back through the club, through the empty coat room, and toward the door. No one stopped me—no one even knew what the hell I was doing there in the first place. As soon as my feet hit the busy sidewalk, I grabbed my phone and texted Rob.

"Got off early, I'll see you soon xo." I laughed to myself, remembering how I did get off early.

Perhaps one day I'd tell my grandkids about the time I almost became a stripper, or kind of *was* a stripper? Until then, I'd leave my short-lived adventure at Club 42 a secret. I'd find another coffee shop job somewhere, or maybe I'd try to work at a bar, or maybe I'd figure out how to actually use my degree, or maybe . . . I'd come back tomorrow and try this all over again.

I headed toward the subway, which would take me to another subway, which would take me home to Brooklyn, to sit on Rob's cock.

Good-bye Club 42. It's been real.

THE END

To go back and follow Melody, turn to page 146.

I followed Melody as she ran down the stairs into the strip club part of the strip club. Yes, she ran down the stairs in her stiletto high heels, and thankfully, because my heels were not nearly as adventurous as hers, I managed to keep up. I had no idea that finding a new friend here would unwillingly enlist me in some sort of Ninja Warrior balance challenge. I panted and took a moment to catch my breath. Melody smiled at me.

"Good job!" she said.

I wanted to ask her why we had to run so fast, but I was catching my breath, which was still full of second-hand bong smoke. She pointed at the DJ booth, which was beaming all of those light colors he'd been previously testing. I guess it's safe to say, they passed with er . . . um . . . flying colors. Anyways, amongst all the proudly working lights I saw the DJ look at us, nod, and scribble something on a whiteboard. What the hell was going on?

"TJ puts the girls on stage in the order of who get down here first," Melody said. "So you always wanna get down here as fast as possible, before all the good guys gets snatched up for a lap dance."

"Got it!" I said, and I nodded even though I still had a myriad of questions, the most pressing being: how did a DJ ever get the name TJ, and was it a coincidence or intentional?

"Fuck! God damn it Natasha. What a hustler. She's always here first," Melody said, looking at a chaise lounge near the bar where a buxom blonde in white thigh-highs rubbed her ass cheeks against the crotch of a dignified-looking businessman. I used my deductive logic and assumed this was a lap dance.

I made a mental note from my quick stripper tutorial. Get down here fast, so you can go on stage fast, so you can give someone a lap dance fast . . . well the lap dance wasn't fast—from the looks of Natasha, it was actually quite sensual—but the selection of a crotch had to be fast. Aside from a DJ named TJ, everything made sense to me.

A rush of men in various well-tailored suits suddenly flooded the room and the next few hours were a blur. I'd go on stage, I'd dance, I'd pick a target, I'd flirt, I'd lap dance. It was like speed dating, but the date was three to five minutes of intense dry humping, and the hobbies you talked about included ass-shaking, seductively dancing to songs you don't really like in front of strangers, and spreading your vagina lips open as wide as they could possibly go.

I was high on myself. As more money littered the stage, my dances became more dirty, more sensual, and less inhibited. I wanted to show these men every last crevice of my vagina, and I wanted them to see it from every possible angle.

I would dance, I would sweat, I would "shower" with baby wipes and Melody's "Japanese Blossom Body Spray" (she told me I could make myself comfortable using it). I gave lap dance after lap dance, and at a certain point I stopped saying, "Would you like a dance?" and started saying, "Come on, you're next, let's go!" Everyone agreed, when ordered, and followed me into the darkness to get dry humped. It was like a day at Fix when every customer loved their coffee, left a tip in the tip jar, and told me to have a nice day—only a day like that never happened, obviously.

I have to admit, I felt victorious when I felt the customers' cocks get hard in their pants. Sometimes they'd get so hard I could get a true mental image of what was behind the curtain. I could feel the girth, the length, I could tell if it curved, I could even tell if it was circumcised by how pronounced the head of the penis was. Some guys enjoyed small talk, some guys didn't. Some treated me like a girlfriend, some treated me like a whore. Some needed love, and some needed a good smack in the face, and I was happy to be of service to anything that got that cock hard.

My Trader Joe's grocery bag was swelling with money. I mean, obviously it wasn't *completely* full, because if you've ever had a Trader Joe's grocery bag yourself you know, it's a big fucking bag. Dollar bills from the stage and twenties from the lap dances accumulated in the same place where I transported discounted produce. If things kept going the way they were, I could possibly upgrade and get my produce from the boutique natural market near the train station . . . or perhaps even from a Whole Foods.

The stream of customers dwindled down as the lunch rush went back to work. I noticed a stream of girls leaving the floor and heading toward the staircase that led to the dressing room. I circled around the same four men, asking them if they would like a dance for the sixth time. Their polite rejections were getting more frank and less polite. "No thank you" was turning into "no," and one guy actually got up and left when he saw me heading in his direction.

Melody walked over. I felt like I hadn't seen her in ages, but it had only been about two hours and we'd been in the same room the whole time. She peeked into my grocery bag. She herself had an elastic garter wrapped around her ankle with a giant wad of cash rubber-banded around it. It didn't look like a safe way to carry your money, and certainly would be an impossible way to carry produce.

"Well, you had some beginner's luck! That's for sure!" she said.

"That wasn't luck. That was skill!" I said.

"Ohhhh right." She smiled and brushed back her mermaid hair. "Well, you came in here blushing over a giant cock on your phone. Clearly you're not a prude! There was a little slut inside you just waiting to come out."

I felt a wave of guilt, and I didn't like it. I'd forgotten about Rob . . . and his dick pic . . . and my entire life outside of this club.

"Well, you'd better go get changed. The night shift girls are gonna start coming in soon, and I'd advise you to get your stuff out of the dressing room if you don't want it drenched in hair gel."

"Really?" I said.

"Oh yeah," she replied. "It's their polite and friendly way of telling you that your shift is over and to get the fuck out."

"But . . ." I stammered.

"But what?" she said.

"But . . . who still uses hair gel?" I said.

"They do," she laughed. "Come on, let's go get changed out of our whore clothes, and we can exchange our singles for big bills up front." She peeked in my reuseable grocery bag. "I have a feeling you're gonna have a lot of them."

She pulled me up the stairs, with my sweaty hand in her sweaty hand, both of us reeking of the same cheap perfume—ahem, I mean body spray—with a bag full of cash on my shoulder, and I guess it wasn't so surprising that I started humming Led Zeppelin's "Stairway to Heaven."

After piles of sweaty crumpled bills went through a money counter, I was handed six crisp one-hundred dollar bills, two twenties, a five, and four singles. I had never made this much money in one afternoon, ever. Was this common? If I made this amount of money every day, I'd be in the same tax bracket as the strip club customers, and then I'd have to find a strip club to go to myself.

I took out my phone and almost cried as I clicked open the Lyft app, something I only used to go a few blocks when it was pouring rain or hailing ice and I was intoxicated in Brooklyn. I was choosing to spend fifty-two dollars over a two dollars and fifty cent subway ride just because I felt like it. This must have been how it felt to be Cardi B.

"What's your address? I'll add a stop!" I said to Melody. We were both sitting outside of Club 42. She was dressed in denim leggings, aka "jeggings," Vans high tops, and a washed-out Iron Maiden tour T-shirt. I would believe she legitimately went to the concert, and didn't just buy the T-shirt at a vintage clothing store or on Etsy or something.

She gave me her address, which was in the slightly more residential side of the neighborhood. "Make sure to share the ride with me so we can split it," she said.

"No! I got it!" I replied.

She paused, and then chuckled to herself. "Ah, you feel rich right now, don't you?"

"Yes. I AM rich right now," I replied, only half joking.

"Well, alright then, big baller, I'll take it!"

A 2019 Toyota Camry driven by someone named Josh pulled up moments later and picked us up. I had multiple unanswered calls and texts from Rob. People always say that if you slightly avoid someone, they chase after you more, a theory I'd never been able to test because I was always the one chasing. Usually, playing hard to get consisted of waiting an incredibly agonizing twenty minutes to answer a text, and then patting myself on the back for how independent and strong and busy I must have appeared in those twenty minutes. I put my phone in my pocket and didn't text him back.

Melody and I sat in the back of the Camry, which was driving .00001 miles an hour in Times Square rush-hour traffic. "We probably could have walked to Brooklyn faster than this," I said, breaking the moment of silence.

"Oh, yeah, well, I take a car home from work so I can just have a few minutes alone to … you know . . . decompress. Also, it's not EXACTLY a good idea to get on the subway with that much cash."

Oh yes. I'd forgotten how rich I was.

"As soon as I walk through my door, I'm taking care of a nine-year-old. Melody disappears and Elizabeth comes to life, with coloring books and crayons and Girl Scout cookies."

I couldn't even begin to process the complexity of being a single mother, let alone a mother and a stripper. Suddenly my conundrum of wondering whether I should tell my not-boyfriend about my day seemed pretty insignificant.

"I'm sorry if I interrupted your alone time," I said.

"A free car ride home is worth more than my alone time," she said with a smile.

"Well thank you," I said, "for all your help today . . . Elizabeth?"

"Oh no. Elizabeth isn't ready to come out yet. You can call me Melody for the rest of the car ride," she said.

"OH! Really?" I smiled devilishly. "Can I get a quick lap dance then before Melody disappears?"

"Fuck you," she said, and we both laughed. As our laughter died down, she put her hand on my hand. It was oddly comforting, and part of me never wanted this car ride to end. Another part of me, the old me, really wanted it to end because I could only imagine what the surge pricing would be like if it went on forever.

I walked into my apartment. It was crazy to think that the last time I'd been in this apartment, I'd had no idea what a lap dance was. Rob was in a pair of black boxers, sitting on my couch playing video games with my roommate, Jessie. There were several boxes of Papa John's pizza, half-smoked joints, lighters, ashes, half-empty ramekins of ranch dressing, and that mysterious garlic butter sauce that only Papa John's offers, all strewn about my coffee table. I had a lot of questions about this current situation, and here were just a few: Why was Rob still here? Why would anyone eat Papa John's at any point earlier than 4:00 in the morning? And, perhaps most importantly, when did we get an Xbox?

"Hey babe," Rob said, barely shifting his head. He was staring at the screen, controlling a character in a full suit of armor who was running through a field, setting everything and everyone on fire with a torch.

"Hi guys!" I said. Jessie didn't respond—she was fully engrossed in the game. Her character was a sexy ninja warrior, with a giant sword in her hands, wearing a skin-tight spandex suit laced up with crisscrossed red straps. I couldn't help thinking to myself: that would be a terrible stripper outfit. She'd never be able to get that thing off.

I awkwardly stood in my own kitchen, which was less than a foot away from the living room.

"Babe! I went to Joe's and picked up my Xbox! Surprise!" He lifted a partially smoked joint from the table and smoked it down to the very end. I was impressed with how he multitasked: playing the game, saying hello to me, and not burning himself all at once.

I noticed a duffel bag near the couch that was unzipped, with men's socks and stained white T-shirts spilling out of it. In the court of "it's complicated" relationship law, is it worse to not tell your partner you're a stripper, or worse to not tell your partner you moved in?

They put their controllers down and each grabbed a slice of pizza from different pizza boxes. Apparently, this stoned operation had inspired them to cater this experience with their own pizza buffet, where they could sample all of Papa John's finest, tapas-style. I took this brief intermission to go through my living room—walking in front of the TV to get to my bedroom. I wanted to stash away my stripper evidence while I had the chance.

I went into my room, threw my Trader Joe's grocery bag in a drawer, took off my sweaty garments, and lay in my bed, naked. I'd spent a good portion of my day naked, but now I felt like I was truly naked. Rob came in my room. Or was this *our* room now? He stood at the foot of my bed with an adorable goofy grin on his face, wearing nothing but a pair of black boxers. His shoulder-length black hair and his muscular body were illuminated by the evening sun peering through the window, and he was . . . holding a box of pizza with four cold slices, a side of garlic butter sauce, and a bunch of leftover crusts inside of it.

"I saved you some," he said. He was just so goofy and handsome that somehow the cold pizza from my least favorite pizza place absolved him of anything he had ever done wrong. I smiled at him, and I pulled him onto the bed with the pizza box. I dipped a sliver of leftover crust into the butter sauce, and I had to admit, it was disgusting and delicious.

"How was your day?" he said.

"Oh! Fine! It was fine. I'm just kinda tired," I said. I still wasn't technically lying about anything. I was just strategically leaving out information.

"Awww. Okay! Just lay down, I'll give you a massage," he said. I was completely okay with that idea.

I lay down on my stomach, and he propped his dense body on top of my ass. His muscular hands dug deep into my back. I was completely naked, and we were separated by only a thin layer of his stretched cotton boxers. It was like I was getting a lap dance. I could start to feel his cock getting hard between my ass cheeks. I couldn't even count how many erections I'd felt pressed against me today. Of course, the other ones had paid me, and this one was squatting in my apartment. It was a little unfair, wasn't it? That all the men who woke up in the morning, took a shower, put on clean clothing, and paid for my attention didn't get to touch my nipples or my pussy, and the one who saved me four slices of cold pizza would inevitably get to stick his tongue, his fingers, or his cock anywhere

154

he damn well pleased? I'd been getting massaged for merely two minutes, and my pussy was already wet. My legs had started to feel like Jell-O, and I wanted to give all of myself to him. I guess in this equation I really was the sucker getting the lap dance.

He leaned down and kissed my neck. "You smell good," he said. Ah yes. The infectious scent of stripper was all over me. This magic potion apparently had the ability to draw in pheromones from all classes of the social hierarchy—from the guy who worked on Wall Street to the homeless guy squatting in my apartment. He moved my hair to the side, licked my earlobe, and grabbed onto the back of my hair as he said: "How about I go down on you? Or maybe you could go down on me?"

To see Rob go down on Naomi, turn to page 156.

To see Naomi go down on Rob, turn to page 160.

I flipped over, and my body said "Fuck yes" without me having to say a word. I admit, oral sex from a broke musician with an insatiable sex drive is always a treat. But today, it felt more deserved than ever. I'd spent my entire day acutely focused on turning people on, and now the universe was karmically giving me what I deserved by transferring this arousal to me.

He moved his hands up and down my body. He grabbed my nipples, he pinched them, I squirmed. He mounted me and kissed my neck in the perfect spot that woke up all the senses in my body. He licked my earlobe in a surprisingly sensual way. I started kicking my legs and trying to physically move his head down. I needed his mouth, I needed his tongue. He shot me a devious grin and said, "Be patient."

"I don't want to!" I replied—in a rather adorable voice, might I add. He ran his fingers down to my pussy and slid two of them inside me.

"Oh yeah," he growled. He was like his video game character, ready for battle, ready to demolish my pussy instead of a field full of . . . um . . . thieves. Or whatever they were.

He licked my left nipple and slid his fingers up and down my pussy lips, teasing them. I could feel everything inside me tensing up and loosening at the same time. He moved over to the right nipple, and he gently used his teeth to nibble at it. I shook, I giggled. The powerful, all-mighty LeClaire had left the building, and Naomi, the horny hipster in desperate need of an unshowered, tattooed man, was here. He looked me in the eyes and gave me a devious smile, which said, "Oh you just wait. I haven't even gotten started."

The nipple licking was just the opening act to the concert that was about to begin between my legs. He moved down to my crotch, and he took a moment to smell every inch of sweat and juices wafting from my pussy.

"Mmmmm. Smells so fucking good," he said. Rob definitely had a passion for pussy, in such a primal and carnivorous way. If my pussy was a piece of chicken, he would pick it up and eat it with his hands without giving a shit if sauce was smearing all over his face, even while everyone else at the table opted to use a knife and fork. He really liked to dig in there without any manners.

I felt his soft tongue moving in slow concentric circles, which grew smaller and smaller as he zeroed in on my clit. My legs started shaking and he held them down. He sucked on my clit, his lips softly drawing out deep moans from my body. He found my hole, which his fingers had visited not that long ago, and he fucked it with his tongue. He darted it in and out of me, entering me over and over. He used his fingers and rubbed my clit as he fucked my hole with his tongue, and then he switched things around and put his tongue against my clit so he could stick his fingers back inside me.

My legs couldn't stop shaking. He aggressively grabbed my long legs and lifted them up. He pushed them backward, close to my head, and moved my arms so my elbows locked around my knees and I couldn't move. I was like a pretzel, waiting to be eaten.

By then, he had a perfect full view of all my holes, and he didn't waste any time. He went down to my asshole and stuck his tongue in there, too. He licked my asshole while he rubbed and fingered my pussy with both of his hands. His mouth went back to my pussy. I mean, my *entire* pussy was in his mouth. His tongue was all over the place, like it was playing the piano and hitting all the right keys. I already knew his fingers were well-practiced, but I was now learning that his tongue certainly had its own set of skills. My arm slid and let one of my legs down for a second, and he threw it back up immediately. He was determined to make me cum in this vulnerable and contorted position, and it was moments away from happening.

I could feel my insides getting warmer, throbbing. I was pushing my pussy so hard into his face, and he was pushing back just as hard. Then he drew back slightly and tickled his tongue up and down my outer lips. My clit still somehow throbbed with pleasure, even though he'd turned his attention elsewhere. He ran his strong tongue from the top of my labia down to my taint, painting me with his saliva. Then he plunged a finger inside, circled his tongue back around to my clit, and there it was. I reached such an intense climax, I felt it everywhere.

He inhaled loudly and would not let go of my pussy. He wasn't going to stop until every ounce of orgasm went directly down into his throat. He moaned, and I moaned back, and I was cumming so hard tears were coming out of my eyes. I couldn't hold my legs back any longer—my body was spent, my arms and legs fell, and I collapsed, which is a funny thing to say when you were already lying down to begin with.

He pulled away from my pussy and regarded it like he was staring at his own kingdom after just becoming the emperor of it. How could I go from feeling so strong to so weak in such a short amount of time? I was fine with him paying his rent in orgasms, if he did in fact live here . . . which I should probably figure out at some point.

To go back and see Naomi go down on Rob, turn to page 160.

To continue with Naomi in this fantasy, turn to page 166.

My mouth started salivating as soon as he said it. I still had the taste of butter sauce in my mouth, and there's no better way to wash down a serving of garlic-flavored melted fat than with a healthy helping of cock. I flipped over and looked at him, with his day-old boxers, and his raging hard-on underneath, and it was beautiful. I know, I know what you're thinking. This guy really had some nerve to give himself an open-ended invitation to stay in my apartment for as long as he pleased, and then to come in and ask for a blow job. But my mouth was already open, my pussy was clenching, and I wanted nothing more than to swallow his entire beautiful penis.

Now that I worked in the field of entertaining penises and such, I wanted to put on a show for him. I got excited at the prospect. I was ready to show off a few of the tricks of the trade that I'd learned today at the um . . . er . . . coffee shop.

I slithered out from underneath him and placed him on the edge of my bed so that he was sitting up. He seemed a bit confused, but happily went along with it. He was getting a blow job after all. I got down on my knees on my floor. It was a nice change of pace from this afternoon to have my knees on a clean floor. I dramatically pulled his boxers down. I took the opportunity to secretly push them into my dirty laundry pile in the corner of my room with my foot, because they absolutely needed to be washed . . . or thrown away.

As I'd done with the men at the club, I looked deep into his eyes. I gave his cock one big long lick, from his balls to the top of his shaft. It was my nice way of saying hello. I worked up a healthy amount of spit from my salivating mouth, and I slobbered it all over his cock. I smooshed my perky *B* cups together and formed a nice tight little envelope for his cock to slide up and down in. He was definitely surprised. Titty fucks are like the long-lost ancestor of the blow job and hand job. They've been around for so many generations, but always seem to get forgotten about.

I continued to stare directly into his eyes as I moved myself up and down on his cock. I could feel it growing thicker and stronger between my breasts. My pussy was dripping onto my carpet, and I wasn't entirely sure how clean it would still be after this.

His eyes rolled back into his head. He wanted more friction, so he took control of the situation and thrust himself into my breasts as I leaned back, holding them in place. From my point of view on the floor, staring directly into his big, beautiful brown eyes, it looked like he was aggressively fucking the air. I loved the carnivorous expression his face made when he was horny. His raging boner really connected him to his true sense of self. He was a sexual beast, and I could smell that on him the first time I met him. Quite frankly, it was dangerous.

A few minutes had passed, and while I enjoyed this homage to the titty fuck, it was time to get his cock in my mouth. I pushed him down onto my bed so he was lying flat, with his delicious large flagpole waving at me. I spread his legs open, and I got in a seductive doggy position, wedged in between them. I licked my lips and put the tip of his cock in my mouth. For a little bit of flair, I started doing a subtle twerk with my ass in the air. I saw him watching it in awe, so I turned my subtle twerk into a slightly more obvious twerk. It was like he and my ass were having their own little love affair while my mouth was on his cock.

I moved up and down the considerable length of him, sucking and licking, my lips never leaving his dick. I stuck it as far down my throat as I possibly could, and then a little ball of collected liquid from the back of my throat spilled onto the rest of his cock, making a wonderful lubricant for me to continue sucking. I tasted a little salt—some pre-cum. I wanted to lick every last drop out of him. Next, I moved my attentions down to the bottom of his shaft and licked his balls. That's when I had an idea. I remembered earlier today when Melody had told me there was a little slut inside of me, just waiting to come out. And she was right, it was out.

I moved my face to the edge of the bed and hung it over it, upside down. I demanded that he get up and fuck my face. Once again, he seemed incredibly surprised, and might I say . . . impressed. Of course he obliged. He stood up and held my upside-down head in place as he thrust his cock in and out of my open mouth. I had never tried this kind of acrobatic face-fucking before, but somehow it all was coming quite naturally to me. I could feel my eyes tearing up, but he wiped away my happy blow job tears and continued to fuck my face. I loved the feeling of being suffocated by his cock. I loved the feeling of being pushed to the point of gagging on it. Who was I, and where did I come from? Was I still LeClaire? Was I Naomi? When did one start and one end? I concluded that I was in fact Naomi, but my good friend LeClaire had given me some tips that helped me get to where I was, which was upside down with a huge cock balls deep in my mouth.

I moved my hand down because something desperately had to attend to my eager pussy. I fingered myself and rubbed my clit, which was already a little swollen from being smacked up against hard cocks inside of clean pants all day. Rob glanced down at my pussy. This interrupted his love affair with my face—he seemed almost furious. Like he was saying, "How dare you use those fingers when I have a giant throbbing cock right here?"

He took his cock out of my mouth, spun my body around, and brought my pussy toward him. The head of his cock slid right in, and the long shaft stretched me open. The thickness of his dick hugged every erogenous zone inside of my pussy, and I was totally full. He was standing up, so I had a good view to watch him fucking my brains out. We were in some kind of deconstructed standing missionary position, and you know, it was times like these when I really thought the missionary position needed a new name. Missionary can be filthy, alright. It's got a bad reputation, but it's actually a great position where you can see someone's face and their cock can slide all the way inside you. I bent my legs back so he could slide in me even further, and then I really felt it. Something about the way I moved my legs back and his angle of thrusting pushed the head of his penis into the perfect fucking spot, and I started shaking.

"Harder! Harder!" I said. I was practically crying. I have to admit, it was really complicated and rare for me to have an internal orgasm without any clitoral stimulation at all. He could feel my pussy tensing up, and he knew what was going on. He used the entire force of his dense body to fuck this one particular spot inside my pussy. He was panting and sweating, like he was getting to the end of a marathon. I was quivering, and then I felt my pussy clench up so tight that I almost pushed him out of me—but he kept fucking harder and fought the force of my pussy.

A powerful and intense orgasm took over my body. I was shaking and squealing and moaning and cumming. I hoped Jessie was enjoying Rob's Xbox on a loud volume so she couldn't hear the insanity going on right now. Or maybe I just didn't care. If she was entitled to leave dirty dishes in the sink for eight consecutive days, then I was entitled to have loud obnoxious orgasms.

He pulled out and let out a loud, sexy grunt, and his semen exploded all over my stomach. Rob barely had the energy to move off the couch to get himself a soda, but when it came to sex, he turned into an athlete. I sat there and admired the large load of jizz on my stomach. I scooped it up into my mouth, and it tasted almost as good as the garlic butter sauce. He dropped down on my bed and passed out. Or was this our bed now? Was he sleeping here again tonight?

These were somewhat major things to be addressed, none of which I had the energy to address. I wiped the remainder of jizz off my stomach and pulled out an extra long D.A.R.E. T-shirt I had in a clothes drawer. Rob was snoring. I didn't know how he passed out so fast. Oh, right, it was the power of my pussy that put him to sleep.

I left my bedroom and plopped myself down on my couch. Messy Jessie was nowhere to be found. I grabbed a controller and did what I felt was the most logical thing to do, what with all my convoluted emotions and life decisions, and that was to teach myself how to play Xbox.

To go back and see Rob go down on Naomi, turn to page 156.

To continue with Naomi in this fantasy, turn to page 166.

I'd been working at Club 42 for a little over a month now. I worked Monday through Thursday, and sometimes Fridays if I wasn't too exhausted. My life became like a nude *Groundhog Day*. I woke up, rode the subway to Times Square, covered my face in makeup, put on microscopic clothing that sparkled, took it off, danced on people's laps, went on stage again, and repeated this several times each day. Throughout the course of a day's worth of dry humps, twerks, and smiles, it accumulated to anywhere from three to seven hundred dollars, depending on the day.

I'd love to say I was paying off all my student loans, or taking care of a sick relative, or putting money toward a security deposit on an apartment that didn't resemble a railroad in any way, shape, or form, but I wasn't doing any of those things. I was spending almost all of my money on Rob.

I'll have to backtrack here. I wasn't exactly *just* spending my money on Rob, I was spending money on the both of us. I'd always lived like a broke college student in New York, and I'd recently realized the joys of being not broke in New York. Every night, we'd eat at different restaurants, high-end gastro pubs, and drink cocktails with multiple ingredients in them.

One night when my air conditioner wasn't working, we simply walked out of the apartment and got a room in a $750-a-night hotel in Brooklyn that overlooked the water and boasted artwork from local artists in the rooms. I couldn't even calculate how many lap dances that hotel room, and the room service we ordered that night, tallied up to. My thighs hurt just thinking about it.

Throughout all of this, I still hadn't told him I was a stripper. I didn't know how he thought the coffee shop salary was supporting this life of excess, but he never asked. Maybe he just assumed I had a trust fund. Maybe he thought I made a ton of money off the documentary film I made that never came out. Maybe he didn't know how much money most people made at jobs because he'd never actually had one. It didn't really matter. We existed in this plane of existence away from reality, where we didn't talk about our relationship status, we didn't address the fact that he moved in without asking me, and we didn't discuss mundane things like where I came up with $1,200 plus in cash to spend in one evening, even though I lived in a railroad apartment with a roommate.

He'd told me a few times that he was going back on tour again "soon." I'd actually looked up his band's tour schedule on social media, and all it said about their upcoming tour was "TBD." That could have been soon, and that could have been never. So, you're probably thinking, well, why didn't you just kick him out? And the truth is . . . I didn't want him to leave.

It wasn't a healthy relationship. I'm not even sure if it was a relationship, or if I was just free housing with pussy included. But whatever it was, I enjoyed it. That is, until a particular Thursday in August. It was record-breaking heat outside. I feel like any day of extreme temperature in New York, they call it record breaking. Perhaps New Yorkers find the shit weather exciting if they know it's legendary on some level. But this day felt hotter than any other record-breaking day of heat I'd experienced in New York, and I had experienced several.

I could confidently say that I was more hungover than I had ever been. My evening before with Rob had consisted of multiple bottles of champagne, countless amounts of whiskey shots, and an assortment of eighteen-dollar cocktails from a bar that looked like a speakeasy where everyone wore three-piece suits. The more expensive the alcohol I drank was, the worse my hangovers got. It's like it was stronger or something. Who knew?

My pussy was so swollen and sore, from so many hours of sex. Truthfully, it was having its own hangover, and it desperately wanted to drink some Gatorade and curl up on the couch, but instead it had to go onstage and look loud and proud so strangers could attempt to refill the large hole in my bank account.

I caked on as much makeup as I could. I contoured and re-contoured my face, attempting to mimic an Instagram video I'd watched in hopes that it would bring some life to my face, but it was as if I was just smearing dirt across it. The other girls in the dressing room were shouting at each other, and it hurt my head. Melody entered, and I turned slightly away. I was embarrassed for my stripper mentor to see me like this. Of course, we were strippers. Maybe she'd be proud?

"Good morning," she said, happily drinking a Capri Sun, wearing a long, soft, black cut-up T-shirt and a sports bra underneath it that squished her large breasts.

I gave her a half-smile back. It wasn't like me to be so dismal when Melody entered the room, but it fully hurt to speak.

"Well you're looking awfully chipper this morning," she exclaimed, taking her T-shirt and sports bra off. She always did her makeup topless to avoid spilling excess makeup on her clothing. She used a lot of liquid liners and loose powders. It was always exciting when instead they spilled on her breasts, and then she'd wipe off the rainbow of leftover makeup with remover wipes at the end. Something was incredibly arousing about the way she wiped shimmery powder off herself in such a clean and calculated way. There was almost never even a drop left on her creamy, white, freckled skin after she was finished, but if there was, she'd rub Pond's Cold Cream into her breasts and then wipe it off again. And that's when things really got exciting.

"Is it that obvious?" I asked.

"Well . . . yeah," she laughed. "I can practically smell the alcohol from here. No actually, I *can* smell it. It's coming out of your pores."

"Great," I said. "Maybe it will work as an aphrodisiac!" I replied. I was hopeful. I mean, this alcohol had inspired some marathon sex last night after inhaling it through my mouth, who knew what affect it could have on people when being circulated back through my pores?

I thought maybe going on stage would literally and figuratively shake this out of me. I put on a sequined zebra-striped dress. I actually thought the dress was hideous, but I was drawn to it for some reason, and this logic seemed to translate to the customers because I always made more money in this dress.

TJ the DJ knew this dress very well, and every time I wore it, he put "Welcome to the Jungle" on. This animal role-play brought to you by '80's metal always got me in the mood. This tune turned every uptight businessman into an air guitar specialist, reminding them of their more wild days when they possibly had long hair and didn't have to wear suits. Or maybe they were just always boring people their entire lives who, at some point while studying for their exams in medical school, listened to this song and felt slightly less boring. But regardless, they all knew this song . . . and I did too. And I felt a different relationship with these men while dressed like a zebra. We were very much in the jungle, baby.

But today, it just wasn't working. I made my entrance. I strutted around the stage, and people even walked away. I leaned against the pole, I smiled, I scowled, I growled, I looked fierce, I looked innocent, I licked my lips, I went through every facial expression I could possibly think of, and my four-person audience was unaffected by any of them. I was a ghost. Could they even see me? I shimmied down the pole and spread my legs open, and no one even glanced in my direction. I got down on all fours and circled my ass . . . still nothing.

TJ could sense the awkwardness on the stage. He tried livening up the customers with banter, telling customers to tip if they loved the jungle. He told them to walk on the wild side, and then he got slightly more crass and he told them to scream if they liked pussy. They did not tip, and they did not scream. They just sat there, painfully unamused as my hangover continued to spread through all the limbs in my body. TJ ended the song early, something he never did.

I glanced up at TJ in the DJ lighthouse, and he shrugged and shook his head. He seemed defeated. I knew he was grasping for straws when he asked guys to scream if they liked pussy. I walked off the stage with zero dollars. But it felt even worse than that, like if there was a way to tip negative dollars, these people would have done it. Perhaps I would be sent an invoice and be billed for the three minutes of time during which I'd offended these people with my naked body.

I walked toward the back of the club, hoping to drain my sorrows in carrot juice. Melody stopped me in my tracks. "Hey, we all have days like this," she said.

"Really?" I replied.

"Yes, really," she urged.

"Will it get any better?"

"To be honest, it usually goes from bad to worse. It's like the customers can smell the desperation on you, and it's their least favorite scent. When you really need them, they don't want you. And when you're really busy, they want you more. I'd just cut your losses and call it a day. Go home, come back and start fresh on Monday."

I couldn't believe the rules of playing hard to get still existed when you showed the inner folds of your labia to someone before even knowing their name. Was Melody right? Was there no coming back from this? Or should I scour the room and search for whatever shred of sexiness I might have in me, in an attempt to channel it back onto the stage?

To see what happens if Naomi goes home, turn to page 172.

To see what happens if Naomi stays at the club, turn to page 184.

"Alright, I guess I'll just go home," I said.

"Trust me. I know what I'm talking about. If you stick around and beat a dead horse, it'll fuck with your head, and then you'll never make money here again. It will curse this place!" she said.

"Alright! Alright!" I replied. "I'm going." I started walking away.

"Call me later, let me know you're alright?" she called after me.

"Well, what if I'm not alright?" I said.

"Well, call me anyways." She blew me a kiss, then she perked up her breasts and walked away.

I left the strip club feeling like a boxer who'd just lost a match. I gathered my things and walked through Times Square toward the subway, sweating profusely from the humidity. I certainly didn't deserve a Lyft, and I didn't even deserve a yellow cab today. Hell, I wasn't sure if I deserved the subway. Perhaps I should just walk forty blocks, eight avenues, and over a bridge to suffer for being a failed stripper today.

I'd flunked a math course in college, and at the time I'd found that quite humorous. I'd also failed my driving test three times when I went to get my license, and I'd thought that was hysterical. But there was nothing funny about today. There was no silver glitter lining on this stripper cloud, and it made it worse that I couldn't go home and vent about it, because no one knew about this aspect of my life.

Perhaps today should be the day I told Rob the truth. I wondered if there was a way I could fast forward this confession, and say, "Hi, I'm a stripper. I have been for a few months now. I like it . . . usually . . . but today was a bad day. Now, please give me a massage and maybe some slow and sensual oral sex and make me feel better."

I sat on the subway and watched my fellow passengers, who were bopping along to music on their headphones, reading on their Kindles, or casually engaging in small talk. All I could think was, *no one else on this train failed as a stripper today.* I mean, I didn't think anyone on this train was a stripper at all, but it was safe to say that if anyone was, they probably didn't fail at it. My parents would have considered me a failure if they knew I was a stripper, but what would they have said if they knew I'd failed at being a failure?

My emotions were all over the place. Between the hangover, the rejection from strangers who stared at my ass, this up and down rollercoaster with Rob, the lying, and a bizarre little side crush on Melody, I felt like I just wanted to melt into a puddle of sequins and body spray.

I got off the train and walked to my apartment. Regardless of the financial logistics, I was happy that Rob would be there when I got back. I could use some familiarity, some affection, and . . . some Gatorade. While Rob never offered to pay for much, he always went and got Gatorade for me at the bodega across the street when I was hungover. Which, lately, was just about every day.

I walked into my apartment and . . . Rob was in his boxers playing Xbox with the other guys I didn't know.

The other guys were thankfully not in boxers. This situation was somehow more offensive, and more confusing, than me walking in on him with another girl. One guy was lanky and pale white, wearing bootcut pants and rocking a shaggy blond haircut. He seemed like he came straight out of the '70s. The other guy was extremely attractive, with black and gray tattoos that looked subtle against his dark complexion, including tattoos on his neck and hands. He had a gray skull cap on and a red and gray T-shirt, baggy pants, and some impeccably shiny and clean silver Air Jordans with a gold chain dangling from the laces. It seemed silly to wear such expensive shoes inside my railroad apartment just to sit on a couch next to a guy with no pants.

"Hello?" I said. The three of them hadn't noticed when I walked inside. They were in a heated argument about what kind of potions and plants to get in some virtual bodega. In the past month, I'd learned to occasionally enjoy indulging in the Xbox. I will admit, I sometimes found pleasure in pretending to be a sexy samurai swordswoman, running through fields and slashing people's heads off. I loathed this particular game, which never seemed to have a beginning or end, just a whole lot of walking around as an anthropomorphic lizard person collecting weird items for a battle that never seemed to happen.

I was still completely invisible. I'd spent the morning being ignored by men while I was naked, and now I was being ignored in my own apartment, wearing clothes. I was starting to doubt my own physical existence.

Finally, after what felt like an eternity but was likely about one minute, Rob acknowledged me.

"Oh, hey babe! What are you doing home?" he said. Did I really need to answer that question? Did I need to explain why I was in my own damn apartment?

"I . . . left work early." I wasn't lying. I still technically hadn't really lied to him since that first morning—I'd just left out a whole lot of information. The two other guys on the couch gave me a half-smile, half-wave kinda thing. I will admit, while I wasn't entirely pleased with strangers making themselves comfortable on my couch, they were handsome strangers. So I supposed it could have been worse. In the club, dancing would boost my serotonin levels so high, I could be attracted to anyone. But at the moment, I found myself incredibly attracted to these men who were definitely more excited about a virtual ogre speaking in talk bubbles than they were about me. I forgot that I actually do have a type. And all three men on this couch were it.

"This is Sean, and this is Digger," Rob said, pointing at each of them respectively. Digger was the shaggy blond one, and Sean was the guy in the skull cap with the tattoos. Ah. I knew these names—they were the other guys in his band. Sean was the singer, Digger was the drummer. There was another guy in the band (a guitar player named Jackson), but I guess he didn't hear about this gathering on my couch, or maybe he was coming later.

"It's nice to meet you guys!" I said. They both smiled back at me and said hello. I was still standing by my door, like I was waiting for a proper invitation to my own couch. I took my bag of makeup, heels, and sparkly clothing off my shoulder and threw it underneath my kitchen table . . . as if that was a way to hide my evidence.

"We just finished up a little band meeting. We had to

go over some stuff for the tour!" he said, with such confi-dence. He definitely wanted me to be proud about the fact that today he got up before noon and, um, "went to a meeting," I guess. I wondered if the other band members cared that he didn't bother to put pants on for the meeting. Or was it just an understood rule that whoever's house the meeting is at doesn't have to wear any pants? Not that this was his house. But that's beside the point.

"I'm about to slay this fucking dragon, babe! Come sit down, you gotta see this!" I had no desire to watch him slay a dragon, and I also knew that with this goddamn boring game, he wasn't going to be slaying any dragons, or any anything at all, anytime soon.

It was apparent that today I was not going to get a massage, oral sex, or even a Gatorade. I barely got an invitation to sit on my own couch. I was sweaty, dehy-drated, and defeated. And I felt like the shower was the most sensical place to solve the bulk of these issues.

"I'm gonna shower. Save some dragon slaying for me after I freshen up."

"Alright!" he said, grinning. He shifted his position on the couch, and I could see his balls spill out from his boxers as he took a giant bong hit. I'd be lying if I said I didn't want to put them in my mouth. He sucked the smoke out of that bong the same way he sucked on my clit, with so much force and determination to get every ounce of goodness into his mouth. That stupid lucky bong was getting all the attention.

I walked in the opposite direction of the "meeting" on my couch, through my kitchen, and into my bathroom (yes, my bathroom was off the kitchen). I closed the door. Today I wore a green checkered summer romper, which I peeled off my body. I stood in my bathroom naked, scrutinizing myself. My legs and arms had developed some new muscles I'd never noticed. My stomach was by no means a six-pack but it was like . . . a one-pack. I felt taller—walking around in high heels and being forced to thrust my small chest out all the time had retrained me to have great posture. I wondered whether my mother would be proud—she always used to yell at me for slouching. Perhaps that would be a good way for me to justify my stripping job to her if I ever decided to tell her. People always seem to villainize stripping as some sort of last resort job, taken only when times are desperate, but I could simply explain that it was the only option I had to improve my posture.

I stepped into my shower. It was mildly glamorous for a Brooklyn apartment. I think the landlord at some point attempted to remodel the shower, but stopped and gave up halfway through. The tiles on the wall were an ugly shade of brown, and several of them were missing. However, the shower had a sleek brass nozzle, AND a removable shower attachment, to boot. The tub was porcelain white, and I guess compared to the tile, it looked pretty modern. Any appliance in a New York apartment that worked and was purchased after 1940 can be classified as "modern" on Craigslist.

I turned the water temperature up. Even on a really hot day, I loved a good hot shower. I took a tube of Tahitian vanilla-scented liquid soap I'd stolen from the fancy hotel Rob and I stayed at. The smell alone transported me from my railroad apartment to an exotic beach. I squeezed the soap all over my body, and I let the liquid run all over my skin. It was creamy white, like the texture of jizz, but a vanilla-scented jizz. I rubbed the soap all over my nipples and down my new and exciting one-pack stomach. The soap suds dripped down my pussy, and I loved the visual of the thick cream running all over my lips. It looked dirty, but in a good way. I never used to get excited by the sight of my own body, but now I was so much more in tune with it.

Sitting with all the guys in their lap dances who unabashedly told me their sexual fantasies, ranging from unique and kinky to straight-up disturbing and illegal, had really helped me unleash my own. Much like these guys in the club, I didn't get to act on most of these fantasies, but hearing them be so forward about them had unlocked a part of me. And while I didn't have anyone to sit and listen to the details of *my* fantasies (unless they were specifically about Rob, then they would get transcribed into text messages to him), the fantasies were now at least free to roam around my brain and get me excited. I had a little Rolodex of filthy images in my brain that helped me get aroused during lap dances . . . and sometimes made subway rides a little more exciting.

Right now, a new one came into my brain, inspired by the Tahitian jizz running down my thighs. I re-enacted a much filthier version of the terribly mundane situation that had just occurred in my living room. In my fantasy, I walked in the door and told Rob that I had a really bad day, and he told me that to cheer me up, he was going to gangbang me with his other bandmates. In this version of the story, none of them had pants on, and there was certainly no Xbox. In this version of the story, I walked straight to the couch, and the three of them tore off my romper and had their way with me.

Rob threw me down and licked my pussy, while the other two guys stood beside me with their giant cocks near my face, and I stroked them with my hands. Rob took a break from licking and aggressively grabbed onto my clit. "See guys, that's her clit. When you get in there, just run on it like this, and she'll go crazy."

It was so kind of him to show his bandmates the way around my pussy. I stroked the bandmates' cocks, one in each hand. They were so hard, and I could see the vulnerability in their faces, the same way I saw it in the guys I gave lap dances to. Only here they didn't have to keep their hands behind their backs or their cocks inside of their pants. Rob lifted my legs up and inched his cock into my pussy slowly.

I slid my fingers inside of myself, thinking of his cock sliding inside me, while the guy who went by Digger started fucking my face. Sean assisted by rubbing my clit, just as Rob had instructed him to do.

My fantasy went to a place I didn't expect it to. Rob pulled his cock out of my pussy, and then Sean took Rob's thick cock and put it in HIS mouth. Sean put his hands behind his back and grunted with pleasure as he eased Rob's cock down his throat. I sat there mesmerized by this sandwich of sexual testosterone that I wanted to bite into. Their connection was so carnal—the image of these two stallions eagerly feeding each other made me want to sacrifice my body to them in some very dangerous ways. Rob rolled his eyes into the back of his head and curled his lip as his cock was swallowed. Sean sucked Rob's cock better than I did, I had to admit. They had spent a significant amount of time together on the road, so it made sense.

Panting from Sean's blow job, Rob eventually stepped aside, and gave Sean a nod. Sean got in between my legs. He slid his length inside me, while making out with Rob and stroking Rob's cock. Digger was still fucking my face, and my saliva was running all the way down my body. "Come on, fuck her," Rob instructed, and Sean thrust himself deeper inside of me. I felt like a guest of honor in this house of gorgeous men.

Digger took his dick out of my mouth, and then he pushed Sean aside, interrupting him mid-stroke. Digger picked me up and put me on all fours on my couch. Then he slid in behind me and pounded me, doggy-style. He slapped my ass. Rob was standing next to me getting his dick sucked by Sean, and I could hear him groaning over the sound of Digger's body slapping against my pussy.

Sean took Rob's dick out of his mouth and got on all fours on the other end of the couch, where Rob started fucking his ass. It was a doggy-style fucking party, all on my couch, and in this fantasy, my couch was a lot bigger and could actually hold two different sets of people fucking at the same time. Rob kept pushing himself into Sean, and I kept getting railed by Digger, as his shaggy blond hair shook back and forth. Rob pulled his dick out of Sean's ass, who was groaning and moaning with plea-sure, and he stuck it in my mouth. I could taste Sean in my mouth, along with the delightful taste of Rob's cock. I could also taste drops of pre-cum dripping out of Rob's cock, and felt spoiled by the snack. It was like an appe-tizer of jizz before my giant entrée to come later.

Rob pulled me forward so that I slid off of Digger's cock, and he lay down on the couch. He told me to sit on his dick. He pulled me toward his muscular chest and whispered in my ear, "Be a good whore for me," and instantly I gushed all over his cock.

At this point, in reality, I was sitting down in my tub, using my removable shower nozzle, hitting my clit with the scalding hot water, with my pussy gyrating in the water as hard as it could. My body was still covered in sudsy soap, and my hair was dripping down my face. I was pinching my nipples and shoving my fingers down my own throat. I guess I was . . . gangbanging myself in whatever way I possibly could.

In my fantasy, as I lay against Rob's lithe chest, I felt the head of his dick searching for my entrance, finally finding it and slipping in easily to the base. Digger then crawled up behind me and slid into my asshole, while Rob was still inside of my pussy. Sean, wanting in on the action, went around and dipped his cock into my parted mouth. I was air-tight with cock. Every opening filled. All the men were looking at each other, but also all focused on me. It was a fantasy, so anything was possible. I was being double-penetrated, cocks were stretching open all my holes. I was sliding back and forth on the two cocks, trying to soak in all the sensation. Digger pulled out of my ass, and Sean and he switched places. Rob stayed deep inside my pussy, pounding away as his bandmates took turns in my ass. It was like my pussy belonged to him, but my mouth and ass were up for grabs. It was romantic, and I liked it.

My pussy pulsated, in both reality and fantasy. The stream of water was pressed hard against my insides, and I stuck a finger in my ass. This was actually the first time I'd stuck anything in my ass while masturbating, but it was also my first time in a bisexual gangbang. Although, since that was only happening in my brain, I wasn't sure if that counted.

As the tension built, and the fantasy cocks pushed harder into every hole, I started cumming. I felt such a strong release inside of me—my pelvis was arched out, fucking the air and the water, while my finger remained in my ass. I was soaking wet with my own orgasm, the shower water, and the milky white soap.

In my fantasy, I came so hard on the two cocks inside of me. As the first wave of orgasm peaked, I crawled off of Rob, got on my knees, and watched as Rob jerked off Sean, Sean jerked off Digger, and Digger jerked off Rob. I was inside a circle jerk, as they all got each other to the point of completion. And then, I was showered in all of their loads, at the exact same time. I would imagine if this actually ever happened (which it never would), the guys wouldn't be able to coordinate quite that well, but since this was my fantasy, perfectly synchronized jizz was completely possible.

I was covered in their cum, aka the white, scented soap. They all patted me on the head and told me I was a good slut. I lay in my "modern" tub, with my body feeling like goo. I'd successfully masturbated away my hangover and my anger, and I felt re-energized and revitalized. I washed the soap off and grabbed a towel, which felt decadently soft against my sensitive skin.

I left the bathroom and walked back to my living room, freshly showered and wearing only my towel. Just as I suspected, Rob, Digger, and Sean were deliberating over which weapon to trade in as Rob's anthropomorphic lizard character argued with the town elf. There wasn't going to be any dragon slaying, and there also wasn't going to be a gangbang, so there wasn't much for me to stick around for. I walked past the couch and continued into my bedroom, deciding the best thing to do right then was to sink into my IKEA bed frame and take a nap.

To go back and see what happens if Naomi stays at the club, turn to page 184.

To continue with Naomi in this fantasy, turn to page 195.

"Thanks for the advice, but I don't want to go home yet. I'm gonna stick it out," I said. Just the thought of walking through Times Square on a Friday afternoon amongst hundreds of tourists in this weather made my hangover worse, and I certainly hadn't made enough money (any money) to justify taking a Lyft. It was worth it to stay here and make zero dollars, if only for the sake of using their air conditioner. I also wasn't sure how I would explain to Rob why I was home early from my job, when I couldn't tell him what my job was, and that kind of pressure definitely wouldn't help my hangover.

"Alright, then you better go drink some electrolytes and suck it up." She smiled and walked away. I trudged toward the "bar" and stared down the odd selection of juices. Green Machine, Berry Blast, Mighty Mango . . . they all sounded way too intimidating for me right now. This was some very aggressive juice.

I signaled for Rachel (the bartender) to come over. Over the course of the time that I'd worked here, I'd seen her wear every color of sparkly Uggs—green, blue, pink, purple, red, silver, and gold—but today she wore a multi-colored pair. I wondered if that pair of Uggs was created from all the residual glitter that had spilled off the other Uggs. I remembered when I used to be so baffled by her hideous shoes, but now, being a consistent wearer of sparkly clothing myself, it just made sense.

"Do we still have coconut water?" I asked. Coconut

water was a hot commodity here. A pallet of juices was delivered to the club every other week, and while there was always a surplus of Mighty Mangos and Green Machines, the coconut water went fast. I'd suggested to Tony before to simply order more coconut and less Mighty Mango, but he didn't take my suggestion seriously. He had a big passion for liquid mangos on steroids, and some kind of bias against hydration and coconuts.

"I'm sorry, we're out. We get some more in on Monday." She looked truly remorseful, even though I knew this coconut issue was way above her pay grade. She handed me a bottle of Mighty Mango, and I thought this day just could not get any worse. I took one sip of the thick yellow beverage, and didn't feel mighty.

I surveyed the room. I tried to use my stripper sight to get a sense of who might want a lap dance. The four customers who had dissed me by the stage were out of the question. There were about a dozen people in here, and all it would take was one single person who was horny, had a credit card, and wasn't totally disgusted by me to turn this day around. If one person got three dances and left a tip, that would be about enough for an electric bill.

Melody walked on stage. Shit. It was pointless for me to even try to get an electric bill out of anyone now. Melody would snare all eyes in the room.

At this point in my stripping "career," I knew I wasn't shy—I will admit I enjoyed spreading my pussy lips open in front of strangers and seeing their reactions. When I threw my legs up in the air, it looked dramatic simply due to the amount of leg that I had—what I lacked in tits and ass, I made up for in leg, and I used this to whatever advantage I could on stage.

I was basically a horny person having some fun up there. Most of the clubs in New York were "topless," meaning the girls just stripped down to a thong. In some places they even wore pasties. Quite frankly, I didn't know how I would survive in one of those establishments, because the reveal of the inner folds of my labia was the most exciting part of my show.

But, unlike me, Melody was an actual entertainer. She knew how to do more than just take her clothes off and spread her holes open. I often saw men who'd been sitting as far away from the stage as possible get up and flock to the stage to tip her. Today, in a vest/belt/thong combo, she made her entrance to "White Wedding" by Billy Idol.

Melody grabbed the pole and spun around it swiftly. She walked around the stage confidently before taking off a single piece of clothing, or even looking at anyone. Her strut sent a message: "I'm gonna put on a fucking show. Watch it or not, I don't care." The same men who may or may not have been alive during my set were now full of life, and full of dollar bills. She climbed up the pole and did a whole number of tricks up there, moving her body weight around the pole and sticking her legs out in different directions, even flipping upside down. As she was upside down, she managed to slide her fingers to her thong and slip it off.

Dismounting from the pole, she got down on her knees and opened her vest, revealing her breasts to the crowd. She did this little party trick where she lifted her arms up and raised each breast individually, then together, then individually. People got a real kick out of this. Melody removed her studded belt and threw it on the back of a customer's neck. She used her belt as a tool to bring the guy's face right into her breasts, and she suffocated him while shaking back and forth. Everyone looked intimidated and turned on at the same time. Myself included.

She spread her legs open in the last few moments of the song, strategically in front of the guy who'd tipped the most. She made a little V shape around her pussy lips, and barely spread them open a little further. The guy's eyes gazed between her lips without shame, his jaw dropped and his mouth watered, and just when he looked like he was about to explode in his own pants, she closed her legs and giggled. She knew exactly how to toy with everyone's emotions … including mine.

When the song ended, someone immediately swooped her up before she even had time to get her vest back on. She was whisked away off the floor and sent directly into the VIP room. Watching Melody's stage show gave me a second wind, or, a wind, since I never really had a first one. Her pole tricks, combined with my now finished bottle of Mighty Mango, gave me the strength that I needed to get that electric bill paid.

I walked toward a cluster of suits with a smile on my face, like I was ready for battle. I sat down next to a bald, portly man. He didn't seem remotely interested in me, but I was ready to flirt. However, before I could, I felt a tap on my shoulder. I turned around and saw Melody behind me. The bald guy seemed a lot more excited now that she was there, but she didn't address him at all.

"Hey, come with me, this guy wants me to bring a friend in." She pulled me in her direction and didn't give me the option to say no. I still wasn't letting this bald guy off the hook. He WOULD get a dance from me later, or the wrath of the Mighty Mango would be coming for him.

Melody pulled me into an area behind a thick red velvet curtain. There was nothing but a plush couch in there, and a little end table. Melody plopped herself down on the couch like it was her throne. I sat down next to her, right in front of an old silver fox, who looked like he was a direct descendant of the Rockefellers. He had on a black suit, a white shirt, and a red patterned tie that had been loosened up by Melody. Why on earth was he sitting on the floor? Did Melody charge extra, on top of the $500, to have couch access in the VIP room?

Melody kicked her dagger heels off, and the guy on the floor immediately started rubbing her feet.

"This is Richard," she purred. "He loves my feet, and he's gonna love yours too! Isn't that right Richard?"

He nodded. He didn't have much of a say in the matter, but I did hope he liked my feet. For the price he paid for this room, he should get a decent pair of feet.

"Hi Richard!" I said.

"Do you want to play with her pretty paws?" Melody asked. I had never heard anyone refer to feet as "paws," and I really liked the term, and the alliteration.

Richard nodded and took my shoes off. My pretty paws were a bit calloused and sweaty, and I was embarrassed. Melody's feet looked incredibly smooth, nails painted in a light shade of pink with a smooth white line on the top. I had clear nail polish on, which was mostly chipped off.

"I know how much you like toes without the polish!" Melody said. Richard nodded and smiled again, and he started to rub my feet. He was fully focused on them—I'd never had anyone inspect my feet like that before. He rubbed the arches, he stuck his thumbs underneath my toes. I heard him moan softly. This was not the worst!

He was giving me a good massage while I just sat here on this bench, and he was getting aroused. I was so used to being everyone's personal orgasm clown—it was always up to ME to figure THEM out, and I had to dance and juggle and make balloon animals with my tits and ass and pussy to please them. Now, I just had to … sit … next to Melody, inhaling her jasmine body spray, and get a foot massage. It was like we were at the spa getting pedicures, only some great-grandchild of an oil baron was paying to massage us.

Melody rubbed my thigh, and Richard now did double duty, and using one hand to rub my right foot and one hand to rub Melody's left foot. There was so much rubbing going on here, it was the most relaxed I'd been in days!

"I told you that my girlfriend had the sexiest feet, right?" Melody said. I will be honest, I really liked hearing her call me her "girlfriend," even though I was well aware that this was by no means official. Kinda funny that Melody used the *G* word on me, when Rob had yet to do so. He lived in my house, and I was technically a guest in hers. But the VIP room was a place to let go of reality and indulge in your fantasies (if you could afford it), so I was going to enjoy my half hour of pretending to be Melody's girlfriend.

Melody stuck her foot into Richard's mouth, and he looked like he had officially gone into a trance, like he'd disappeared to his happy place. Some people think a foot in the mouth is a negative expression, but to Richard, it signified bliss. He got carried away sucking on Melody's foot, and his hands sort of forgot about my foot, focused now on rubbing his crotch over his pants. Melody grabbed my legs, and then SHE started massaging my feet, all while keeping her foot in his mouth. I caught her eyes and she smiled at me. She continued to press into the arches of my feet, massaging each of my toes.

She was naked with her legs spread open—Richard wasn't going to let go of her foot, and that gave me the perfect view of her pussy as she rubbed my feet. I could swear her pussy was airbrushed straight out of *Playboy* magazine. It was soft and smooth, and everything sort of just fit compactly into a tight clamshell of a vagina. She had a little tuft of trimmed red pubic hair above her lips, slightly larger than a landing strip but smaller than a fully grown bush.

"I like watching you play with your girlfriends," Richard said. I did not like the use of the plural "girl-friends." I didn't like the thought of some other stripper bitch getting her foot rubbed in here, but I had to ignore that for now. I only became her girlfriend about forty seconds ago, so it was too early in the relationship to start fighting.

"Oh yeah! You like that?" she said, and she giggled. It was so endearing to see the girl who flips her hair and lands in splits on stage giggle. She then started to actually lick my feet, while Richard licked hers. She licked the arches, tasting my sweat. She tasted my heel and massaged my calf. She seemed to really enjoy herself doing this, pushing her pussy forward, gyrating on the plush bench. She was getting turned on, or at least doing a convincing job of pretending. Wait a second—I think . . . Melody ALSO had a foot fetish! It was evident her reaction was real. She and Richard were like a match made in strip club heaven.

She took my foot and pressed it into her thigh. She started moaning. Richard switched back and forth between rubbing and licking her right foot, as I slid my own foot up her left thigh. Slowly, it crept up toward her vagina. When I finally pressed my foot against her pussy, she pushed her pelvis into the arch of my foot. Richard watched us intently. He was an extremely well-behaved customer, content to admire and rub his own crotch on the floor.

I moved my foot up and down her pussy, and I could feel it getting wet. She grabbed my foot and licked her own juices off my toe. She delicately tickled the bottom of my feet with her fingers. It was a sensual tickle that I felt run through my body, making me aroused, rather than the type of tickle that makes you burst out laughing. She moved my foot back to her pussy and used it like her own personal toy. She rubbed her clit against the arches of my feet, and I could feel her getting more and more wet up against my "paws." I wanted to give her more. I wanted to give her everything, but I honestly didn't know how to give someone an orgasm with my feet.

She laid me down on the couch and put her big ass and her perfect pussy on my face. I went to work with my tongue like I never had before. I wanted to taste every last bit of her, to make her cum.

"Richard!" I heard her yell from my position underneath her ass. "Rub her feet while I sit on her face!"

I couldn't really see what was going on, but I felt my feet getting massaged again. I really enjoyed the foot rub, but right now I was focused on the feeling of Melody's soft folds against my lips. She gyrated around my face—my tongue desperately tried to keep up, but her pussy knew how to get what it wanted, and it was going to do its thing with or without my tongue's help. I reached my arms up and I grabbed onto her hips. I tried to lick her pussy in the same way Rob licked mine, taking every inch of it in, using every bit of muscle in my tongue. Richard, meanwhile, continued to press his thumbs against my heel. He rubbed my calves, then used both hands and rubbed each of my toes individually while Melody rode my face. I could feel her entire body weight on me, and I was excited and lightheaded from the suffocation. If I did in fact run out of air, this would have been a decent way to go.

Moments later I could feel her pussy tremble. I saw her thighs shaking, and she started breathing heavily.

"Oh yeah, come on," Richard cheered her on.

She continued to quiver on my face, so I stuck my tongue into her pussy hole, and I could feel it tense up, like it was going to bite my tongue off. She tasted so good, with a soft hint of that cheap body spray, and the inside of her pussy was so slick and soft. Her shaking slowed down, but I managed to move my tongue back onto her clit, and she started moaning again! I was giving her an orgasm encore. I'd had a whole lot of orgasms in the very recent past, and I knew when there was one little one left in there. I licked, and I got it. She quivered and moaned, and I think she was a bit shocked, and even impressed, with my ability to find orgasm number two.

She got off my face, and I licked my lips, tasting whatever residual juices were left on me. Richard continued to rub my toes. I could see a boner underneath his pants, and the harder he rubbed my feet, the larger the bulge in his pants grew. Melody sat next to me, and I put my head on her thigh. Richard massaged my feet, and I felt so incredibly accomplished and relaxed that I never wanted this moment to end.

But it did, moments later, when a blonde, tan woman with large breasts in a black blazer came into the VIP room. I had never seen this woman before, but I had also never been to the VIP room with Melody before.

"Richard honey! Did you want to do another half hour?" the blonde woman said.

Richard looked torn. His mind was saying yes, but his wallet was saying no.

"I gotta get back to work," Richard admitted. "Goodbye Melody! And nice to meet . . . you." He didn't know my name. Quite honestly, I didn't even know my name anymore, so, it was okay.

He handed the tan blonde woman $1,200 in cash and walked out of the curtain. The woman handed me $500, gave Melody $500, and kept the $200 for herself. That was a generous tip for opening up a curtain.

I had no idea what to say. I had so much to thank Melody for at this moment, and I wasn't sure if the one and a half orgasms I gave her made us even.

"Well, I'm glad I didn't go home," I said. She laughed.

"Yeah. Me too."

We sat on the couch naked, holding each other for a few more minutes, before the tan, blonde woman came back in with a much less friendly demeanor and told us to "get the fuck out because someone else needed the room." And . . . well, we did.

We put our respective stripper outfits back on and returned to the not so important area of the club. The bald guy was still sitting there, and he now looked magically happy to see me.

"Hey, are you free for a lap dance?" he said. I could feel the energy of the room back on my side. My hangover was gone, I had several months of electric bills paid, and a bald man's crotch had my name written all over it.

To go back and see what happens if Naomi goes home, turn to page 172.

To continue with Naomi in this fantasy, turn to page 195.

I'd gotten so comfortable with lying to Rob, it didn't feel like lying anymore. It was just my truth. When I was in my apartment, I was not a stripper, and when I was in the strip club, I was. When I was home, my stripper life didn't feel real, and when I was at the club, anything outside of the club didn't exist. Club 42 was like its very own self-sufficient ecosystem, surviving off of cash and carrot juice and frozen pizza.

The summer was coming to an end. I wasn't sure if Rob or stripping was my summer fling. Were either of these things permanent fixtures in my life? Was this my career? Was he my boyfriend? Did I love being a stripper, or did I just love being around Melody? I was unsure of a lot of things, but this ecosystem had to keep surviving, and it was time for me to go to work.

But this morning was different than others. While I was in the shower, Rob did something he normally didn't do at 9:00 a.m. He . . . woke up.

"Morning!" he said, as he comfortably walked into the bathroom without knocking, dressed in his boxers and nothing else.

"What are you doing up?" I asked.

He reached inside of his own toiletry bag, home to various strongly scented peppermint soaps, cologne, a toothbrush, and also little toothbrush wisps that served as a substitute when he didn't have a toothbrush. He was oddly obsessed with hygiene for someone who showered one to two times a week. He grabbed his own tube of black charcoal toothpaste and began to brush his teeth.

"I've got a meeting today! With the management. Tour stuff. You know," he said while brushing, and black goo poured out of his mouth. This type of toothpaste always stained the sink. It was one hipster craze that I simply couldn't get behind. The completely non-natural white toothpaste that was definitely tested on innocent bunnies in a lab made my teeth feel a hell of a lot more clean.

"Oh?" I replied. I had just finished showering. I grabbed a towel and patted down the droplets of water on my breasts and torso. He spit black goo into the sink and gargled water a few times. He looked at my naked body and smiled with freshly charcoal-scrubbed teeth.

"Where are you going?" he asked.

"To work!" I replied. He always seemed confused when I told him I was going to work. He truly didn't understand that some people did have to go to work on a regular basis, at the same time, on multiple days in the same week.

I gave him a kiss on the cheek and put my fingers through his greasy hair. He gave me that look. I knew that look. When he gave me that look, I disappeared into a vortex. Is it possible to be addicted to someone else? He grabbed me by the back of my wet hair and dragged me in front of him. I saw myself in the mirror—no makeup on, with a clean, dewy face. I had started using some vitamin C serum because I could afford to use serums now. I'm not sure if any vitamins were actually penetrating into my skin, but it certainly did glow.

Rob moved my legs with his knee. I was standing in front of him, getting double teamed by him and the bathroom sink. He licked his fingers and stuck them inside of me. It was a formality, really—he was just poking around to make sure my pussy was wet enough to slide his cock into, and, well, it was.

He slid his boxers down and stuck his morning boner inside of me as I looked at my vitamin C–filled face in the mirror. I didn't know how I could be so physically connected to him, while mentally I was a million miles away. My pussy knew his thick cock so well. He continued to pump in and out of me, pushing his length a little farther each time. I leaned back on him so we were pressed together into one horny human. My head was against his neck. He licked my ear, and it made the rest of my body shake. Occasionally, customers at the strip club would lick my ear, and I found it rather revolting, but when Rob did it, it made me shake. Perhaps he knew his way around an ear better than they did. Or perhaps I just liked everything his tongue did. I was sure I'd have an orgasm if he licked the bottom of my toe. Or, if I licked the bottom of his.

"I'm gonna fucking cum," he growled into my ear. Like an animal hunting for prey, he was a penis, hunting for a place to cum.

To see Rob cum inside of Naomi, turn to page 198.

To see Rob cum on Naomi's face, turn to page 200.

"Cum inside me, cum inside my pussy, cum inside me," I whispered. I don't even know why I whispered anymore. My roommate had heard us having filthy sex so many times, all over the apartment. Last month I'd handed over double the amount of rent in a stack full of singles. I figured it was the right thing to do, since I sort of had an extra person living there, but the good thing about having a messy roommate is that they don't get offended by things like . . . remnants of spilled semen, squirt, and sweat all over the couch. Jessie liked Rob—he was a partner to smoke weed with during the day, and she certainly appreciated the Xbox. She told me not to worry about him chipping in, but she still pocketed the money I gave her and didn't question why it was all in singles.

Regardless. I whispered and begged for Rob to cum inside of my pussy.

"I want your cum inside me, Rob." I wondered if all the substances in my body and lies in my brain would counteract my birth control. Was this a bad idea? I didn't even care. I wanted Rob's cum inside of me, and I didn't care about the consequences. I could feel his cock throbbing, like a dragon breathing fire inside of a castle, and yes, that castle was my pussy. His thrusts became slower and slower. I was pushed so hard up against the sink, I was eye to eye with my own reflection, who looked so helplessly addicted to Rob's cock. LeClaire would never act like this. LeClaire would never beg for cum. LeClaire had everyone wrapped around her finger, and didn't take orders from anyone . . . except Melody. And, I guess, TJ. Especially if he played Guns N' Roses.

Rob's eyes rolled into the back of his head. He pressed himself into me, as far as he could go, as he deposited a giant load of semen inside of my pussy. I could feel myself filling up with it, warm inside. He pulled his cock out, and his cum dripped down my leg, onto the bathroom floor. He smiled and said, "Okay, now you're ready for work."

He pulled his boxers up and left the bathroom. I cleaned the jizz off my leg and wiped away any remnants of cum that I possibly could with some baby wipes. I looked in the mirror and said goodbye to Naomi. I would see her later. It was time to snap out of this lusty trance and let LeClaire step in and take over.

To go back and see Rob cum on Naomi's face, turn to page 200.

To continue with Naomi in this fantasy, turn to page 203.

Rob continued to thrust himself into me—I could feel his cock throbbing inside of me. He had such a huge cock as it was, and I swear it had gotten bigger over the course of the summer. Every time he thrust into me, I felt my insides stretch, and every time he hit my G-spot, it felt like he'd found a new G-spot with more G in it than ever before. With me standing up all squished against the sink, he was hitting a brand new angle. I couldn't control myself. My legs couldn't stop shaking. Rob had to hold me in place so he could keep his cock snug in my pussy. My body was a rollercoaster and his chiseled arms were my seat belt, holding me in place, making sure I wouldn't stop cumming and his cock could continue to throb to the point of explosion.

I was dripping wet, the towel having long ago fallen to the floor. He moved his arm so he was holding my neck in place in a headlock, like we were engaging in some kind of wrestling match. I couldn't take it anymore—my pussy was a super saturated solution of orgasms. Wait . . . could I have one more? Okay. One more. Yes. I felt an incredible release of tension inside of me, a wave of tingling pleasure rippling up my spine, and then the muscles inside of my vagina physically pushed his cock out of me. I did say before that we were in some kind of figurative wrestling match, and my pussy was now fighting back, going for a TKO. I mean, pushing a cock out of you that just gave you a zillion orgasms isn't exactly a polite thing to do, but I justified it to myself that my pussy was not just my pussy anymore, it was an asset, and it didn't need to have manners. It had its own hoard of admirers, who paid to stare at it in the afternoon, in place of eating lunch.

I turned around and got down on my knees. While my pussy had been fucked to the point of no return, I had other holes and limbs to milk the semen out of Rob. I opened my mouth, stroked his cock. I could taste my creamy juices all over him, and I was turned on by my own scent. I stroked his cock deeper into my mouth.

"I want to swallow your cum. Give it to me," I said. I wanted to swallow it, and I also wanted to know that I could always make him cum. I'd become such an expert in arousing other men this summer, I felt like the empress of all boners in NYC. But when Rob glanced in my direction, even in the very apartment I paid for him to live in, I was just a puddle of helpless, horny goo.

So it made me feel slightly (and I stress *slightly*) empowered to get on my knees and beg to swallow his load. My hands and my mouth controlled the load, and I had the ability to release it however I liked. I stroked his throbbing cock, and felt the dirty cold tiles under my knees. I could see his face, so vulnerable and desperate. I stroked and sucked, my tongue running rings around the head of his cock, my hand clutching at the base.

"Give me your cum, Rob!" I said. He went from moaning to gasping, his long, sweaty dark hair moving from side to side as he jerked his head. Finally, he produced a giant delicacy of warm, delicious sperm into my mouth. Like my orgasms, it kept going. First a big stream, then a little stream, then little left-over trickling cum came as an aftershock. I swallowed every drop, and felt it run down my throat. As he swayed in post-orgasmic glory, I got up and kissed him on the cheek.

"Now I really have to get ready for work," I said.

"Yeah, I gotta get ready too." He chuckled. He was always chuckling. It was both adorable and infuriating.

I had a giant load of cum for breakfast, and now it was time serve my pussy to the public for lunch. So long Naomi, hello LeClaire. It was time to get to work.

To go back and see Rob cum inside of Naomi, turn to page 198.

To continue with Naomi in this fantasy, turn to page 203.

I sprinted down 8th Avenue with my stripper duffel bag on my shoulders. This really tested the structural integrity of the thick, padded shoulder strap, but the bag somehow stayed in place.

While I wasn't in any danger of missing a morning round-table on the subject of bagels and multiple selections of coffee and juice, I did hate being late because it would mean that I missed sitting side by side with Melody as we transformed from Brooklyn locals to strippers. My home life was filled with chaotic cock-crazed obsession, and my work life was a whirlwind of highs and lows, glitter and nudity, and cash. The morning routine Melody and I had—caking on foundation and dousing ourselves in Rite Aid body spray—created some sense of calm in my nonsensical life. I'd say it was the calm before the storm, but it was more like a calm between two different storms, in two different boroughs. My impromptu morning craze for cum put me behind schedule, and now I'd be contouring my face alone.

Melody was always on time. She had her whole routine timed to the second. She woke up at the crack of dawn, she walked her daughter to school. She walked back home, gathered her things, without fail took the 8:43 G train uptown, then the 9:17 train across town. She got to the club around 10:05, ate some yogurt, put her makeup on, and then immediately went to the floor and started her hustle. My college graduate friends could barely make it to their jobs at the coffee shop on time, even when their shift started at 4:00 p.m. Melody had no formal education whatsoever, but was by far the most responsible person I knew. She made me want to do better in life, even if that life was inside of Club 42.

I plowed through the club's door and ran up the stairs. The dressing room was empty. I stripped out of my yellow Maxi dress and flats, and I did an abbreviated version of my stripper makeup. Fortunately, with the vitamin C serum I'd been using, my glowy face required less makeup. Or at least, that's what I liked to tell myself. I brushed foundation on my face, made a thick, distinct line of liquid liner on my eyes, glued long lashes onto my shorter lashes, highlighted my cheeks with a forty-seven-dollar shimmery stick from Rihanna's makeup line, slid on some black thigh-high boots, a short red dress, a sparkly black thong, a leopard print garter around my thigh, and I took a deep breath. I proceeded to head downstairs, into the abyss of intermittent multi-colored lights, fake smoke, and nonalcoholic beverages.

I saw Melody on stage, doing one of her infamous boob tricks for a small crowd of mesmerized men, to the beat of "Talk to Me" by Peaches. There's not a lot of music that makes just as much sense in a strip club with yuppies as it does in a warehouse filled with beards and tattered vintage cardigans, but Peaches successfully defied that. It was dance music mostly for people who weren't strippers, but when an actual stripper danced to it, it was awesome.

Melody saw me from the stage, and it was as though her left boob was waving at me, going up and down and up and down.

I circled the room, and all the customers who weren't

hypnotized by Melody's breasts were shacked up with strippers on their laps. It was a complete violation of all stripper codes to even glance in the direction of customers who already had a lap dance claimed. I walked up the ministaircase to TJ the DJ's little lighthouse.

"Hey, get me on stage whenever you can. I'll dance to whatever I don't care—I just need people to know I'm here!" He half listened to me with his headphones on, and he scribbled "LeClaire" on his whiteboard. TJ nodded his head to the music, which I took as my cue to leave. Sometimes TJ seemed to want to indulge in small talk, and sometimes he seemed to really want you to get the hell out of his booth. If the headphones stayed on, it meant "go away." But just as I was about to leave, TJ pulled one side of his headphones up.

"Why you late?" he said. I found that odd. I knew TJ had authority over what songs to play and held the power to make the stage purple or blue, wish someone a happy birthday, or announce drink specials, but I didn't know he had any concern for what time we began our shifts. That seemed above the whiteboard's pay grade.

"I . . . don't know? Subway . . . um." I stumbled on my words and TJ started laughing.

"Just playin'! Ruby just went to VIP, so I can put you up next?" Before I had the chance to reply, or thank him, or pretend to laugh at his horrible attempt at sarcasm, he erased Ruby's name off the whiteboard. He put Ruby's name down at the bottom, and then wrote a bunch of roman numerals next to it. Every time I thought I was coming closer to understanding the logistics of how this whiteboard worked, he would throw in an asterisk or a roman numeral, and I'd be back to square one.

Regardless, I could deduce from this interaction that TJ and I were on a joking around basis, and that he was doing me some kind of solid by letting me skip the line while Ruby worked on . . . roman numeral seven. I appreciated this new camaraderie.

I waited on the side of the stage as Melody collected her dollar bills and her various pieces of neon string.

"Gooood morning everyone! Let's give it up for MELODY! Put your hands together for Melody. She's available for lap dances and VIP rooms. Coming up next on stage, it's LeClaire! LeClaire, coming up to the stage." Melody winked at me as she left the stage. While I wished nothing but the best for her, I hoped she'd had a truly miserable and empty morning without me in the dressing room. Okay, that might have been a bit dramatic, but I did hope she missed me a little bit.

TJ put on a Nickelback song. I have to admit that . . . I did not hate when this song came on. I had developed a unique relationship with it, where I fully acknowledged that my hipster friends judged it, but I found myself enjoying stripping to it. It took me some time to be honest with even myself about this, but I couldn't deny the scientific phenomenon that occurred when it came on. The song starts off all slow, and then it kicks in, but not, like, too much. When the chorus kicked in, I flipped my hair, threw my legs up in the air, and found myself thrusting my pelvis. I got emotional and sensual, and I got a big rush of adrenaline that made all the customers infinitely more attractive.

At this point, I had become complacent about the fact that I was going to lead a double life forever, where hipster Naomi and Nickelback-loving LeClaire never needed to cross paths. My two personalities could exist on different planets, in different boroughs, without anyone ever knowing about my double life.

That was, until right now.

I was lost in my own moment, crawling around on stage, basking in the joy of the predictable guitar riffs that felt so comforting. I slid my short red dress off and slithered around the stage in my thigh-high boots. I wrapped my legs around a bald man in glasses who was sipping on root beer, and I pulled his tie toward me. From his expression, I knew I had pre-sold one lap dance. Everything was going smoothly, dollar bills were flying onto me. The big chorus was about to come up, and I was going to do an epic hair flip. This hair flip completely disrupted the slow and seductive tone of the dance and turned me into some kind of stripping sex goddess. I pointed my head down, strategically collected all of my hair to the front of my head, and then I would BAM, FLIP! It was almost time to get up, do a twirl, and tease my panties off—

"What the fuck? Naomi?!" I heard from underneath my own hair. It felt so bone chilling, so invasive, and so intrusive to hear the name "Naomi" in here. My two lives could not intersect. I was Superman right now, and Clark Kent wasn't allowed in here. Naomi was sitting in a small bathroom in Brooklyn, happily content with a load of Rob's jizz.

What the hell was going on? Was someone else here named Naomi? I couldn't let this ruin my hair flip. At least four customers had been waiting for this moment, and more importantly, I had been waiting for this moment.

I flipped, and felt the ends of my hair fall back into place down my spine. And then I found myself looking straight into the eyes of Rob, standing near the stage with the rest of his band members and another guy who was slightly older, maybe in his mid-forties. Melody ran over to the guy in the suit—it was apparent that she knew him—and if she went out of her way to talk to him, he had to have been a regular customer of hers with multiple expense accounts and a credit card that matched the color of my thigh-high boots.

I stood on stage, frozen, missing all the good break-downs in the Nickelback song.

"Hey Jerry! I was JUST thinking about you. You're looking sexy today!" Melody said to the guy in the suit. Melody had impeccable selective memory. Anyone who spent over $1,000 on her remained etched in her brain, and whenever these big spenders made a return to the club, she could sense their presence, and she had always, without fail, "just" been thinking about them.

"Melody, this is the band I manage. I want you to take good care of them." He handed her a fresh stack of cash, with hundred-dollar bills that looked so clean and sharp, I was mildly concerned she'd cut herself on them.

"This should be enough to get you started," he said. I had no idea how much was in that stack ... but I didn't have time to do the mental calculus at the moment. Rob was standing a foot away from mostly naked LeClaire.

"Are you fucking kidding me right now? Really? You're a fucking stripper?" Rob ignored his bandmates and the other customers, and even Nickelback. I didn't know how to respond. Was there a point in responding? Melody watched the exchange with concerned eyes, while shoving her tits in his band member Sean's face.

I glanced up at the DJ booth, and TJ looked confused.

I couldn't let him down. I knew TJ took his whiteboard very seriously, and he didn't just reorder names for anyone. If I messed this up, he might lose trust in me, and I'd never jump to the front of the line again. I crawled over to the other side of the stage, acting as though business was usual, even though there was nothing at all usual about this business. I was well aware that the chorus of this song repeats itself a few times, and I was going to do another hair flip—nothing was going to stop me.

The customers on the opposite side of the stage from where my life was crumbling to pieces were completely oblivious. They sipped their nonalcoholic drinks, loosened their ties, and made themselves comfortable. I did my flip, I squatted against the pole and bounced my knees up and down. I got down on all fours, I kicked my legs back and forth, I thrust my pelvis in the air and basked in the moment. This was my moment, this was my stage, and no one could take it away from me. That was, until the end of the song, when the moment would literally be taken away from me as TJ called another girl to the stage.

I felt like I was dancing harder and better than I ever had, like I had something to prove. I realized, I wanted Rob to see this side of me. I wanted him to gawk at me the way all the other customers here did. I wanted him to stare up at me like a goddess, I wanted him to get a lap dance where he could worship me but not touch me. I wanted him to clank his own bottle of root beer against his "manager's" and say "That's my girl up there," while Digger and Sean showered Melody with money from that stack of cash they'd been handed. I played this fantasy in my head as I continued to shimmy my legs for the small crowd of customers in front, men who handed me bill after bill after bill until their own ministacks were done.

The song ended (and might I add, this particular Nickelback song does end rather abruptly), and I smiled at the assortment of men in khaki suits in front of me. A man with dark combed-over hair came toward me and told me to see him when I get off stage. I smiled and nodded and pretended to act like everything was completely normal, though it wasn't.

I peeked back at the other side of the stage, and Rob was gone. Melody was sitting on the lap of the "manager," and Sean and Digger sat with their arms folded in chairs, incredibly uncomfortable. I walked off the stage, threw my dress on top of my sweaty body, and sloppily rubber-banded the stack of singles around my garter belt. My hands were shaking, my stomach was racing—I wasn't entirely sure who I was and what was real at this moment. This summer had been a whirlwind summer camp romance between me and Rob, and me and stripping. Rob showing up was as if my parents came to pick me up from summer camp a day early, before I had time to say goodbye to all my friends. But in this instance, was I saying goodbye to Rob? Or the stripping?

I walked aimlessly through the club in my existential crisis, and then Rob stopped me dead in my tracks, close to the nonalcoholic bar.

"You fucking liar," Rob said. "I thought you worked at a coffee shop! What the hell was that?"

"I did work at a coffee shop. And then . . . I didn't work at a coffee shop. And I don't know, everything kinda happened so fast, and I didn't know how to tell you. Does it really matter? What's the big deal?" I looked up at him with pouty eyes, which on most occasions shortly led to his cock down my throat. "Did you like seeing me up there?" I asked.

"Do you know how fucking embarrassing that was? To walk in here, and see you up there looking like some dumb slut, in front of my band, and my manager? Are you fucking kidding me?"

My jaw dropped. I was in complete and utter disbelief. The same guy who'd fucked my ass on the floor of a public restroom and maybe changed his socks four times in the past three months had some kind of prejudice against strippers? A guy who relied on couches to crash on and pussies to penetrate in lieu of signing a lease and paying rent anywhere, ever, had just referred to me as a "dumb slut." Could I even begin to explain that the dollar bills being thrown at me all summer had paid for everything, from the electricity that powered his Xbox to the Plan B pill I took just the other day?

No. There was no need to explain any of that. I had truly learned the power of my own body language while working here. I spoke to people through my movements on stage, and this conversation expanded to grinding our crotches against each other in a lap dance. Actions spoke louder than words here at Club 42, and for that reason, I decided that I should—

To see what happens if Naomi slaps Rob in the face, turn to page 212.

To see what happens if Naomi kicks Rob in the balls, turn to page 214.

T HWACK!

I smacked Rob across the face. I have dainty hands, and I'd never hit anyone in the face before, so as much as I would like to report to you that this smack gave him massive amounts of physical pain, it didn't. I did not possess the physical capabilities to actually hurt Rob.

I had tears in my eyes. He didn't seem to give one shit. I was furious. There was truly nothing worse he could have done to me than absolutely nothing.

So I did the most logical thing I could think of, and I slapped him across the face again, harder. This time his hand jumped to his cheek. I wouldn't go so far as to say this one hurt, but it certainly hurt more than the first one. This time he started laughing. I said that there was nothing worse he could to do me than absolutely nothing, but I was wrong, laughing was certainly worse than nothing.

"You crazy fucking bitch!" he said, and he continued to laugh.

I felt humiliated, I felt small, I felt degraded. I felt all the things the general public assumes strippers feel every day just because they are strippers, but this severe disempowerment had nothing to do with the choice I made daily to exploit my own body for executives on their lunch break. This feeling was a direct result of me falling for someone with a giant cock and a bass guitar.

I stood there trembling, unsure of what to do next,

and unsure if what I just did (twice) was the right thing to do. Then I saw Melody, the guy who called himself their manager, and Tony, who actually was a manager, walking straight toward me.

To go back and see what happens if Naomi kicks Rob in the balls, turn to page 214.

To continue with Naomi in this fantasy, turn to page 216.

213

I'd learned several fighting moves from the countless hours I'd spent playing Mortal Kombat on Rob's Xbox this summer. I just never thought I'd attempt to try one on him. In my black boots and my red sparkly dress, I did have a strong resemblance to a Mortal Kombat character. Granted my tits were a mere *B* cup, and I had no swords or flames to throw at anyone, but I did have enough rage inside me to be more powerful than most weapons. Kitana was my preferred Mortal Kombat character, and in her backstory, spelled out on the game's select-a-player menu, it explained that she was on a quest for revenge, to take back what had been stolen from her. That was me, at this moment. This was my strip club, my Nickelback song, and my stage. I belonged here, not him. I needed to take it back!

Hi-yah! I did some kind of half-spin kick, lifted my leg up, and aimed right for the very cock that had given me earth-shattering orgasms all summer. The very same cock that penetrated every hole of my body on a nightly and daily basis. I wanted to destroy it.

I tripped over myself mid–spin kick. I'd like to blame my heels, but I'm not sure how smoothly it would have gone in any of my shoes. It was a lot easier to hold down the *A* and *X* button repeatedly on my couch than it was to use my actual leg. I didn't fall completely—I found my balance and re-positioned myself in the same fighting stance Kitana appears in on the main menu.

I shifted to the side, and kicked him right in the crotch. Unfortunately, Rob had reacted when he saw my failed spin kick, so this was a rather glancing blow. From the corner of my eye, I saw the juice bar girl spill a bottle of carrot juice all over the counter. Rob just stood there, shocked. I'm not sure if it was fortunate or pathetic that I'd clearly caused him absolutely no physical pain whatsoever, after all this effort.

"You're fucking insane, you know that? Seriously. You're fucking insane. What the fuck do you think you're doing?"

I was about to explain to him that I was on a quest for revenge and I wanted to take back the strip club that was rightfully mine. But then I realized this would only prove his point further, because that would be literally insane.

I stood there, trembling. I had tears in my eyes. I'd had a routine all summer, strategically coexisting in two separate worlds, and it was crashing down right before me. I didn't want to even begin to explain myself, I just wanted to get back to work. The dark-haired man by the stage had already found another stripper to shack up with. I was losing money as I stood here, and while it was worth taking a pay cut to kick Rob in the crotch, it was not worth losing money to stand here and cry and make apologies for things I wasn't sorry for.

Then I saw Melody, the guy who called himself their manager, and Tony, who actually was a manager, walking straight toward me.

To go back and see what happens if Naomi slaps Rob in the face, turn to page 212.

To continue with Naomi in this fantasy, turn to page 216.

"This dancer is assaulting my client! I'm a VIP customer here, and I demand she be removed from the club!" Jerry frantically said this to Tony as the group surrounded me and Rob. What kind of a joke was this manager? He couldn't even handle the situation himself, he had to outsource his dilemma to another manager.

Melody stepped in and attempted to out-manage the other managers (and me).

"Jerry, this is LeClaire, my girlfriend. I told you about her. I told her your guys were into BDSM, she's just warming him up—isn't that right sweetie?" She gave me an exaggerated kiss on the cheek.

"Wow," Rob said. "This just keeps getting better. Are there any other lies you want to tell me, *Naomi?*"

Melody snapped out of stripper mode for a moment—the tone of her voice and her entire facial expression changed. "Alright dude, I don't know how you two know each other, but you can't come in here and shout people's civilian names. It's fucked up. So cut it out," Melody said.

Tony was completely flustered. Jerry's eyes had started wandering, and he was obviously scoping out the other strippers walking by instead of paying attention to his "guys."

"That's her fucking name. Naomi. She never told me she had another name. SHE told me she worked at a coffee shop," Rob snarled.

"She did work at a coffee shop!" Melody replied, pushing her face closer to his.

Even though I was surrounded by coworkers, I couldn't overcome my hurt at Rob's disdain, and tears poured from my eyes as I said, "You've done nothing to deserve the truth. You've had every part of me from the moment I met you. I liked having this piece of me for myself." I truly spoke from my heart, but I don't think Rob heard a goddamn word I said, because the exact moment that I mustered up the strength to speak was also the exact moment TJ announced a two-for-one lap dance special, which was accompanied by a crowd cheering sound effect and the sound of fireworks. He was passionate about the two-for-one lap dance special today. I mean, rightfully so. It was a really good deal.

Tony stepped in, utterly annoyed. The only time I ever saw him was when I went to trade in my singles in the office, and he was always, without fail, on the phone, so the two of us never spoke. This confrontation was disrupting his soda ordering schedule, and for a club that didn't sell alcohol, I knew how important the soda delivery was around here.

"Sir, I'm very sorry for the inconvenience. I'll have my hostess set you guys up at a VIP table and anything you want is on the house," he said to Jerry. I found it funny that he had no inclination to apologize to Rob, the person who had been assaulted. Just to the person who allegedly was "managing" the victim. Anyone who came in here and wasn't in a suit was like subhuman to the staff. Also, I'd like to point out that I'd heard every table in this club referred to as a VIP table, and there was definitely no extra cost to sitting at any of them. They were technically just tables. But Jerry nodded and gave me a smug look, as if he'd really showed me who had more power in this situation.

Tony snapped his fingers, and the club's one "hostess" immediately came over. I'm not entirely sure what this hostess did, aside from stand around in a revealing black pantsuit and walk people to and from the VIP rooms. Tony gave her a nod, and she immediately knew to take them to a fake table. Well, the table wasn't fake, but the notion that there was anything important about it was.

Tony pulled me and Melody away.

"I don't know what just happened. Melody, I know you've always been good in my book, and you . . . uh . . ." He glanced at me. "Well you seem fine. How about I get you guys a car home? Take the rest of the day off and come back tomorrow, so it looks like I did something. Okay?"

"I'm sorry, Tony, this was my fault. Melody didn't do anything wrong," I said. Once again, TJ decided right at that moment to announce yet another two-for-one lap dance special, this time with the sound effect of a honking horn. I looked at Melody, and she smiled at me and took my hand.

"Everything's gonna be fine," she said.

I'm not sure if she heard me or not. Regardless, I sincerely found comfort in her response and held onto her hand as tightly as I could. I could feel our sweaty stripper palms pressed up against each other. Tony shrugged his shoulders.

"Alright, now get dressed. I'll have a car outside in five." He walked away. Melody continued to hold my hand as she pulled me in the direction of the dressing room.

"Wait, this way," she said. She shifted directions and took me on a slightly more scenic route that involved walking around the dark perimeter of the club to purposefully avoid crossing paths with Rob's table. I stopped in my tracks when I saw them, comfortably sitting at a table with an ice bucket full of root beer and a piping hot pizza, fresh from the freezer, sitting in front of each individual band member. Two different girls were grinding on Jerry's lap as he sat there with his eyes closed.

Rob was deeply engaged in a conversation with the hostess, who was sitting at the table next to him. This definitely wasn't part of her job description, but then again, I had no idea what her job description was. I could tell by their body language that sometime in the very near future, he'd be in her bedroom ripping off her pantsuit and plowing his fingers into her cunt. And you know, I was pretty sure she lived in Staten Island, so he would have to sit in a whole lot of shitty Verrazzano Bridge traffic or take a goddamn ferry to get there. I wondered if this would be the last time I ever saw him. I wondered if this meant I got to keep the Xbox.

Five minutes later, Melody and I were sitting in the car, holding hands in dead silence. We were in an actual "black car," not a Lyft or an Uber. This was a legitimate town car, driven by someone who specifically drives people for a living and took pride in it, not a recently unemployed millennial with a clean Honda Civic and a good driving record.

"So, I'm guessing that was your boyfriend?" Melody broke the silence. I never talked about Rob with Melody.

I never talked about Melody with Rob. But she knew I had some kind of complicated relationship situation back in Brooklyn, just from eavesdropping on phone conversations in the dressing room.

"I mean . . . he was my something," I said. "But whatever it was, it's over now," I added.

"I gotta say, I never saw you as the type to . . . you know . . . fight people. You surprised me with that one!" she laughed.

"Oh yeah? Were you intimidated?" I replied, in a bit of a flirtatious way.

"Um, no. Not at all," she laughed. "But be proud of yourself. He tried to manipulate you, and you rejected it. You believed in your own instincts, you were unapologetic, and you fucking did it. That kind of thinking will make you a very good stripper."

"What do you mean?" I said.

"The customers come in thinking their money and their suits are gonna control you, but you flip it around, and you control them, by taking every situation and making it yours," she said.

"Well, I had a good teacher," I said.

"You didn't need a teacher. Just a fellow Brooklynite to make you feel comfortable."

"You did a lot more than just make me feel comfortable," I said. Since she seemed to be such a champion of going with my instincts, I decided to obey them and move closer to her. I slid down the smooth leather seat until I was right next to her. The temperature-controlled car was perfect for getting close to someone. Normally the ventilation in the Lyft vehicles made it a constant battle between too cold and too hot, until you gave up on the temperature completely and tried to open the window, which left you smelling the scent of garbage and listening to loud car horns.

Melody and I had met under the guise of two fake names, in a place where we were both pretending to be someone else. But where were we actually pretending? Was my life in Brooklyn the real me? Was Naomi the real me, just because that was the name on all my legal documents? I'd never thought my feelings for Melody could be real, because our relationship and our interactions existed in a place that wasn't supposed to exist. But in this moment, everything I felt was very real.

The release of Rob from my life was like quitting an addiction cold turkey. And while an addiction fills a lot of immediate voids, I knew I wanted to kiss Melody in a way that I'd never wanted to kiss Rob. I didn't want her to reach inside of me and pull an orgasm out—I wanted to run my fingers through her hair, and I wanted to caress her creamy skin and count her freckles and make her laugh and wrap myself around her . . . and reach a simultaneous, beautiful orgasm. I wanted to run through a field with her, but in Brooklyn we don't exactly have fields. We do have a nice botanic garden. I'd have to check out their membership prices.

I was going to do this, I told myself. I was going to submit to my instincts and kiss Melody. But, like always, she was one step ahead of me. She kissed me before I had the chance. It was beautiful to know that in this moment we both felt the very same thing. Melody and I spent so much time with our naked bodies rubbed up against each other, with our hypersexual stripper personas aggressively flirting with one another, and at times we'd even given each other exaggerated, over-the-top orgasms that customers paid to watch. But this moment was real.

We'd worked backward: we met each other naked and wound up kissing clothed. The moment was so intimate, but so innocent. Our professional driver caught sight of us in the rearview mirror and he turned up the music, which added the perfect soundtrack. Because guess what coincidentally came on the radio? Nickelback.

I kissed her more passionately. This song was directly associated with the sexual beast inside of me, and it brought just the right amount of filth into this innocent kiss. We sucked each other's faces in the back of the town car—I held on to the back of her hair, and we slid ourselves into each other like puzzle pieces. The car came to a stop in front of Melody's apartment. We'd shared a car home many times this summer, and we'd always stopped at Melody's place first and said goodbye as she disappeared into her own second life as a mother.

"Well since I'm off early, Sophia won't be home for a few hours." She looked at me seductively. "So . . . you coming in?" I was already shutting the door to the ever-so-luxurious town car before she could even complete her sentence.

Melody and I couldn't keep our hands off each other. I followed her inside, walking and kissing at the same time.

Her apartment was less than two miles from my apartment, but two miles in Brooklyn is like an entire city away. Her part of Brooklyn was known to be more family oriented. I was lost in the heavy make-out session, but in the brief moments when I opened my eyes, I noticed some sleek appliances from this decade, an assortment of well-maintained plants against an exposed brick wall, a teal velvet couch that looked intentionally vintage, an assortment of multi-colored throw pillows, and a coffee table with actual artistic coffee table books on them. It had all the charm of a Brooklyn apartment, but, like, for grownups. And I thought that was fucking hot.

She threw me down on her teal couch and continued to kiss me. I'd only been with a few women before, and I wasn't sure how much they counted. I'd been in college, and I'd wanted to experience being with a woman, so I'd agreed to a few one-night stands with the first few women who expressed interest. While I'd enjoyed the physical experience, none of them were women I had any emotional connection with. They were just kind of . . . there. I'm sure they all thought of me as a very forgettable lesbian, if they ever thought of me at all. This, with Melody, was different.

We were inside of a dream, and this velvet couch was a big sea of clouds that we were floating around in. It felt like the most innocent first date, which was ironic considering we were two people who'd spent the summer naked together, listening to men talk about anything from wanting to get urinated on to fantasies about their aunts. Melody was my mentor in losing any shred of innocence I'd ever had, but somehow, right now, she brought it back.

We couldn't stop touching each other, we couldn't stop smiling. She was on top of me, still fully clothed in black leggings and a Led Zeppelin T-shirt. She smothered my body with her voluptuous breasts, and I couldn't stop staring at her freckled skin peeking through the intentional holes in her leggings, and her soft pouty lips, shining with remnants of strawberry flavored lip balm. I was in a short, patterned summer dress, which slid up and down my thighs as we kissed. We pressed ourselves into each other, fully clothed. It was like we were giving each other a mutual lap dance.

She pulled me up so my legs were wrapped around hers, and I was straddling her. She slid my dress up over my head with ease. It was safe to say we were both very good at taking off clothing. She kissed my neck. She moved her hands up and put her arms around my back, pulling me close to her. We released for a moment just to stare at each other.

"I can't believe this is really happening," I said.

"I can," she replied, and immediately she put her lips back onto my mouth. I was covered in goose bumps— cold on the outside and warm on the inside. My cotton panties were getting moist. I pulled off her Led Zeppelin T-shirt and the gray sports bra she wore underneath it. We pressed our breasts against each other, though hers were about twelve times the size of mine.

She pushed me back down onto the couch. She moved down my body and licked my right nipple. My pussy thrust up toward her, eager. She caressed my torso while she licked my nipple with the very tip of her tongue. Then she moved to the left nipple, but used her fingers to caress the right, keeping both nipples nice and hard.

The foreplay was getting less innocent, and I was beginning to moan heavily. My panties were in dire need of coming off. She let go of my nipples and kissed me again, sucking my face with more passion that she had before. She slid fingers under the band of my wet cotton panties, exploring my body as if she hadn't already seen it naked a hundred times. She gently rubbed my outer labia, using a delicate circular motion with her fingers around my pussy. It was such a gentle, slow movement, like she was waking up my erotic senses from a midmorning nap. I let out another moan.

"Melody . . . fuck," I said. "You're so fucking hot . . ." She put a hand on my mouth and shushed me, which was convenient, because I was completely ready to say "I love you." Seriously! I was! I know. It was too soon for that. But in the thrill of this encounter, I was completely in love with her, and it had a little to do with the way she moved her fingers around my pussy, and a little to do with how fucking beautiful and incredible she was.

She moved her lips down my stomach, and then her lips met my other lips. She licked up and down my vagina. My body could barely handle the intensity, and my legs tried to close. She opened them up, with one hand on each thigh, and she kept my legs spread wide open and my pussy in her mouth. My pelvis thrust against her dainty mouth as she rotated her tongue around and around. She merely brushed against my clit with her tongue, and I shook.

"Ah! There it is!" she said. I felt like I had, like, twelve clits. Everything she did everywhere was heavenly, and every touch felt like it could have led to a climax. This felt like a tantric experience, like I was cumming the whole time, even while we were kissing.

But while everything felt amazing, once she found my clit that amazing feeling multiplied exponentially. She put more pressure on my clit with her tongue, and used her fingers to spread my pussy lips open so she could get more acquainted with it. My insides were tensing up, my toes curling. She sensed my body edging toward completion, so she sucked on my clit even harder. Harder and harder she went—her tongue felt like it had a twenty-pound weight on it. The pressure of her tongue against my completely wide-open pussy was just incredible. And then, she slowed it down . . . she licked ever so gently and . . . god damn. Holy shit. I exploded.

My body convulsed as she continued to gently kiss between my thighs. Who knew such a gentle grazing of the clit could cause such intensity inside of me? This was one giant orgasm. It had many layers. But Melody wasn't done. She moved her tongue just slightly to the left, and it felt like a whole other orgasm. She moved it ever so slightly again, and I could not control myself. My entire crotch was flopping up and down, and somehow her tongue was able to follow. She licked all over my pussy, and it felt like some kind of grand finale, where every little part of my pussy was cumming at the same time.

"Fuck, fuck, FUCK! Melody!" I couldn't speak, my brain was mush, I was quivering and shaking, and I could see a puddle of wetness beneath me on her velvet couch. She pulled away from me for just a moment and gave me a sinister smile.

"I've just gotten started with you," she said. I was still shaking on her couch as she got up. A minute later, she returned with what looked like a large jewelry box. Wait. Holy shit, was she going to ask me to—

No, come on. Just kidding. That's not where this was going.

She opened the box, and inside of it there was an assortment of sex toys. A flesh-colored cock connected to a harness, Hitachi vibrators, butt plugs, handcuffs, and more. She had an impressive little stash, neatly organized in a beautiful vintage box.

"What do you want to play with?" Melody asked. She picked up a strap-on with one hand and a titanium butt plug with a shiny blue crystal with the other. *Hmm . . . which one do I choose?*

To see Naomi use a butt plug, turn to page 228.

To see Melody use a strap-on, turn to page 233.

Well, I'd already had cock this morning. As much as I was sure Melody could work a cock better than anyone born with a cock could, I wanted to enjoy her femininity, and I wanted to celebrate the purging of the toxic cock in my life by having penis-free sex. I mean, even though the cock was made out of silicone, who knew. I could wind up supporting it and letting it move in with me, if I liked it too much.

So I chose the shiny butt plug. It looked exciting. Was I supposed to use it on her? Was she going to use it on me? I'd already had a giant orgasm, so I was ready for anything. My body was so insanely sensitive, I felt like I could fit anything inside of it. Truthfully, just about anything Melody did would have made me cum again.

But more than wanting to cum again, I wanted to make Melody cum. I wanted to press my quivering body against hers and feel her shake. She was standing up now. I took the strap-on and put it back in the box, but I put the butt plug and the Hitachi momentarily on her coffee table with all the art books. I landed on my knees on her Persian rug in front of her couch.

I took my hands and I slid off her skin-tight leggings. They slowly rolled down her big and beautiful thighs. Her leggings made it down to her knees, and then she took control and grabbed my face, stuffing it between her legs. It was an incredible feeling—the elasticity of the leggings made it so her legs could only open so wide, and my face was stuck in between her thighs. I thrust my tongue out and licked between her pussy lips in any way I physically could. I could faintly hear her breathing as she grabbed the back of my head and pushed it harder into her vagina. I moved my tongue up and down and sucked on her meaty pussy lips while I was happily trapped between her thighs.

She slid her pants entirely off, pushed me down on the couch, and grabbed the butt plug. She joined me on the couch, lay back, and moved her legs toward her ears, in kind of a pretzel position. I'd seen her do this on stage, but I never thought I'd get to experience it next to her, on her very own couch. She handed me the butt plug.

"Here. Put this inside me. . . . Slowly. And keep licking me." She giggled. *Yes ma'am!* I was ready.

Then she put her hand out.

"Here! Spit in my hand," she said. I worked up some spit and did as she said. She reached underneath herself and spread my saliva around her asshole. I loved being used as her own personal bottle of lube. My pussy was still soaking wet as I watched her moisten up her ass with my fluid.

I slid the plug in slowly with one hand, while I licked her vagina with the flat of my tongue. She had a thick, meaty pussy, and I loved it. I had seen so many men mesmerized by the layers of her labia. You could really get lost in there. I licked up and down her various flaps— each of them had their very own personality. I circled my tongue around while slowly working the shiny plug into her ass. She started moaning more loudly, and I knew I had found a good spot close to the top of her pussy.

I licked harder in that very same spot, and then the butt plug slid right in. She grinned.

"Good girl!" she said.

Now that the butt plug was in, my hands were free. I used one hand and slid my finger into her now slippery pussy. I slid a second finger in, but it felt like it needed another one. I licked her clit as I slid my fingers in and out, grazing the shiny butt plug that remained stationary in her asshole. As I said before, I didn't have a whole lot of experience with women, but I felt like I knew exactly what to do with her body. Perhaps because I had been staring at it all summer, or perhaps because of the intense desire I had to make her cum, I just kind of knew what to do. I couldn't explain it. Everything came to my tongue so naturally.

I could see her eyes rolling into the back of her head. She groaned from somewhere deep in her belly, and I picked up the pace with my fingers. The slick inside of her pussy was getting warmer. I took my fingers out for a second so I could lick the juices off of them. My greedy mouth wanted to taste her insides. My fingers tasted so good, so warm and creamy and moist.

She caught my eyes. I'd seen her give this look to people on stage. It was just a rule—you had to give her whatever she wanted when she locked on you with her hungry wolf eyes. Whether it was all of the money in your wallet, or your entire bank account . . . or, in my case, a giant orgasm, you just had to give it to her.

I could see the butt plug just lightly puckering in and out. It was so hot to see all of her erotic zones working together, and it was an incredible feeling to know that I was capable of making this happen.

"Fuck yeah, come on! Make me cum!" she said. "Come on baby, make me fucking cum!" She was panting. It was so hot to hear her talk to me like this, like we were in a fantasy. To think, just about an hour ago, I was assaulting someone in a strip club, and now I was in complete orgasmic heaven, tasting the wonderful wetness of Melody's insides in my mouth.

I continued everything I was doing, but bigger and better and stronger. My fingers and my tongue were hard at work. I sucked and licked every part of her pussy, from her lips to her clit, and I curled my fingers inside of her until I found her G-spot.

"Yes! Right there! Right there!" she cried when I found it. I was overjoyed at my success. Her pussy was tensing up on my fingers, but I kept curling and thrusting them. Her vagina was getting hungrier in my hands, it was speaking to me. I slid one more finger into her, and her eyes widened. Her pussy was so tight, it was going to cut off my circulation, and I was perfectly fine with that happening. I would have happily donated my fingers to make her cum harder.

"Yes! Yes!" I heard her softly say. Her thighs shook. I could tell she was having an internal and clitoral orgasm at once. Her clit swelled up, and her pussy spit my fingers out. I'd never used a butt plug on anyone before—I'd never even used one myself—so what was I supposed to do? I continued to lick her clit while she was still mid-orgasm, but my fingers rested unsure on the plug.

"Pull it out, pull it out!" she said. *Yes. Thank you.* I was waiting for further instruction. I didn't want to, like, use it the wrong way? Even though there was . . . only one way to use it. I pulled it out slowly as she continued to convulse and shake. I took my tongue off her clit and rubbed it with my fingers to put more pressure on her pussy. I needed my eyes to be fully focused on the plug in her ass, not only because it took a bit of concentration and coordination on my end, but also because it REALLY turned me on to watch.

I could see her asshole stretch to the shape of the plug as I pulled it out, hugging the sides of the wider ends. She breathed heavily as I slowly pulled it out, with a smile so wide, she looked like she was possessed. I licked the butt plug, reasoning I had tasted all her other parts and this was the last part of her I needed in my mouth. It tasted like fresh warm skin, if that makes any sense. I placed the plug back with the art books on the coffee table, and I got on top of Melody. My lips found my way to her mouth. We returned to making out furiously, our freshly orgasmed pussies pressed up against each other. Sucking each other's tongues and licking each other's lips. I could have kissed her forever, and I was going to keep kissing until she made me stop.

To go back and see Melody use a strap-on, turn to page 233.

To continue with Naomi in this fantasy, turn to page 239.

I'd spent the summer physically addicted to Rob. It was like a drug. As someone who had recreationally indulged in a variety of drugs in my lifetime, I can say the addictive feeling I experienced with Rob was far worse, and that includes the time I went on a four-day coke bender in Columbia.

What was it about him? When I thought about it, there was nothing particularly grabbing about his personality. Come to think of it, I barely knew his personality. I found myself rolling my eyes at half the things he said, if I even paid attention to them. I hung onto every last word Melody said. She made me laugh, she taught me things I truly wanted to know about, I found her fascinating, I respected her, and I thought she was beautiful.

And now . . . she'd just given me a giant orgasm. If Melody had a cock, would I go from enamored to addicted? I wanted to pine over her the same way I did for Rob. She deserved my addiction, so I chose for her to strap-on a cock and fuck me. I reached for the leather harness with a dildo attached to it. She gave me a sinister smile and said, "Well . . . now you're really gonna get it." I thought I'd already gotten it—but I was definitely ready and willing for more.

I sat on the couch obediently, with a swollen, freshly orgasmed pussy, as she slid on the leather harness. She fastened the buckles on both sides and tightened up the straps surrounding the ring that held the dildo in.

I suppose it was my first time with a strap-on. I say "suppose" because I had obviously used dildos before, and I'd had sex with women before, and I'd had a woman use a dildo on me before, so I felt like this combination gave me a little too much experience to consider myself a total strap-on virgin.

I had to admit, simply the visual of her standing there with a strap-on was incredibly arousing. With her large perky breasts on top, and a couture accessory around her waist and hips attached to something large and phallic, it was the perfect combination of everything that could possibly turn me on. Cock and breasts and expensive leather, mixed with the scent of flavored lip gloss and perfume. I ogled her the same way her customers ogled her on stage as she stood in front of me, looking like a fucking goddess. But I got to see her with a cock, and they didn't.

I started touching myself. My hand was like a magnet that was pulled to my pussy—I didn't even know my hand had snaked down until it was already there. I felt so lucky. Her customers wanted to stroke their own cocks so badly when they watched her on stage, and here I was, touching my pussy while I watched her.

She sat on the couch and smiled. "Come here and sit on my dick," she said.

I was expecting her to throw me down on all fours and fuck me from behind, because that's normally what Rob would do once he knew my pussy was wet enough. In retrospect, it's like the goal of the sexathon for both of us had been to get aroused enough so we wouldn't have to look at each other anymore and could just focus on our own selfish orgasms.

She squirted a bit of lube onto her cock, and I got on my knees and straddled her, facing her. She ran her fingers through my hair, as I'd seen her do to so many smitten men in the club, and I understood immediately why they loved this attention. I ever so slowly began to descend my pussy onto her cock. It was thick, but I knew I could handle it. I'd learned this summer that once I was aroused, I could fit just about anything inside of any hole of mine.

She never broke the intense eye contact, and she moaned heavily, as if she could really feel my pussy. This cock was an extension of her, which was truly a unique experience for me. I wasn't entirely sure logistically how my pussy on this dildo caused her to moan like that, but it did, and while I didn't get it, I liked it.

The cock still had a ways to go. I wasn't even halfway down, it was so thick and so hard. She reached down and started rubbing my clit. Now I was moaning, and she was moaning and encouraging me. "Yeah come on girl, get it. Get my fucking cock!" she said, as she rubbed my clit, and now I began to open up and slide down the dildo faster. Hearing her talk about her cock just opened me right up. She grabbed my face and kissed me as I got the remainder of it inside of me. I was balls deep on her cock, or . . . leather strap deep on her cock? The end was attached to leather, and quite frankly that was so much sexier than . . . balls.

She penetrated me deeply. She took her hands and started moving my pelvis back and forth. Holy shit, what a good feeling that was. As she maneuvered my body to grind back and forth, I could feel her deep inside me, pushing against the walls of my pussy, and I could feel my clit gently rubbing against the leather as an added bonus.

She knew exactly how to move my pelvis, exactly how to penetrate my mouth with her tongue. I held onto her breasts and caressed her nipples, rolling them under my thumbs. I kissed her neck, her ear. Then I gently began to unfold my knees and move my pussy down her cock.

My juices served as enough lube for me to ride her harder and faster, up and down and up and down. We were both breathing heavily inside each other's mouths. These were not the same orchestral noises I made when Rob railed me, these were breaths of genuine passion. I ran my fingers through her long red hair. I pulled her face toward my small, perky breasts, and she sucked my nipple as I continued to ride her. She licked my left, she licked my right, and then she gently bit my left nipple, just hard enough to add a speck of pain to the pleasure.

I switched back to grinding, and I could feel the dildo inside me hit my G-spot. My pussy tightened up on the dildo, building pressure inside of me. Melody grabbed onto my pelvis again and ground against me. My pussy was so tight I was worried I'd snap the thing right off, which was a unique issue I'd never had to worry about before.

"Come on, cum on my fucking cock!" she said. I furiously switched back and forth between grinding and riding, all while sticking my tongue in Melody's mouth and grabbing onto her breasts. I was so deeply entranced by her body that my pussy was about to explode.

She grabbed me aggressively, in the most ferocious and sexy way, and she threw me down on the couch. She lifted my legs up as far as they could go (she knew I was never exactly all that flexible), locked eyes with me, and said, "Lay back. I'm gonna fuck the shit out of you."

Now the mood had changed from sensual to filthy. My eyes widened. That was it. I was hooked. I hoped she was prepared for Naomi the cock-crazed sex fiend to enter her life—a side of me she had never quite met. I submitted to her, feeling simultaneously weak and wonderful.

She did exactly as she said. She placed her palm on my clit and pounded my pussy. It was so fucking hot to look up and see her tits bouncing, and then to look down and see my pussy getting pounded by her dick. Just when I thought her cock had reached the edge of my cervix, she would rub my clit, and somehow more inches of the cock would disappear inside me. My hole belonged to her, and it would do anything she wanted. My G-spot was being hit with intense pressure, my clit was being rubbed with her left hand, and my right leg was being held down so she could hold me in place and fuck me on her terms. She started cackling. This strap-on session seemed to have unlocked a sex demon inside of both of us, and it was the perfect union of dominant and submissive stripper debauchery.

She moved her hand off my pussy and thigh, and *whack!* She smacked both of my tits. Fuck. Yes. The sting of her slap hurt in an incredible, sensual way, and somehow it inspired her to pick up the pace of her already fast fucking. She smacked my tits again, and now I was moaning loudly. Everything in my body tensed up.

"Cum! Come on, let it out girl!" she said. And then . . . I did. My G-spot tensed up and I felt the ultimate release as she pounded away at me.

"I'm cumming, I'm cumming," I said, my mind unable to form other words. She was moaning and shaking as if she was cumming too? Maybe somehow she was? Was there a way to have a mental orgasm from being the dildo disher in the strap-on equation? I had never worn one, so I didn't really know. All I knew is that I was cumming really hard, and if she wasn't, she was feeling something, because the look on her face was of pure ecstasy.

We both crescendoed and then came down. She slowly dragged her cock out of me. We both began to laugh.

"Holy shit. That was awesome," I said.

"No, you're awesome," she said. We started kissing again on her couch, and I was going to continue kissing her forever . . . or . . . until she stopped me. Whichever came first.

To go back and see Naomi use a butt plug, turn to page 228.

To continue with Naomi in this fantasy, turn to page 239.

Melody and I spooned on her couch. She was the big spoon. She held me tightly and played with my hair, and we both lay there smiling, coming down from the intensity we'd just shared.

"Well, I'd love to sit around here naked all day, but Sophia's gonna be home soon," Melody eventually sighed. She sat up and began putting her leggings and T-shirt back on. I grabbed my dress from underneath the couch and slid it back on, but even clothed, I couldn't stop smiling.

"Here! Don't forget these." Melody grabbed my panties off the ground. I laughed and slid them back on. I figured this was my cue to leave, and I certainly didn't want to overstay my welcome here, but I also . . . kind of wanted to overstay my welcome here. I didn't want to go. Then again, I also didn't want to "Rob" her . . . so to speak.

"I promised Sophia I'd take her bowling if she got an *A* on her test today. And, I'm guessing she got an *A* on the test because she's a fucking genius. Do you . . . wanna come with?" Melody said.

I paused mid–purse collection. "Really?" I replied.

"Yeah!" she said. "I mean literally just yesterday she was asking me why I don't have any friends . . . so this is perfect timing."

"So that's what I am? Your friend?" I replied.

"Oh my god." She laughed. "Are we seriously having

this conversation three minutes after the first time we had sex?"

"I'm sorry," I said. "I just want to be . . . more than a friend." The words just slipped out of my mouth. Hey, she was the one who'd told me to go with my instincts.

She smiled and kissed me again . . . and our kiss was interrupted by the loud beeping sound of a school bus outside.

"I'll go get her. I'll be right back!" Melody walked outside.

I sat on her couch and let the moment soak in. It all felt so surreal.

I'd spent this summer as LeClaire by day, and Naomi by night. I'd tried to keep the two personalities separate, never able to quite decide which part of me was actually *me*, and which part of me was just pretending to be something. LeClaire was not the name I was given at birth. She started off as nothing but a name for my nudity, but she became the source of my strength and independence. She was an exhibitionist, and a hustler. She was my sexual inner animal, who specialized in witty, horny banter with men in suits.

But both parts of me had sex with Melody. The stripper and the hipster—the nerdy and clumsy film school graduate and the graceful and desirable dancer, the Brooklyn and the Manhattan. Every aspect of both of my personalities had come together and joined forces in the name of having mind-blowing orgasms on this very adult teal couch. It felt peaceful. It felt wonderful. It felt . . . like love. A broken American flag bikini had led me to find that special someone that I hadn't even known I was searching for. Now, I couldn't get too ahead of myself

. . . but I knew that together we were in this for more than just one lap dance.

THE END

To go back and choose another fantasy, turn to page 13.

Rob closed his eyes and soon drifted off to sleep. The minutes passed, but I was wide awake. He began to breathe in that way that isn't exactly a snore, but almost could be. I wanted to drift off to dreamland with him, but I also wanted to tell him the truth.

"Hey. So, tomorrow, I'm not going to work at the coffee shop," I said. I didn't know if he was actually sound asleep or if I'd woken him up and he was ignoring me. I sat up. It's hard to speak sternly when you're snuggling.

"ROB!" I said louder, and I shoved him with my hand. Now that I was mentally prepared to tell someone I was a stripper, there was no going back. He had to wake up. His eyes opened, startled. He looked around to collect himself, and then he realized he was in the same exact place that he'd been not even five minutes ago.

"Yeah, hey, um what's up? You okay? I figured it was cool if I stayed here, but I can go if you—"

He started to get up. He seemed so nonchalant about this situation he thought was happening. If I'd had sex with someone and passed out in their bed, I'd be furious if they woke me up to kick me out. He must have been very used to getting kicked out of beds. I wasn't sure if I found this concerning or not.

"No! Don't go, you don't have to go anywhere. Sorry. Um, I just wanted to tell you something."

"Do you have a boyfriend or something? It's cool. . . . Don't worry, I go back on tour in—"

"No! I don't have a boyfriend!" I laughed, and now wondered how many of my friends in committed relationships might also be sleeping with Rob.

"Look, I told you I didn't have to wake up at five . . . and I didn't tell you why, and I just want to tell you, so you know," I said.

"Okay . . ." He looked really confused, and rightfully so.

"Today I got fired from the coffee shop I worked at, and . . . well, on my way home I kinda sorta stopped at this strip club in Times Square, and . . . I got a job there. As, you know, a stripper." He had an innocent, confused expression on his face, but then the confusion turned to a neutral nod, and then the nod turned into a smile.

"Cool! So . . . you're a stripper now?" he said.

"Well, I just auditioned today, and I go back tomorrow to officially start." I made quotation marks with my fingers when I said the word "auditioned," even though it literally was an audition. I just felt like any of my friends who used the word audition referred to trying out for Broadway musicals and such, and I wasn't sure if applying for a job to work at a strip club warranted the same word.

"Hmm . . . have you ever done it before?" he asked.

"No, never. Nothing even close." I wasn't even sure what was "close" to stripping, but the only jobs I'd ever had were working at coffee shops, and for a short while a bookstore, and it was safe to say that neither of these were close to stripping.

"So, wait you just walked in? What did you wear on stage?" he asked.

"Um . . . the same clothes you saw me in?" I shrugged my shoulders, and he broke into a laughing fit.

"Fuck, really? Are you serious? You just walked in and stripped in that?" He pointed at my pile of clothing on the floor, still laughing. I didn't understand. Coming from a guy who changed his jeans maybe once a month, how was he some kind of Tim Gunn for strippers?

"Well yeah, I didn't really plan this. Alright? It all kinda just happened." I was starting to regret telling him.

"I'm surprised you even got the job!" he said, patting my thigh.

"Hey, fuck off!" I shoved him jokingly, but also kind of seriously. "I don't know if you noticed, but I had a very nice matching pair of bra and panties that was just . . . lovely up there, and, you know, vintage dresses are becoming a real thing at these clubs. Just you wait." I paused, realizing how ridiculous I sounded, but it was too late to take it back. "Anyways, I start at 11:00 a.m. tomorrow!"

"Yikes. The day shift?" he said. Here I'd been worried he'd judge me for taking my clothes off for money. But instead, he was judging me for taking off the wrong clothes at the wrong time for money. I was speechless. He must have seen my face contorting, half in surprise and half in indignation, because he held up his hands.

"Hey, babe. I'm no stranger to strip clubs, or strippers. I'm in a band. I've been to nudie bars all over the country, and I've definitely dated a whole bunch of—"

"Alright!" I interrupted. "Thank you. I don't need to hear about all the strippers you've fucked. Wait, did you fuck any strippers who work at Club 42?"

He thought for a moment. "Only like three," he said.

"What!" I threw a pillow at him . . . once again, half joking and half not joking at all.

"I'm just fucking with you. No. I've never even heard of it. But I also never go to strip clubs when I'm home." He held his arm out and pulled me toward him. "Come here!" He held me close to him and kissed me on the cheek. I think this was his polite and loving way of saying sorry for calling me a crappy stripper, and also telling me he fucked a lot of non-crappy strippers.

"So how about I help you out a bit? I don't want you going in tomorrow like you went in today. If this is what you wanna do, babe, you gotta go in and kill it!"

"Really? How can you . . . help me?"

Rob drew his arm away and pointed to the small square of empty floor space by my bed. "Well, why don't you show me what you can do, and I'll give you some pointers!"

"What do you mean?" I said.

To see Naomi do a strip tease for Rob, turn to page 246.

To see Naomi give Rob a lap dance, turn to page 253.

"**A** strip tease?" I said.

"You heard me! Show me your routine! Let me see it!" he replied. He moved back to the corner of the bed and placed a pillow flat in front of him on the covers, and did a "ta-da" shake with his hands. I wasn't sure how this pillow made it any more practical for me to turn this bedroom into a strip club. "This is the stage, and I'm a customer, sitting here!" he said, pointing at the bed to demonstrate that the bed beyond the pillow was the stage, and anything behind the pillow was the customer. I started to shimmy my naked body around awkwardly, laughing.

"Well that's no way to start. Come on! Put on an outfit and dance for me. Or then I won't believe you that you actually became a stripper today." He folded his arms, all smug. Sheesh. These strip club customers can be so demanding!

"Okay, if I'm gonna do that then you have to put on some clothes too? You can't be naked by the stage. What kind of establishment do you think this is?" He nodded and pulled on his boxers. Rob did not graduate high school, or go to college, or adhere to most rules in life. It was nice to know that he did, however, respect the rules of the fake strip club.

I didn't have actual stripper clothes, but I did have a burlesque outfit, which I'd purchased for a burlesque-themed brunch I used to frequent every Sunday at a bar in my neighborhood. After wearing it once, I'd realized it was a terrible outfit to eat poached eggs and drink mimosas in. Luckily, it was far more suited to wear while dancing in your bedroom that was also coincidentally a strip club.

As I found the red and ruffly outfit, Rob was patiently waiting by the um . . . stage/pillow. He grabbed his pants off the floor, reached into his pocket, and pulled out his wallet. He threw a few singles onto the pillow. I had better hurry and get this outfit on—I had customers waiting!

The outfit consisted of a red corset with black ruffles, matching ruffled panties, and red satin gloves. The corset was an idiot-proof one that thankfully had a zipper down the front. It cinched around my waist and it pushed my perky *B* cups together, making them appear slightly more like *C* cups. I pulled on the ruffled panties and then put on the satin gloves, which extended up to my elbows. I immediately found myself caressing my own exposed skin on my neck and chest. The gloves felt silky and smooth, and got me in the mood to take all this off.

And now . . . of course. I needed a song. I'm not gonna lie, I was starting to believe we were in a strip club now. I could see it. I was committed to this. I pulled out my phone and cued up a Christina Aguilera song. You know, the one from that movie *Burlesque* that was about . . . burlesque. It seemed appropriate. As soon as I pushed play, Rob perked up.

Shit. It was a commercial for Geico. Maybe the first thing I would do with my stripper money would be to get an actual paid subscription to Spotify. Now it was very awkward in the strip club. Rob started laughing, and then a Spotify announcer came in and assured us that we would now have thirty minutes of music.

Finally the song began. I started by standing on my bedroom floor. We never discussed if the stage was only the bed or if it extended onto the floor, but I took it upon myself to use my own imagination since, after all, I did work here. Christina's powerful voice came in with a big belting sound, and I used this opportunity to get in a committed stance. I took my gloved hands and ran them through my hair, then brushed them across my face, slowly. Rob nodded in approval. My outfit and the song, combined with the fact that I was incredibly attracted to my one audience member, helped this all come to me quite naturally.

I climbed onto the bed. The song shifted tempos drastically, and it felt like that meant it was time for me to move drastically. I stood on the bed and I began to slowly draw my silk hands down my satin corset. This naturally led me into a crouching position, where I continued to feel down my thighs. I repeated this same motion again, sliding my hands up and down my body.

"Take it off! Wooohoo!" Rob yelled, and he threw a single dollar bill at me. I slowly began to unzip the corset, exposing more cleavage, my nipples, and eventually my navel. I threw the corset at him—it landed on his head and we both smiled. He was quite adorable in his boxers with a corset on his head, sitting behind a pillow at this bedroom strip club.

I crawled toward him, and let him get just close enough to want more. Even though I'd had his entire cock inside me less than an hour ago, I really enjoyed role-playing in this "look but don't touch" tease. I put my boobs incredibly close to his face, and then I backed away, turned around, got on all fours, and began to shake my ruffly butt. I was more or less dry humping the bed, and after several moments of that, I decided it was time to take my panties off.

I put my face down on the bed and my ass up in the air. I reached behind me and managed to slowly pull the panties down. Rob had a perfect view of my ass and pussy, and with my face down where it was on the bed, he could see that too. He stared, mesmerized, right at my pussy . . . the same way the customers had earlier today. He had a whole different admiration for my pussy from this angle. I mean, before, he didn't have the opportunity to get a good look at it. He'd been too busy pushing his cock into it and trying to make it cum. Before, it was like his musical instrument—now it was like his very own oil painting.

He threw the three remaining dollar bills at me. And then, breaking every strip club rule that I assumed existed, he leaned in and stuck his face in my pussy, while I remained face down and ass up. He licked my exposed lips, and I shuddered.

"So, since you're the stripper expert, is *this* what happens at the end of every song?" I giggled.

"No! Just at this club. This one's different," he mumbled, lifting his mouth just barely from my skin, and then he got right back to licking my pussy. I still had my satin gloves on. I'd never found an appropriate time to take them off, and I liked it. It made this whole little pussy-eating session feel . . . fancy. I could feel him breathing inside me. He worked his tongue as far into me as he could go, which sent electricity spiraling through my chest. He spread my lips open ever so slightly, and then sucked on my clit.

From my upside-down view I could see my left satin glove clenching the organic navy blue sheets in a fit of pleasure. He stopped and came up for air, and I wanted to scream. How dare he choose oxygen over my pussy? I needed more. I looked back and saw his rock-hard bulge inside of his boxers. He swiftly pulled down the already stretched-out elastic and his eager penis slid right inside of me.

"Fuck!" I yelled, in anger and in pleasure, like I was cursing him for making me feel this good. His cock penetrated me so deeply from this angle, I could feel him all the way to my cervix. He pushed himself all the way inside me as the walls of my pussy stretched open to fit every inch of his cock. He thrust in and out, and smacked my ass, and it felt dangerous. I wanted him to rip my insides apart and destroy me.

Instead, he paused mid-stroke and his cock stopped moving. "Come on," he said, and he gave me another good smack. "You want this cock? You better get it!" He laughed, in the most manly but immature way. I couldn't believe he was going to make *me* do all the work after working three jobs today—a coffee shop, a strip club, and a make-believe bedroom strip club—but alas. I did want that cock, and I was going to get it.

I scowled and pushed my ass back and forth, getting every last inch of cock I could possibly get. My ass cheeks bumped up against his pelvis, and I slid back and forth, from the tip of his head to the bottom of his shaft. His cock was so thick that every time my pussy came off it I worried it would never fit back in, but my soaking pussy solved this physical mystery, and he slid right in every time.

I got into a good back and forth rhythm, riding back on him. He moaned and kept saying "Ohh yeah" in approval of my ass. I liked his encouragement and decided to try to add some flair to my ass-riding by throwing some twerks in there. It fucked up my flow, and I'm not entirely sure what it looked like from his point of view, but quite honestly it felt ridiculous. This was probably too advanced for a person with little to no twerking experience. We both immediately started laughing.

"Cute," he said. *I'll take it*. He smacked me again, pulled my ass cheeks apart, and then reclaimed control of the thrusting as he plunged himself in and out of me. I moaned in ecstasy. "Yes!" I kept yelling. He was destroying me, just as I had wished for earlier, and I couldn't have been happier that my wish was coming true. I could feel his cock throbbing, pulsating. He thrust faster and faster, hitting my G-spot, and my legs quaked. I was in orgasmic tears. And just when I thought I couldn't possibly cum anymore—I came again.

I yelled, a loud broken moan, interrupted by the rapid thrusting. Spotify wasn't lying about its half hour of uninterrupted music. It had taken us down a rabbit hole of all the Christina Aguilera hits, so my orgasm moan harmonized quite well with one of her belting choruses. He pulled out of me and covered my ass crack and some of my cheeks with his semen. While I couldn't exactly get a great view of it from where I was, it felt like an impressive load, especially being his second one for the evening. I reached my hand back and scooped up whatever droplets of cum that I could get, and then licked my fingers clean. I loved the way every part of him tasted. I got out of my doggy position and lay my head on his chest. I needed a moment to collect myself, to return from the other orgasmic dimension I'd been abruptly transported to.

"So, how did I do?" I said.

"Well, I guess you can work the day shift in Midtown . . . and the night shift here." He laughed.

"Oh, thank you. I've always wanted to work the night shift at the strip club in my own bedroom, I just never thought I was good enough!" I threw off my satin gloves, and we resumed our snuggle position. I shut my eyes, and this time I fell asleep soundly, knowing that honesty truly is the best policy. It had turned my bedroom into a strip club, and had gotten me multiple extra bonus orgasms. I was ready for Club 42.

To go back and see Naomi give Rob a lap dance, turn to page 253.

To continue with Naomi in this fantasy, turn to page 261.

"Well, why don't you give me a lap dance? Let me see what you can do!" Rob said.

"A what?" I replied.

"A lap dance," he repeated.

"Excuse me, I dance on a stage. *Not* on people's laps. Maybe they do that sort of thing at your trashy hole-in-the-wall clubs in Pennsylvania, but this is in Times Square—it's very classy, and Cardi B used to work there."

"No she didn't. She worked at Lace. And the dancers definitely do lap dances there, I know because I've gotten several . . . not from Cardi B." I had forgotten that I completely made up the fact that Cardi B worked at Club 42—I'd gotten so excited about my own lie that I'd forgotten it wasn't true.

"I thought you didn't go to strip clubs when you were home?" I replied, with a little more edge in my voice.

Ha! Now he was the one caught in a lie. He looked unsure of what to say. "Well they had a really good steak dinner. So that was different."

This still didn't entirely get him off the hook, but I accepted his answer.

He pulled his phone out of his pants and quickly found Club 42's website, which clearly stated in large letters on the homepage that there were "Two-for-one lap dance specials" every Friday. Today was a Thursday, so not only did this mean I would have to give a lap dance tomorrow— this most certainly meant I would have to give two.

"Did you think you'd be dancing on stage the entire shift? What did you think you'd be doing when you weren't on stage?" he said.

"I don't know . . . getting ready to go on stage again?"

He laughed. "No, that's not how it works." I was starting to wonder when Rob would flip this conversation and admit that *he* was actually a stripper, because he seemed to know a suspicious amount about the logistics of stripping.

"You basically . . . get on my lap, and you give me your own special dance! Every girl's got her own way of doing it. In most clubs, the guys have to keep their hands behind their backs, or to their sides, so you gotta move your body around and, you know, get things going." He started to get visibly excited as he said this. He was definitely a lap dance connoisseur. How strange that just moments ago, he had his entire cock inside of me, and now the thought of me dancing on his lap with his hands behind his back was turning him on.

"Well, alright! Sounds like fun. I guess I better get some practice in," I admitted.

Rob grabbed his boxers and put them on. Before I could even finish my sentence, he was sitting on the edge of the bed with his hands beside him, already in his assumed lap dance position. I jumped on him and straddled him. I moved my body around a little, but was more or less ready to just rip his boxers off and have sex with him again. It seemed more efficient than doing this whole lap dance thing.

"Hey! You gotta slow down! And you need to put on an outfit," he said.

"Oh! Okay . . . we're like, really doing this aren't we?" I replied.

"Yes. I want the full lap dance experience. Don't you have some high heels? Or some lacy panties? Or something?"

Okay. He may have been the expert on strippers, but I refused to take any fashion advice from him. This was exciting, though, because not so long ago I had purchased a beautiful La Perla lace teddy that I found on a discount designer app, and I never knew when I'd have the occasion to put it on. I also had a pair of designer stiletto heels sitting in my closet that I never wore because they were far too uncomfortable to walk more than a few feet in. I'd tried wearing them once on an evening I knew I'd be Uber-ing to my destination, and I literally couldn't even make it through my kitchen. But it was safe to assume I could probably wear them while sitting in someone's lap, on a bed, in my room.

I pulled the teddy out from my drawer. I knew exactly where it was—I gazed at it often just to admire it. It was lacy and cream colored, and completely open down the middle, just barely covering the nipples on the sides. It was so dainty and feminine and beautiful, I instantly felt sexier the second I slipped it on.

I grabbed the heels and put them on my freshly pedicured feet. These high heels really tested the endurance of the arches of my feet. This had to have been good practice for being a stripper, right? I stood up in front of Rob, now with a brand new persona.

"Would you like a lap dance, sir?" I felt like this classy lingerie paired nicely with a classy pronoun like "sir." Even though I was speaking to a man with stained boxers and bed head.

"Yes, yes I would. I've been waiting for you," he replied,

his voice low. He even said it with a twinge of a British accent. But only a slight one. The word "sir" somehow set that off. We were clearly role-playing in a very upscale strip club here, which was possibly in the UK.

Rob picked his phone back up and cued up a song. I knew it from the first few chords—it was "She Rides" by Danzig. A classic stripper song, so classic that even I knew that ... and I knew very little about strippers. And after just seconds of the song, I knew exactly why. The beat of the song told my body what to do.

I shimmied toward him while still standing on the ground. I slid my hands up and down his thighs. Then I turned around and brought my ruffled ass right between his legs, grinding it to the beat of the music against his cock. I was getting the hang of this now. Surprisingly, I even liked it! It was like a dry hump and a slow dance mixed into one. I could feel his cock growing inside of his boxers, and I liked the sensation of his growing excitement against my fancy lingerie.

He arched against me. "Yeah, you got this!" Yeah. I fucking did.

I jumped up on him and straddled him, with my knees locked around his thighs, bouncing against the thin fabric that held his eager cock in place, and I rubbed his tattooed chest as I slowly grinded against his steadily growing boner. He started to thrust toward me while I pushed my pelvis back into him . . . but I was in lingerie, and he was in boxers. It was so sexy how dirty we could get without actually doing anything dirty. We weren't kissing, and we weren't fucking. This wasn't oral sex, this wasn't foreplay. This tease wasn't on the typical "baseball field" we all learned about in middle school—it wasn't any base.

I followed my instincts and did what the music told me to do. I unhooked the buckle on the back of my neck and let the two sides of the teddy fall to my waist. My breasts hung out. He licked his lips, which told me how badly he wanted to lick my nipples, and even though I had absolutely no qualms with him licking my nipples, I had to abide by the rules of the strip club bedroom. I mean, really, imagine how embarrassing it would be if I got fired from here.

I decided to tease him by pinching my own nipples, while continuing to grind on his cock.

"I bet you wanna touch them, don't you?" I whispered.

"Oh yeah, I really do. Mmmm. Lemme see you lick them," he said.

I stretched my tongue out of my mouth and lifted my breast as close to my tongue as possible, and I licked my own nipple as he sat there writhing with jealousy, his mouth parted. I got off his lap, stood on my floor, turned around, bent over, and slowly slid off the teddy, showing off my ass as I took it off. He kept his hands on the bed and gripped the sheets. I could see how hard he had to restrain himself, and it was such a turn-on. I was tempted to just give in—take his hands and put them all over me—but I also enjoyed watching him resist.

The teddy came off, and I was now in nothing but incredibly uncomfortable pointy heels. I strutted over and straddled him again, but now I was rubbing my bare pussy right up against his boxers. I could feel him rock hard against my lips. I held onto his neck and pushed myself into him. The fabric between us, tempting and restraining us, amplified his desire, and he started to moan. I licked my lips and breathed heavy breaths of passion inches from his face. Danzig continued to serenade us with the perfect song to grind on someone to. The song shifted tempos a little for the . . . I think this part was the bridge? I wanted to do something drastic for this part. It called for something exciting.

I had to think fast. I knew the bridge didn't last for that long. I locked my legs around his waist and did some kind of gymnastic move, throwing my torso upside down. I arched backward, with my legs secure around his hips and my head near the ground. I put my arms back and morphed into, like, a handstand. I had a plan here, I swear. I was going to move my legs around his neck, and get his head as close to my pussy as possible. It was a test to see how well he could restrain himself, and if he would give in and lick it. I was secretly hoping he would. I put the plan into action, and I raised my legs in the air. I kicked my legs around and then—

"OUCH! WHAT THE FUCK!" Rob yelled and jumped back, which made me completely lose balance and fall to the floor. I got up, and Rob was yelling in pain. His face was scratched and bleeding profusely. Holy shit—I'd kicked him with my heels.

"OH MY GOD, I'M SO SORRY!" I said. "God damnit!" I turned on the overhead lights so I could inspect the wound. There was a very deep scratch on his face. The blood was dark and thick. These heels truly were dangerous. "She Rides" ended, and another Danzig song I didn't know came on. With all the blood on his face and me naked in heels, we sort of looked like a hot Danzig music video. But unfortunately this was not stage blood, and something real had to be done about it.

I threw my deadly shoes off and I grabbed him. He definitely didn't have a boner anymore.

"Come on, we gotta wash this. I'm sorry, I'm sorry," I kept repeating.

"Fucking Christ, what did you do?"

I didn't want to answer the question because I didn't really have an answer to the question. I rushed him out of the bedroom and took him into my bathroom. On the way to the bathroom we passed my roommate, Jessie, who was smoking weed on the couch. I was completely naked and he was in boxers with blood on his face. Jessie looked up and did a double take.

"Um . . . what the hell are you guys doing in there?" she said. I didn't answer. I pushed Rob into the bathroom, sat him on the toilet, and furiously opened the medicine cabinet, trying to find anything that would make sense to use. I took out the Neosporin and the rubbing alcohol. I had absolutely no idea what I was doing—I wasn't a nurse any more than I was a stripper. I took a washcloth and tried to run it under hot water, but it took at least five minutes for hot water to come on in this goddamn apartment. Was it even supposed to be hot? Was it supposed to be cold? I had no idea! I settled for lukewarm, because that's what was coming out of the sink. I washed the blood off his face, and it just kept bleeding. I washed it again as he continued to wince in pain. I doused the washcloth in rubbing alcohol, and I put that directly on his cut. He screamed.

"FUCK! OUCH THAT HURT!" he cried out.

"I know, but it's hurting in a good way! I think that means it's getting better!" I said, with absolutely no idea what I was talking about.

He looked incredibly frustrated, and he got up and pushed me out of the way.

"I'm getting out of here. I'm going to the emergency room before this gets infected. I have to go on tour soon, I can't risk this shit."

"Do you want me to go with—"

He slammed the door before I could finish the question. I was alone on my toilet with half a bottle of rubbing alcohol and a travel-sized tube of Neosporin.

I heard Rob walk out my front door. It was safe to say he wouldn't be wanting another lap dance.

This morning I'd burned someone with coffee, and this evening I'd stabbed someone in the face. I was a disaster, and a liability. I was dangerous, but not any kind of sexy.

In a flash of a few metal chords, my relationship with Rob and my career as a stripper had both ended . . . which was impressive, since they'd both barely started. I wasn't sure what to do next, but I knew I should find some occupation that didn't involve hot beverages or high heels. Perhaps I should go work in an office somewhere, in a very private cubicle, at a bare desk with no sharp objects anywhere on it, and nothing but a water cooler near me (with only the light blue lever for cold water, of course). It was time to hang up my barista apron and my lingerie, and figure out what was next for me in life.

THE END

To go back and see Naomi give Rob a striptease, turn to page 246.

My alarm went off at 8:30 a.m. I woke up next to Rob, curled up as the little spoon. It's a good sign to be able to successfully spoon with someone for the duration of the night. I admired his muscles and his array of unfinished tattoos, taking a moment to creepily stare at him as he slept. I lifted the covers and saw a raging morning boner. I wanted to stick that beautiful large thing somewhere inside me, but I had some serious stripping to do.

Rob's enthusiasm for this career path made me want to be the world's greatest stripper, though I wasn't entirely sure if the world has a designated best stripper? Did people vote on that sort of thing? I needed to get ready for work, but I also realized I had no idea how to get ready for work. *What should I even bring with me?*

I pulled out a black mini-duffel bag from my closet and stared at it blankly. What bags do strippers even bring to work? Do they bring suitcases? Do they bring backpacks? Is this like a one carry-on allowed type of situation? These were all things Tony hadn't bothered to explain to me, and I had no one I could call to ask about this problem. The internet was no help either. I mean, I did a Google search on strippers while sitting in bed early this morning, and a whole bunch of images came up—but none of them described how big or small the suitcases were that they took to work. As I stood in the corner of my room staring at the empty duffel, Rob woke up. He stretched and grinned at me.

"What are you doing?" he said.

"Well, I'm trying to decide what the hell to take to work!" I said.

I know this was a foolish thing to admit to him, but I'd officially learned that Rob knew more about strippers than I did.

"Well, bring like . . . your makeup and stuff."

"Oh yeah! Okay. Good idea." This was easy because my small collection of makeup lived inside of a compact travel bag anyway. Not because I was some jet setter or anything, but because when you live in New York, you live by buying small supplies and putting everything inside of travel bags to conserve space wherever you can. I put my makeup in the bag, and then threw in that same burlesque outfit, since it went over so well at the strip club bedroom. He watched me collect this outfit and nodded in approval. This was a good idea, according to the local expert.

I stared blankly at my shoe collection of flats and incredibly modest heels, before turning to Rob for help.

"Um, what shoes should I bring?"

"You shouldn't bring any of those." He laughed. "Where's your club again? Times Square?" He casually scratched his exposed thigh, which was peeking out from the sheets.

"Yeah, on 42nd," I replied.

"Oh there's plenty of stores in that area that sell the kind of shoes you need, and they're all open twenty-four hours." He winked.

To see what happens if Naomi and Rob go to a store together, turn to page 263.

To see what happens if Naomi stops in one of the stores on her way to work, turn to page 308.

"Come with me?" I asked. Rob didn't strike me as the kind of guy you go shopping with, but this was a different kind of shopping. While I had passed these kinds of open-twenty-four-hour stores many times, I'd never been in one. But from the window, I could tell they wouldn't be anything like Bloomingdales.

We took a subway to another subway, which took us to Times Square, and we walked into the first shop we saw as soon as we got off the train. Neon blue lights in the window spelled out the word "Exotic." I wasn't sure if this was the name of the store or . . . just a sign celebrating all things exotic. Either way, I was fine with it. I just needed some shoes to strip in, like any good film school graduate.

We walked inside. The store was small, but I'd call it "efficient." With just a quick glance, I saw a selection of lube, dildos, vibrators, pornographic movies, stripper heels, lingerie, and a handful of role-playing costumes and shiny bikinis. It was nice to know that if you're in a pinch and you really need to be a French maid or a Catholic schoolgirl at three in the morning, this store could help.

Rob picked up a pair of basic clear stripper heels. I don't know why I just called them basic—all the shoes I'd ever owned were more basic than these—but it was basic compared to the other shoes here. A pair next to it had a titanium heel that looked like a gun, one pair had fake goldfish swimming inside the clear base of the shoe inside of blue liquid (well . . . I hope they were fake), and one had a design of a giant marijuana leaf on it. So in that regard, this six-inch clear heel that Rob had selected was, in fact, basic, and possibly . . . classy?

"What about these?" he said triumphantly, holding up the clear heel. I was mostly just relieved that he hadn't picked the marijuana leaf shoes, because that could have been a deal breaker in this relationship. I don't have anything against marijuana, unless it's painted on shoes.

I was about to agree to the clear heel selection, but then I noticed a knee-high PVC boot that really caught my eye. Classy and basic were my MO for my wardrobe in real life, but maybe I didn't want to be basic and classy in the strip club. Maybe I wanted to look like a badass. I grabbed the boots.

"I like THESE better," I said. Rob seemed surprised.

"Well, if you're gonna get those . . . you gotta get something like this," he replied, pointing at a mannequin dressed in a matching black PVC skirt and top, a leather choker with a giant dangling O-ring on it, and leather gloves.

"Yes," I said. "I'll take all of it!"

"Really?" He seemed caught off guard by all of this. I had no idea why he would assume that a girl who normally wears vintage dresses and moccasins wouldn't want to occasionally dress like a member of Judas Priest.

"Yes, really!" I said.

"Well, you should really try it on first." He stood there with a goofy smile on his face. He definitely wanted to see this on me. I also definitely wanted him to see this on me, but also, for practical purposes, it was a good idea to try putting this on and taking it off, since that was about 80 percent of my new career.

I saw a fitting room in the back of the store. I found this odd—it didn't seem to be the type of establishment where you showed someone your garments, and a bored employee handed you a bigger size. As far as I could tell, there was only one employee who worked here, sitting near the register with headphones on, and they didn't seem to want to be bothered. Rob managed to locate all the pieces of the mannequin's outfit in the store in a matter of seconds—truly, it was impressive how quickly he found it all, and I found myself wondering again whether Rob might secretly be a stripper.

I walked back toward the dressing room, but it was locked. I had no choice but to disrupt the employee with headphones and ask him to do work.

"Excuse me, can you unlock the room for me? I have some things I need to try on," I said.

He angrily shifted his headphones behind his ears. "I don't care what you do in there, but you pay for it and it unlocks itself." And then his headphones went back on his ears. I didn't understand. What kind of shady fitting room hustle were they running over there? But I suppose you can't expect the same customer service that you'd get at Bloomingdales in a store whose featured film on their shelf was titled *I Creampied my Stepmom.*

I glanced back toward the fitting room, and Rob was there giggling, putting dollar bills into a machine right next to the fitting room door, still holding a handful of PVC clothing.

"Come on! Get in here!" Rob motioned me toward him. I walked back over to the unethical fitting room, where Rob rushed me in and shut the door. The room was small and weirdly dark, with nothing but a large red leather chair and no mirror at all. There was a television screen playing what I believed was their featured film. It was the same stepmom and son combo I'd seen on the box cover . . . though we weren't at the creampie part quite yet. The mother was currently consoling the son, who'd apparently had a bad day, with a sloppy, passionate blow job. Suddenly, everything made sense. I mean, the mother giving her stepson a blow job didn't make a lot of sense, but it suddenly clicked that we were not in a fitting room, we were in a jerk-off booth. Rob gave me a sinister smile, and he sat in the red leather chair. "Put the outfit on. Lemme see it on you!"

"Don't worry, mommy will make everything better," said a blonde, busty woman on the TV, as she stroked the younger man's cock. I turned the sound off. This particular selection of pornography did not match with my outfit at all.

I quickly removed my summer dress and my flats. I put on the PVC skirt and its matching top. I stepped into the high-heeled boots. I was now eight inches taller than I normally was, and I will admit, it felt powerful.

I stood in front of the TV, hoping the porn would serve as a backlight and illuminate me. I stood there, tall and proud, with a fierce expression on my face. Rob was in the chair directly across from me, doing what was intended to be done in this booth. He took his cock out of his pants and stroked it while he watched me.

"You like it?" I said. It was a redundant question because it was pretty obvious that he liked the outfit. Unless this boner was inspired by the stepmom. If that was the case, then we simply were not meant to be.

"Yeah, you look fucking hot," he said as he continued

to stroke his big beautiful cock. He squirted a glob of complimentary lube on his cock, which was conveniently placed right next to the couch. Maybe this room wasn't so unethical after all. His cock glistened as he stroked it slowly. I stood there and moved my hands down the PVC outfit, which felt slick and smooth against my skin.

"Mistress, am I allowed to cum?" he said.

To see what happens if Naomi doesn't allow Rob to cum, turn to page 268.

To see what happens if Naomi allows Rob to cum, but only if he changes the movie, turn to page 272.

Oh wow . . . holy shit. I didn't know that's where this was going, but I was quite happy to be there. I'd never been anyone's mistress in any sense of the word. I had never had sex with someone who was married, and I had never stood in front of anyone jerking off while dressed in leather and PVC. I had no idea how to embrace this moment of unexpected empowerment, but I had to think quickly. We were paying by the minute here, and we'd only purchased ten minutes.

"No, you may not cum. You haven't earned it," I ordered.

"What can I do to deserve it?" he begged. Hmm. That was a very good question, and the answer definitely needed to involve me getting an orgasm. How could I achieve this? If he bent me over and fucked me, I wouldn't really be in charge anymore. Also, there was nothing to really bend over in here. I took a moment, and instead of overanalyzing the situation, I thought to myself, *I am your superior. Your cock is there to please me. You do as I say.* I became the character I'd invented, and it felt fucking good.

"Take your hands off your cock, and I will use it like the sex toy that it is," I said sternly. He obediently took his hands off his cock and it stood there, rock hard and tall. I deliberately walked over to his chair, unzipped my skirt and threw it on the ground, and faced away from him in the reverse cowgirl position. I slowly lowered myself onto him, my vagina stretching around his large, hard shaft, and I felt a sense of power inside my full pussy. I rode up and down on it like it was my own personal dildo. His curvy cock hit my G-spot almost instantly from this angle, but I didn't want to let him know how fucking good it felt. I could hear him breathing heavily, and I could feel his cock throbbing inside of me. I rode him harder, heard the sound of skin against skin, felt his legs trembling under my hands.

"That's a good boy," I said.

"How can I please you, Mistress?" he asked. While his cock alone was doing a damn good job of pleasing me, I figured I'd indulge in the moment and make him do a little extra work. I grabbed his hand and put it on my clit.

"Rub my clit while I use your cock to cum," I said, and he did exactly as I instructed. I was surprised at how well I could balance myself on his cock in these giant heels, but it was safe to assume that these shoes were not made for walking, but for fucking. He licked his fingers and rubbed my clit while I rode his cock, rubbing it at the perfect pace, not too fast but not too slow. He had already proven himself to be quite knowledgeable when it came to clit rubbing. What a good sex slave!

"Am I pleasing you properly?" he asked. I smacked his hand away and pulled my pussy off his cock, even though I didn't want to. I was committed to this character, and she didn't tolerate forgetfulness. "How do you address me when you speak to me?" I shouted at him. I hope he knew the answer, because I was close to cumming and I wanted to jump back on his cock immediately.

"Am I pleasing you properly . . . Mistress!?" he said. Thank fucking god.

"That's right. Yes. Now continue!" I replied, and I slid my wet pussy back onto his lubed-up cock. He went right back to what he'd been doing so perfectly. I could feel the inside and outside of my pussy tensing up. I rode his dick fiercely, and his hand obediently kept up with my pace. I changed my stroke to a grind, pushing my pussy all the way down his length, pushing it as far inside me as it could go. He still managed to find just enough clit to rub from this angle. I was about to explode.

My body started shaking. I was cumming so hard, cumming from the inside of my pussy and the outside of my clit. It was like a two-for-one special, an inner and outer orgasm double. I kept his giant cock deep inside me until I couldn't possibly cum any more. I wanted to lie back against him, but I remembered I was still his Mistress. So I got up and stood in front of him, looked him right in the eyes, and said, "Now, you may cum."

I watched him stroke himself, while grunting and moaning. It didn't take long, and after just a few strokes, beautiful white icing came out of him and covered his entire hand and cock. It was such a big, juicy load, just dying to get out. He smiled and sat there, covered in his own cum, adoring his Mistress. The lights started flashing in the room, which I guessed was a courtesy reminder to get the fuck out.

Rob reached down for the box of tissues on the floor and noticed it was empty. My anger for this room returned. Why was there only *one* box of tissues in here, and why the fuck was it empty? That's bare minimum maintenance for a jerk-off room. Sheesh! Did he really want people purchasing things at the register with jizz filled hands?

I took it upon myself to turn lemons into lemonade here, and by lemons I really mean "ejaculate." I crouched down and licked up all the jizz on Rob's hand and cock. It broke my character because this wasn't really a dominant move, but this Mistress logistically needed to drink Rob's cum.

"Oh fuck yeah," he said as I slurped up his cum. "You're such a dirty girl." I smiled and continued to search for any last drop of cum I could find on his chiseled stomach.

Rob truly brought the slut out of me. I might make a good stripper after all.

To go back and see what happens if Naomi allows Rob to cum, turn to page 272.

To continue with Naomi in this fantasy, turn to page 277.

"Not yet," I said.

I watched him stroke his cock, and he even started tugging on his own balls. I made a mental note of that—I would remember to pay more attention to his balls next time he was in my mouth. He stared at me, his mouth open, saying, "Please Mistress, I want to cum so bad," and I could really see it on his face. He was suffering from severe pain, and my permission was the only antidote. I reveled in this powerful moment.

"Son, I love you so much, I want you to put a baby in me!" I heard from the TV behind me. I cringed, and while I tried to remain focused on Rob's throbbing cock, I couldn't help but snap out of character. In the past twenty-four hours I'd discovered parts of my own sexuality that I never knew existed, but nowhere in that new sexuality did stepsons impregnating their mothers excite me.

"Change the channel, then . . . maybe you can cum," I said.

"Are you serious?" Rob replied. I couldn't believe this early on in our relationship we were already arguing over what to watch on TV.

"Yes! Change the fucking channel!" I said. I was on the verge of going from "sexy dominatrix pissed" to "actual pissed." Rob continued to stroke his cock with his left hand while he frantically pushed buttons on a remote with his right. The first one made the volume louder, and I was starting to feel ill. And then, thankfully, a different button switched to a sexier, and much more relatable fantasy for me, and this was all about pleasing me anyway, right?

"Hey! I'm the neighbor next door, and I need you guys to keep it down, I'm trying to study," said a petite, skinny brunette in jean shorts and a red crop top to three incredibly buff men. She was standing in the doorway of what appeared to be a mansion. I mean, I hear my neighbors all the time, but we share a wall so that's to be expected. I thought that in these alternate universes where neighbors had yards between their walls, you could yell as loudly as you wanted. Apparently, not in this neighborhood.

"But there's a game on! And, my friends are here! Come on. Why don't you just come in and watch it with us, and study later?"

The girl hesitated for about half a second and then shrugged her shoulders and said, "Okay! Sure!" She walked into the mansion, past various modern art sculptures and paintings scattered throughout the living room. I could only assume that the homeowner spent all his budget on art and skimped on proper wall insulation.

The girl had flawless skin, dark brown hair, and a perfectly contoured face, with all the bronzers and highlighters in the right places. I mean who puts bronzer on to study! Clearly she had other motives here.

Rob continued to stroke his cock and whimper at me in despair. I was caught up in the, um, plot here, and my eyes were glued to the TV. But I walked back toward his corner of the room, took his hand off his own cock, and started stroking it. There's something so innocent about giving a guy a hand job when you're watching a movie . . . even if the movie is about three burly, handsome men running train on a college student who is supposed to be studying with bronzer on.

I squirted some more lube on his cock, and I enjoyed the slippery gushing sounds my hand made as I jerked his cock off. "Fuck yeah," Rob muttered. I moved up and down his penis slowly, feeling every part of his shaft. I knew it wanted so badly to explode, but I just wasn't going to let that happen until I saw how these three large men would fit inside this incredibly petite woman.

Fortunately for Rob (and me), we wouldn't have to wait that long. The brunette started masturbating after giving the game about a forty-second chance and stating it was "boring." She had a tight, compact clamshell pussy, which her French-manicured fingers spread open and rubbed in reaction to the boring game. Her jeans skirt was hiked up to her stomach. The three men looked at each other and shrugged, and moments later she was on her knees with three giant cocks swarming around her face. She took turns vigorously sucking them, her tiny mouth barely able to fit around the heads of their cocks, keeping one dick in her mouth and two in her hands.

Her eyes opened wider, and suddenly her horny super-powers kicked in and somehow . . . she deep-throated an entire cock that looked bigger than her head. It went from barely in her mouth to all the way down her throat in one solid gulp. Her eyes watered. She pulled back, and long strings of saliva dripped out of her mouth and onto the beautiful cock she'd just devoured. The other two guys cheered them on with an equal amount of excitement for both the neighbor and their friend getting his dick swallowed. I have to admit, I got wet watching this.

I continued to stroke Rob's cock, and it was clear,

his eyes were on me. Neither a studying student nor an impregnated stepmom could take him away from me, and that certainly was a devotion I never thought I'd have, in a jerk-off booth nonetheless.

I leaned against the wall and I pulled up my PVC skirt. "Come here. Fuck me," I said, and he complied, sliding his cock inside of me, pushing himself into me, furiously grabbing onto my breasts. With just one little snap I undid my top, and . . . it was good to know this thing was, in fact, easy to take off! He held onto my breasts, pulling against them to get his cock further inside of me. I felt so full of his cock.

And speaking of feeling full, the petite girl was now completely full of cock herself. She had one giant handsome man underneath her, in her ass, one guy in her pussy, and one guy balancing himself on the couch and plunging his cock in her mouth. She handled all three cocks beautifully. They slid in and out of her, and she seemed hungry for more. Her pussy somehow still looked like a barely opened coin slot. She was like a vaginal unicorn of sorts. I loved the way this girl handled all these men with such elegance, and such filth. I would definitely have to channel her energy while I was on stage.

Rob continued to fuck me. I wanted to go to work with his sperm tucked deep inside me, in some secret compartment of my pussy that only belonged to him. And . . . I guess one of these guys on the screen, if they ever wanted to be invited. I glanced back over to the TV, and the girl was now taking turns on all the guys, who sat side by side on the couch, politely and patiently waiting for their turn with their neighbor's pussy. She rode each cock—a few good pumps on each one, then onto the next. She started moaning loudly, and so did I. I was sure the entire store could hear me, and I was sure her whole neighborhood could hear her, because apparently that house had terrible acoustics.

"Mistress, can I please cum NOW?!" Rob asked, in between deep plunges into me. I had to say yes. I wanted his cum more than anything. I was his Mistress and his little cum dumpster mixed into one. He pushed me hard against the wall, and I felt a warm gush of goodness in me. He clenched, his fingers dug deep into my shoulders, and he shook inside me. And then suddenly the TV went off, and some lights started blinking. I assumed this meant our time was up, and while I would have loved to see how the rest of the story panned out, I think I had a pretty good idea of how it ended.

It was now time for my own adventure to begin. And with the power of proper clothing and Rob's jizz, I knew I could do anything. *Club 42, here I come!*

To go back and see what happens if Naomi doesn't allow Rob to cum, turn to page 268.

To continue with Naomi in this fantasy, turn to page 277.

"I can't believe you're really leaving tomorrow," I said to Rob. It was 8:00 a.m., and Rob and I just had a hot session of morning sex. The sunlight blasted through my window, illuminating his muscles and the load of jizz on my stomach that was slowly starting to disintegrate into my skin. Rob was leaving for a three-month tour tomorrow, and I was legitimately upset about it. The downside of dating a rock star is that, inevitably, they had to at some point go be a rock star. He had to go and entertain people in arenas across the country, and this would mean he wouldn't be able to entertain my pussy the way he'd successfully been doing for the past month.

And speaking of my pussy, that had also done a fair amount of entertaining this month. Spilling coffee on someone was the greatest mistake I ever made. I enjoyed my job, and coming home and hanging out with Rob with a purse full of cash, telling him about how much I turned everyone on all day, was truly the fairytale romance I never knew could actually exist. I'd practice my routines for him, and he'd occasionally surprise me with sparkly, stringy thongs that I'd wear to work, so it felt like a piece of him was close to my pussy all day.

I know I wasn't a seasoned professional, but I had come a long way from the girl who wore her street clothes on stage. I had a handful of "customers" who came in to see me regularly, I had a small collection of different stripper outfits, and these outfits coordinated with different songs and routines that I came up with. And oh yes! I had a stripper name. I called myself "Indica," after . . . okay, after the strain of marijuana that Rob smoked and I'd occasionally indulge in. I always thought this was an elegant name for something that inevitably led you to giggle and eat entire bags of potato chips.

"I know babe," Rob said. "Don't worry, I'll be back . . . and while I'm gone, you have to send me pics and videos from work to keep me entertained. I want lots of fresh material for spank sessions in my bunk!"

While it definitely turned me on to think of Rob playing to a giant crowd of people, then getting off stage and jerking off in a tour bus to my photos somewhere in Albuquerque, it turned me on a lot more to think about him jerking off into my mouth in my bed in Brooklyn. I also felt like stripping just wouldn't be as fun without coming home to tell him about it. Sending my stories of how I turned people on all day in a text message wouldn't be the same, without seeing the excitement he'd get on his face . . . and in his pants.

I gave him a kiss and left reluctantly for work. I contemplated taking a day off and spending it with him, but I reasoned that would actually make this whole goodbye a lot harder.

I sat in the dressing room of Club 42, overlining my lips with a lip-liner trick I'd just learned, which made my mouth look more plump. This, combined with lip plumping gloss, gave me the perfect pout. I contoured my face, I highlighted my cheekbones . . . things I never did before I worked here. I'd learned to paint my face to the perfect shade of slut. The daily transformation from

Naomi to Indica felt rather zen, now. Smearing different shades of brown on the different parts of my face like war paint, and blending them all together with a beauty blender was my own form of meditation. But today, the blending of my whore paint just didn't give me the same sense of tranquility it normally did. I couldn't stop thinking about Rob.

I looked through my selection of outfits, and it made me frustrated. Everything in the bag reminded me of Rob—everything had some kind of sentimental filthy memory. There was only one outfit that *didn't* make me think of Rob, and that was the Catholic schoolgirl one. I bought this one at some point because I figured it should be a staple to have in my collection, but the few times I'd pulled it out, he'd laughed and told me to put something else on. He said it was "corny." He did drop out of high school, so I suppose he had rejected all forms of school at a young age, and he wasn't going to make an exception for one whose uniforms spelled out "Sexy High" on the emblem.

Rob had an insatiable sex drive. Just the other day, I'd met up with him at a bar wearing an off-the-shoulder oversized T-shirt, and he somehow got turned on by the sight of my shoulder displayed in that particular way, and he'd dragged me to the bathroom and fucked me before we could even order a drink. But for whatever reason, the schoolgirl outfit was where his penis drew the line.

I slipped on the tiny red plaid schoolgirl skirt, along with the matching bra, a miniature clip tie, white knee-highs, and a little white crop top that tied in between my breasts. I put my hair in pigtails and matched this with black Mary Jane stiletto heels. I looked in the mirror, admiring my long legs, my pouty lips, and my "corny" costume, and I thought I looked fucking adorable. A red-headed, large-breasted stripper acquaintance I'd made this summer who went by the name of Melody noticed my get up, and handed me a giant red lollipop.

"Here, take this. It will go with your outfit," she said.

"Oh my god, thank you! It definitely goes with it. What a good idea!"

"You're welcome! I always have a stash of candy in my locker. If I keep it in my house, my daughter will eat it when I'm not looking and then keep me up all night on a sugar high," she laughed.

"Alright well, I'll remember that if ever I need more candy," I replied.

"Make sure you use it to"—she used her hand to make quotation marks—"'sucker' all the money out of everyone down there." She laughed at her own play on words. I had no idea she was a mother. That explained why she was so supportive of my enrollment at Sexy High.

I left the dressing room and went out onto the floor, where I sat down next to a customer to see if I could get a few private dances in before I got called to the stage, something I was usually able to do. The guy had dark gelled hair and a scruffy face.

"Hi! I'm Indica! What's your name, sweetie?" I asked.

"Oh uh . . . hi. I'm Rob."

What the fuck. Was this some kind of sick joke? Of all the names in the world, did it really have to be Rob?

Hoping to hold back the tears, I presumptuously decided to sit on this Rob's lap. Before I was able to ask for a dance, or even ask him anything, he pushed me off of him and said, "Sorry I'm waiting for someone else."

I had now suffered rejection from two different Robs today. It was not a good day at school.

The room could sense my insecurity. I tried to mingle with customers, but they all seemed disinterested. I made my rounds, asking several people if they wanted to buy a private dance from me, and they all rejected me, one after another after another. People got up and walked away as soon as I sat down. What was I doing wrong? I sucked on the lollipop and pouted in the corner while all the men spent copious amounts of money on people who weren't me.

The DJ announced that I was next on stage. I walked over to the small waiting area behind the stage, wiping tears away from my face with the miniature tie around my neck. I walked onto the stage, and the DJ played "Oops! . . . I Did It Again" by Britney Spears. How clever. He must have seen the schoolgirl outfit and thought this would be a good fit. I glanced up at the DJ booth from the stage and gave him a nod of approval. Unlike Rob, this DJ understood the appeal of the schoolgirl.

And just as the beat of the music kicked in, something flipped inside of me. I couldn't quite explain where it came from. I pranced around the stage and sucked on the lollipop. I channeled my bratty rollercoaster of emotions into this dance. I pouted, I pulled my pigtails, I stomped my feet, I lifted my skirt up and went directly over to the Rob that had just rejected my lap dance, put my ass in his face, took his hand, and made him smack my ass. The customers clapped. I got down on all fours and made some of the other men spank my ass while I sucked on the lollipop. People were showering dollar bills on me, and I felt alive. I slid the skirt off, untied the top, rolled it up, and put it in my mouth like some kind of ball gag, while I smacked my tits and pinched my nipples. I was having fun!

When the song ended, I walked off stage feeling like a million dollars, but actually more like eighty to one hundred dollars, if I had to guess what was in this wad of sweaty bills.

I quickly collected myself backstage and threw my outfit back together. I normally went up to the dressing room after a stage session to reset myself, but today I didn't want to leave the floor. I had a fire burning in me, and I had to keep going until it went out. I could feel the energy of the room, and I knew it was a good time to ask people for a dance.

I walked out on the floor with my now slightly disheveled schoolgirl costume and a half-eaten lollipop that was getting sticky. Tony stopped me in my tracks as I was heading to the sea of suited men to see who I could get to buy a dance.

"Hey, you've got a guy waiting for you up in VIP," he said.

"What? Really?" I replied.

"Yup. Half hour. Room four. I got his credit card. So go on and get up there." He motioned to shoo me away with his hands, like I was some mosquito buzzing around his ear. I'd never been to the VIP room before. I seemed to be a one to three lap dance kinda gal here. I hadn't quite figured out how to charm someone intensely enough that they'd want to whisk me away for a half hour to the land of very important things. Perhaps everyone was waiting for me to get my diploma from Sexy High before letting me back there.

I walked past the bar, turned the corner, and went down the VIP room hallway. There were only four VIP rooms total, so I was in the last one down the hall. They had red lights on top of each door that indicated "in use" or "vacant"—you know, like the bathrooms in the airplane.

The doors in the hallway were all black, with silver handles and a stark number on each door painted in gold. I opened door number four. A handsome guy with tattoos and slicked back long hair, wearing black pleated pants, a white collared shirt, and a tie, sat on a plush purple couch next to an ice bucket full of root beer. I did a double take. This mysterious guy was Rob. And not the guy who'd rejected me and then later smacked my ass, the other Rob, who'd fucked my brains out all summer and was leaving tomorrow.

I was in shock. I blinked my eyes a few times to make sure I wasn't having weird delusions of Rob. I wouldn't put it past myself in this mental state to hallucinate him. Just the other day, Rob posted a bunch of photos on Facebook from his sister's wedding, and he'd worn a T-shirt and a leather jacket. Somehow the strip club was the only thing that had the power to make him put on a tie.

"Well, hello Indica! I've been waiting for you!" he said.

"Are you fucking kidding me right now!" I whispered, closing the door behind me.

"Excuse me! Miss! I paid top dollar for the VIP experience, and I don't want to be talked to that way." He shook his fingers at me in disapproval.

"I can't believe the one time you came to see me at work, I'm wearing the schoolgirl costume. Do you still think it's 'corny?'" I laughed.

"You don't know what I like. You don't know anything about me! I'm just a customer who saw you out there, and I liked what I saw . . . so I got a VIP room." He smiled a sinister smile. The depths of Rob's kinkiness never ceased to amaze me, and the fact that I always enjoyed going right there with him amazed me even more.

So, Rob got a VIP room with Indica, not Naomi. I had to leave Naomi out of this, but if Naomi didn't exist, then Rob wouldn't have ever come in here. Or would he? I suppose that didn't matter. Indica had different person-alities on different days, and sometimes her personality changed by the hour if she felt like changing outfits between shows. But right now, Indica was a bratty attendee of Sexy High. The type of student who specifi-cally got herself into trouble because she enjoyed the punishment. I sucked on my lollipop in an exaggerated way. Rob grabbed his crotch.

"Your management told me that 'extras' could be available here, but that would be up to you," he said. "Are you a bad girl? Do you offer extra services here for a VIP customer?"

Did I? Was this a trick question? Normally, if I was confused about something at the strip club I'd call Rob and ask him what to do, but I couldn't exactly do that right now. "Yes, I am a very bad girl," I replied. "And I'd be happy to be your little whore in any way you want me to be for the next half hour—as long as you pay the price," I said in between taking very long licks of lollipop. I raised my voice to a higher pitch, about an octave higher than my usual tone, and I giggled in between my words.

"So what will it be, Daddy?" I said. "What do you want?"

To see Naomi give Rob a hand job, turn to page 286.

To see Naomi and Rob have anal sex, turn to page 292.

A hand job! This was . . . exciting. Much more exciting than the usual over-the-pants rubbing that went on in here.

"Just a hand job? How about I replace this sucker with your cock?" I suggested.

"You bad girl . . . No Indica, it's not safe to put a stranger's cock in your mouth." He gave me another "tisk tisk" motion. I forgot—in this fantasy I was an untrustworthy stranger, and giving a hand job was the "cleanest" way to interact with a stranger's penis.

"How much?" he said. He was dedicated to this role-play fantasy, and part of me was turned on while part of me was incredibly flustered. I wanted to carry it out properly—I'd never been to the VIP room, and I'd never done any extras here in the strip club. It had never been offered to me, and had it been, I would have politely declined because it felt like doing extras would be cheating. But in this instance, Rob was cheating on me . . . well, um . . . on Naomi. With Indica. Luckily Indica strictly adhered to client confidentiality. She didn't even know Naomi. This split personality existential crisis was definitely veering away from the sexy and "safe" hand job I had to begin.

"Um, $500!" I replied. I truthfully had no idea what to charge. Five hundred seemed like a nice round number.

"Well that's a lot more expensive than the other girls," he replied.

I got frustrated. Was he comparing me to the other

girls in other strip clubs that he got hand jobs from? Is that what he was planning to do on tour? Go from club to club getting less than $500 hand jobs, while I cried and sent him sexy text messages? I didn't know how I felt about that. But that was Naomi's problem.

"Well, I'm better than the other girls," I replied, with the perfect bratty inflection in my voice, if I do say so myself. He seemed impressed with my answer. He nodded in approval.

"Alright, well let's see what you can do," he said. He took out five hundred-dollar bills and placed them on the small end table next to the couch. He did tell me at one point he got some kind of advance before he went on tour, for whatever supplies he might need for the road. I felt a bizarre sense of pride knowing that this money was being spent on me, and not socks and toothpaste.

I put the lollipop down and balanced it on top of a bottle of root beer. I got down on my hands and knees and I crawled toward Rob, who was sitting on the couch with his arms folded and a smirk on his face. I truly got off on this challenge to see if I could be his perfect little prostitute.

I felt the bulge of his cock under his dress pants. I could tell he wasn't wearing any underwear beneath them—it was just a thin layer of whatever blended fabric this was. He'd never seen me in a schoolgirl outfit, and I'd never seen him in suit pants. We were truly two different people. The gel in his hair gave him an entirely different scent. His tattoos just barely peeked over his shirt collar, leaving so much to the imagination. He looked so dark and mysterious, like Keanu Reeves in *The Matrix*, and admittedly also kinda like Christian Bale in *American Psycho*. There was something so dangerous about his dominance in a suit, and I wanted to take every risk imaginable with him.

I touched his cock over his pants. I bit my bottom lip. I could feel the outline of his shaft and balls getting bigger and bigger.

"Mmmmhmm. It feels like such a big cock! I want to play with it!" I said, continuing with this schoolgirl fantasy, but with someone less than two years older than me.

Like most suit pants, this pair had a button, a zipper, and a little metal hook on a flap that covered the button. I dove between his legs and unhooked the flap with my teeth, and I growled, kind of like a cat, but mostly like a really horny human. I thought of trying to unbutton the entire thing with my teeth, but quickly realized that would be time consuming and most likely wouldn't even work. So I unbuttoned the button, and I unzipped the zipper.

I pulled down the pants to his knees, revealing his growing cock. I saw a small bottle of lube fall out of his pocket, and I giggled. He really came prepared! I picked it up off the ground and squirted a bunch in my hand, and then squirted a dab on the tip of his cock. I knew he was extra sensitive at the tip. Maybe getting inside information from Naomi wasn't fair in this game of role-play, but Indica the overpriced hand job giver would instantly know her way around any cock.

I spread the lube around the tip of his cock in a small circle, slowly, around and around and around. He nodded and groaned. I took my lubed-up hands and began to stroke his cock, up and down the shaft, slowly. I worked up a healthy amount of moisture in my mouth and spit on his cock. It took some skill to have it land on the tip of his dick without actually touching his dick with my mouth.

A little bit of spit mixed with lube makes everything so much more wet.

I stroked his cock, and it was so sloppy, if someone overheard us they would think I was giving him a bath or something. He unbuttoned his shirt, revealing his toned abs and his soft, un-groomed happy trail. I felt like a lucky stranger, admiring his tattoos and his pecs as if for the first time. His dick was rock hard in my hand, and I felt it pulsate like a beating heart. It was as if I'd sculpted a tall, beautiful cock statue right in front of me. I could see his eyes getting wider and hear his breaths getting deeper.

"How am I doing, Daddy? You like your messy hand job?" I stared up at him with pouty lips and puppy dog eyes.

"Oh yeah. Good girl. Keep stroking Daddy's cock," he said. I fully intended to do that!

I untied the impractical white crop top from my chest and threw it on the ground. I attempted to unhook my bra, but my fingers were too greasy with lube and I couldn't. Fuck it. I took the straps down off my shoulders and just pushed the bra down my stomach. The important thing was that my tits came out.

I leaned closer into him and pushed his cock in-between my tits. I put my hand over his cock and over my tits, like I was making some type of boob bridge with my hand. I moved up and down on his cock, with my hand in place. This was how I was still able to get some friction on his cock.

"Push your fucking tits together," he commanded, and I obliged. He leaned back and thrust his cock toward me, in-between my breasts, as I held them together. Lube dripped down my chest, and I spit on my tits and his cock to keep it flowing. My bra and my skirt were beginning to get drips of lubey grease on them, and I didn't care. I'd replay this filthy hot memory of escorting for my own boyfriend whenever I touched myself for the next few months while he was gone.

After a while of some intense titty fucking, I got on the couch next to him, spread his legs open further, and leaned over his chest to stroke his cock. I felt the heat of his body against my hardworking arm. The mere touch of his skin brushing up against mine made me shiver. I stroked him with pressure, going faster and harder, pointing his cock at me like it was a loaded gun. I could see his dick bulging, so I licked his ear and nibbled on his muscular neck.

"Lemme see that pussy," he panted. I slid my panties off and spread my legs open next to him on the couch. I could see him staring at my pussy with hungry eyes, and I felt his cock get harder in my hands. I took my left hand off his cock but continued to stroke with the right hand. I had a good steady grip on it. I spread my pussy lips open with my left hand, giving him the perfect view of my open vagina, without allowing him to touch it. I stuck my fingers inside of me and gathered up the accumulating moisture. I mixed it with some more spit and then placed my hand back on his cock. I was pumping faster and faster, and I could see that he was getting close. I had an idea.

I grabbed the lollipop off the root beer bottle, got back on my knees, and put it close to his cock.

"Cum on my special sucker!" I said. I had to pat myself on the back for how naturally the slutty schoolgirl thing came to me. I guess all that time in school had paid off in some way. He smiled and took control of his own cock.

It was hard for me to properly hand job him and hold the lollipop at the same time. With my knees on the ground, a lollipop in my hand, and a giant smile on my face, I patiently waited for cum. I mean, I wasn't lying when I said I was a good girl.

To go back and see Naomi and Rob have anal sex, turn to page 292.

To continue with Naomi in this fantasy, turn to page 299.

Oh wow. I was not expecting him to say anal. Rob and I hadn't had anal sex before, and I had very little experience with the act in general. I wondered if doing this for the first time with Indica would be cheating on me with other me?

But of course I would give Rob my asshole. I would give him any hole, anytime, anywhere, and I firmly believed that all attendees of Sexy High took it in the ass, anyway. He sat there with his legs and arms crossed, waiting for an answer.

"Of course, I'd be happy to offer the full service to such a sexy VIP customer." I winked.

"And, how much will that be?" he asked. Was he really going to pay it? I suppose he did already pay to get into the VIP room. How much was he willing to spend on the fake me? Last night we went dutch when we ordered pizza. Naomi was really getting the raw end of the deal here. I honestly had no idea what to charge or what the standard rate was for this type of thing, and I still didn't know if this was a trick question, or if I was on an episode of *Punk'd* right now. Was the real Rob in dirty jeans and flannel going to come out from behind a curtain?

"One thousand dollars," I said. It sounded like a good round number for anal. I mean, I was a "student" after all, so the money obviously would go into my education.

He folded his hands. "Let me see your ass. I need a better look at my merchandise first."

The amount of dedication he put into this role-play was sexy, scary, and admirable all at once. His demeanor in here felt like a mob boss, but I was happy to submit to this handsome client no matter his "business."

I turned around and lifted my miniature skirt up, showing off the tiny thong stuck inside my ass crack. I sucked on the lollipop for good measure—it made sense in this particular pose. I arched my ass and showed it off, and he scoped it out like he'd never seen it before. I couldn't imagine what I would do if I was rejected in this role-playing scenario—that would lead to a unique relationship issue between me and Rob that I didn't think I could begin to explain to my friends, or a therapist for that matter. From the serious way he considered my ass, I feared there was a chance of that rejection actually happening.

I can't lie. This panicked feeling turned me on. I wanted to be the best filthy little slut for him that he'd ever had . . . and I also didn't want to think about how many he'd had. I pulled my thong to the side and I spread my ass checks open for him.

"Come on, Daddy, it's ready for you!" I said. Rob smiled on the couch, and he rubbed his thighs. He reached inside his pocket and took out ten hundred-dollar bills, putting them on a small table next to the couch. I knew he'd just gotten some kind of tour advance, and I felt privileged to know that he chose to spend it on my asshole instead of extra phone chargers and mouthwash.

"Thank you." I smiled coyly. So many mixed emotions swarmed inside of me. The blurring of what was real and what wasn't made me nervous, and excited, and confused . . . and wet. This was my first time escorting, but not really. This was me and Rob having sex, but not really.

I had no idea if this was allowed or not. I spotted what looked like a security camera in the corner of the room on the ceiling. Would I get fired if I was caught? The thrill of all the uncertainty, the way Rob looked in that god damn sexy suit, and the sheer filthiness of this little plaid skirt that just barely covered my ass crack made me so fucking hot. Rob had such a big cock, and I had very little experience with anal—that went for both of my personalities—but in this moment, I wanted him to hurt me. That's just how dirty I felt.

I got down on all fours. The floors in the VIP room were significantly nicer than the floors in the rest of the strip club. I supposed there was some routine vacuuming done in here, just in case someone had to get ass-fucked on the floor. My skirt hiked up to my chest. I put my hands behind me and pulled my thong down to my ankles, though my cropped white top, my bra, and my minitie were still completely intact. Fully exposing my asshole to him without any kind of foreplay, and without even showing him my tits, made me feel like such an ultimate little fuck doll. I really was a bad schoolgirl.

"Use me," I said. "Use my holes, Daddy." My face was on the ground, my ass in the air, and the god damn lollipop was in my hand.

I had to find something to do with this lollipop. I should have put it on the table before I got down on my hands and knees, but it was an essential part of my outfit, my act, and maybe my entire existence at the moment. I didn't want to throw it down on the ground because, as I said before, this was a very clean ground, and I didn't want to mess things up for the next girl who got fucked on the floor. If I got back up, I'd ruin the whole "use my holes, Daddy" vibe I'd so proudly created. For the price I was charging here, I shouldn't mess up any moments.

I stuck the lollipop back in my mouth, but it was admittedly awkward to suck on a lollipop with my face on the ground. Then I had an idea.

I took the lollipop and stuck it in my ass, with a big smile on my face. This wasn't a cheap lollipop with a small white paper stem, this was a fancy lollipop, and the ball of sugar was connected to a plastic tube with rainbow-colored glitter bling inside of it. My asshole was now literally sweet as candy, with a tube of glitter and a ball of sugar sticking out of it. I couldn't stop giggling as I waited for this sucker in my ass to be replaced with cock.

I could see Rob's dress shoes walking step by step in my direction. He crouched down, lifted my head off the floor, and grabbed my cheeks. "Oh, you're really in for it today," he said softly, but sternly. He unzipped his pants but left the top button closed. He pulled his hard cock out of the zipper, remaining fully clothed with just a hard cock sticking out.

He then removed a skinny leather belt from his pants. He folded it and made it into a kind of loop. He slowly walked behind me and . . . *whack*. He smacked my left ass cheek with his belt. It stung in the most incredible way. I wanted more. I let out a painful and pleasurable moan. *Whack!* He did it again, even harder, on my right cheek. Now my cheeks felt unevenly punished.

"More! I want more!" I cried, and I spoke from the heart. Obliging, he smacked me on my right, then my left, then my right, then my left, all while the lollipop remained stationary inside my asshole.

"You want one more?" he said.

"YES!" I cried. He unexpectedly swung his belt at a different angle and managed to whack underneath me, smacking my pussy.

"FUCK!" I screamed. This hurt, but it was a good hurt. Tears came out of my eyes, but I truly felt like I was about to cum, and he hadn't even touched me.

"Give me your cock," I moaned. This feeling of submission and desperation was so intense—it was a place in my brain that I'd never visited before. I never really liked anyone telling me what to do, but my issues with authority seemed to disappear when there was a lollipop in my ass and a belt on my pussy.

I could hear him fidgeting around with something behind me, like he was ripping something open. I waited patiently, crying and begging, with my head on the floor. I felt the lollipop come out of me. I wasn't sure where he was going to put it, but that wasn't my concern at the moment. He spread my ass cheeks open, and I felt a warm splash of lube. I could feel it drip down to my pussy, which was already incredibly wet.

"Give me your ass," he grunted. He grabbed my hips, and slowly but firmly pushed me down his cock. It felt . . . smooth. I lifted my head and looked back at his cock, which was inching into my ass, and I could see that he had a condom on.

This was the first time I'd seen a condom on his cock. Yes, I will admit . . . we were mere strangers when we first met, with a completely irresponsible trust in each other's body parts. After the first few irresponsible sessions, we both went to get a full panel of STI testing, and we both came back negative . . . at which point we joyfully cheered and returned to our irresponsible fucking. I didn't know if there had been any other Indicas in his life (or on his cock) since I met him, but it was nice to know that if there was, he'd use a condom.

While the friction of a condom isn't ever as good as bare skin inside of you, the role-play of me being a complete stranger whose asshole couldn't be trusted without protection made me so fucking hot that the rubbery texture going in and out of me didn't bother me at all. It turned me on even more.

"Yes!" I shouted, pushing my ass back on his cock as far as it could go. "I want it all the way inside me!" I said. He continued to thrust toward me with his wrapped gift of cock. I could feel the curve of him slowly push through me. I could feel my asshole stretching, his cock growing. One more little thrust from him, and I felt my pussy against his suit pants. He was all the way in.

"Good girl!" he said, and he pushed my head back down onto the ground. And then, there was no mercy. Now that he'd slowly pushed his way in and knew I could take it, there was no looking back. I mean, literally, my head was back on the ground, so there was no looking back. He spread my ass cheeks and fucked me hard. I moaned and yelled in ecstasy. I had never felt like such a filthy whore in my life. I'd been having sex with Rob all month, and this was unlike anything we'd done before. I was his purchased fuck toy in here, and he was a mysterious sexy stranger. The fantasy and the reality of this scenario pushed me mentally and physically in ways I'd never been pushed.

Just keep fucking me. Keep pounding my ass. Keep using me. Keep taking me.

He smacked my cheeks and pounded my asshole,

switching off between calling me a good girl and a bad girl, depending on the thrust. He smacked me harder, he fucked me harder. I felt nerves inside my ass that I'd never felt before. He lifted my head up toward his head, so I was arched all the way backward, while he continued to rail my ass. He put his arm around my neck and fucked me with abandon. My eyes teared up again—I could barely breathe . . . and then . . . I came. I came so fucking hard from my ass. He released his arm from my neck, and my head dropped to the ground. I gasped for air and my whole body shook. I felt myself get tighter and tighter, and I felt his cock bulging inside me.

"Did Daddy make that asshole cum?" he asked me. I mean, it was a rhetorical question. He knew.

"Yes! Yes, yes," I wept.

"Stay right there, I'm gonna fucking cum," he said, holding me still, pounding away at my tight, sore asshole, using me for his pleasure. I obediently stayed in place, only going where his hands told my hips to go. He thrust a few more times before he pulled out of me, walked around me, and brought his cock close to my face . . . with the lollipop in hand. I smiled. It was time for my treat.

To go back and see Naomi give Rob a hand job, turn to page 286.

To continue with Naomi in this fantasy, turn to page 299.

"Alright, tell me what you want!" he said.

"I want your cum. Give me your cum," I kept repeating. And then a giant load of semen spewed from his cock directly onto the lollipop. I took the lollipop and stuck the whole thing in my mouth, sucking it eagerly. His jizz mixed with sugar was such a tasty snack.

He breathlessly patted me on the head. "Good girl," he said.

"Yeah, I know!" I giggled. He zipped his pants back up, and then there was a knock on the door, and Tony entered.

"Hello! Sir, are you interested in getting another half hour?" Tony asked, barely sparing a glance for me on the floor.

"No that's all I'll be getting today! Thank you," he replied politely. Rob really was the ultimate classy gentleman when it came to the process of getting extras from a stranger.

"How did she do?" Tony said to Rob, as if I wasn't sitting right there, naked with a jizz covered lollipop in my mouth.

"Great! She's great." Rob smiled at me, and then Tony gave me a thumbs up.

"Alright, you guys take a few minutes to collect your-selves, then, get the fuck out," Tony said, laughing at his own joke, which wasn't really a joke.

I swallowed. "Got it!" I said.

Rob winked at me and said, "Your money is on the table." Something I certainly never thought I'd hear from someone I was madly in love with.

I attempted to count my money in the cab ride home from work. I stopped after $1,800, and there were still stray singles that needed to be counted. After my VIP room stint with Rob, it was like the customers could smell my happiness, and the requests for private dances kept coming in. My stage shows were a nonstop barrage of dollar bills, payment for my slick and seductive moves, and my witty, campy interactions with all the customers by the stage. I pulled people's ties, I deep throated their root beer bottles, and at one point, I took off a man's eyeglasses and rubbed them on my pussy. It's fascinating how different the same room feels, depending on how many people reject you.

I had been on a high, and I slowly came down in the leather back seat of a black car. I told Rob to meet me at my apartment for one last goodbye. Were we going to address what had happened? Or would that ruin the fantasy? Perhaps I could keep it going . . . by one day, in a moment of suspicion, going through his credit card statements and seeing that he spent his last day before leaving for a tour in a VIP room at a strip club. I could start a whole fight about it, and scream at him about his excessive spending and infidelity with a stripper.

I got home, and Rob was there waiting for me on my doorstep, smoking a joint in his ripped black jeans and a flannel cuffed up to his elbow. His hair was back to its greasy, free-flowing form, and his tattoos were fully visible through the opened buttons on his chest and the lower part of his arm. It was bittersweet to see him sitting there, so handsome. Happy to see him, but devastated that this would be the last time I saw that sexy, stoned man on my doorstep for the next few months.

I got out of the car, and he took my duffel bag stuffed with stripper clothes and cash, which had mostly come from him. He finished his joint and we went inside. We sat on my couch in silence and loaded up my roommate's bong with more marijuana. He sucked a giant hit, coughed, and then we began to talk.

"I don't really want to say some epic goodbye. I don't want to cry and shit. Let's just go grab a beer and hang out like it's any other night, and I'll say goodbye when you leave," I suggested.

"Well, I had an idea," he said, exhaling another large puff of smoke. I wasn't sure where this was going. Since he was getting stoned, I assumed the idea would have something to do with getting ice cream instead of a beer.

"Okay. Hear me out. I think . . . you should come with me!" he said.

"Um . . . what? Come with you on tour?" I replied.

"Yeah!" he said. I was stunned. I did want to jump in his arms and say yes, but logic and logistics quickly entered my brain.

"Rob, I don't have time to find someone to sublet my apartment in the next few hours . . . I mean, I *did* make a decent amount of money today, but it's not enough to cover me and bills and rent and everything for the next three months!" I was trying to do the math in my head of how much I had and how much I would need, and I was coming up with an impossible answer.

"No, hear me out. When I was at the club today, I snuck in a few minutes of filming your stage show," he said.

"Wait, YOU were at the club today? I had no idea!"

He rolled his eyes and continued. "Yes, yes I was. I was way in the back, by the bar, when you were on stage, and I filmed some of it on my phone. I got in touch with a few of the club owners I know across the country . . . I sent them your video and . . . they all said they'd have you dance there when you're in their city."

"Wait . . . really?" I replied. I shifted my position on the couch so I could face him. We sat in a moment of absolute silence, which says a lot, because it was never silent in this apartment. His eyes were shifting around the room, his hands fidgeting in his lap. It was like he'd just proposed to me, but instead of crying and jumping in his arms, I'd hesitated.

"Really," he said, breaking the silence. "You'd be on your own tour while I'm on tour. And your tour sounds like a lot more fun. Maybe I'll ditch my tour and hop on yours, you know, if you need a bass player while you strip. Ha!" He laughed at his own joke and exhaled clouds of smoke. And then I laughed at the image in my head—me stripping and him playing bass behind me, naked of course. Could I really do this? Follow him across the country?

To see what happens if Naomi decides to go on tour, turn to page 303.

To see what happens if Naomi decides not to go on tour, turn to page 306.

"YES!" I blurted out, without even giving myself any time to think about it. Traveling the US, stripping in different cities, and touring the country with Rob sounded too good to be true. But it was actually going to happen. I imagined myself spreading my legs open on a stage somewhere in the middle of Oklahoma, while Rob serenaded a stadium full of people somewhere nearby. And then we'd meet up after our respective shifts of entertaining and share a giant plate of pork ribs, and we'd have sex in a truck stop somewhere, and snuggle up in a bunk bed on a tour bus. This sounded like a real modern romance. Like a movie. Which . . . gave me an idea.

"Rob, could I bring my video camera and document this experience on the road?" I asked.

"You have a video camera?" he replied. I pushed him and laughed.

"Rob, you know I went to school for filmmaking right? Do you ever listen when I talk?" I teased.

"Sometimes. I'm usually just busy looking at your butt," he replied, with an adorable smile, and I couldn't be mad at him for having no idea what I did for a good portion of my adult life.

"But seriously, would you be into that? Would the other guys in the band be cool with me filming them too?" I said.

"Yeah, totally. In all seriousness, I know the label has been trying to relaunch our YouTube page, and they could use some of this stuff. Hell, maybe I can get you paid by the label to do it!" His eyes brightened at the thought.

I screamed with excitement. I can't even explain how happy I was at this moment. What I thought would be the most dismal fall of my life would now be full of memories that would last forever, and hell, might literally be there forever, on YouTube.

"Well fuckin'-A dude. I have to pack. I have to call the club and tell them I'm not gonna be there . . . I have to tell my roommate . . . I should probably tell my mom? Where do I begin?" I seriously had no idea how to pack for a three-month trip. I took a whole suitcase with me on a weekend getaway . . . did that mean I'd need twelve suitcases?

"I'll help you pack. Don't worry. We can get shit on the road. But right now, I wanna see that video camera. I need to test it out . . . you know, to make sure it's, uh, good for the documentary and stuff." He smirked.

"ROB! It's a 4K Sony camera I got from the university. Of course it's good enough. Are you serious right now?"

Rob continued to laugh as he took one more bong hit, stood up, and threw me over his shoulder, carrying me into my bedroom. He pulled off my denim dress and threw me down on the bed.

"Come on, get the camera!" Rob said. This portion of the documentary was certainly not going to comply with the YouTube terms of service.

On my first day of film school at NYU, I was told that when it comes to documentaries, you shouldn't follow any traditional rules of filmmaking. So I applied my college degree in this moment of passion and took it upon myself to film Rob's mouth licking my pussy. I turned the camera on to film the very first shot of this movie, a POV shot of me opening my legs and taking my panties off. It felt appropriate, to set the tone for all the leg spreading and panty removal I'd be doing all over the country these next coming months. My professor told me that through filming a documentary, I would discover the world and myself, and that's exactly what I planned to do. Through my lens of strip clubs, rock shows, and orgasms.

God damn it, Rob looked so good eating my pussy. I was gonna cum.

And then I really needed to pack.

THE END

To see what happens if Naomi decides not to go on tour, turn to page 306.

"Rob, I appreciate the effort you've put into this, but I can't just pick up and leave for three months," I said, as kindly as possible. He was clearly confused. I don't think a woman had ever turned him down for anything before.

"Seriously," I added. "I mean, what do I do about Club 42? I feel like I just got a good thing going over there. I've got regular customers that come in to see me, and Tony has finally warmed up to me. The other day he said hello when I walked in AND goodbye when I was leaving. That's a big step!" I said, trying to lighten the mood.

"Dude, who cares?" Rob pushed. "They'll let you work there when you get back. If no . . . there are so many other places you can go. You really want to stay home to work the day shift at some shitty strip club?"

I was shocked and offended by his arrogance, and I answered him honestly when I replied, "Yes. Actually, I do. I like it there."

We sat there in silence, and he folded his arms, pissed off that things didn't go his way. He was used to getting whatever he wanted . . . especially with me.

Rob had been such an integral part of my career so far as a stripper, and this morning, when I felt that slipping away, I'd felt helpless. If I went on the road with him, I'd become entirely dependent on his presence in my life to continue my job. I felt so empowered on stage, but my power was too intertwined with Rob cheering me on. I had to prove to myself that I could really do this without him. While I dreaded him leaving, I was excited to have my next few stripping months without him around, to further my self-discovery.

"Alright well, I gotta go meet up with the guys for band practice. I'll see you later, I guess." He got up off the couch. I stood up to kiss him, and he turned his head away.

"Alright, fine, be like that. But I love you, Rob. I mean it," I said. He nodded and gave me a patronizing half-smile, and then he walked out the door.

I wasn't sure if that would be the last I'd ever see of him, or if I'd hear from him in a few hours. But either way, I'd be back on the Club 42 stage tomorrow, shaking my ass in the afternoon for sober men, completely happy with my own decision. My first pair of stripper heels will always have his name written all over them, and his jizz will forever be ingrained in the soles. But it was time for a new thong, and a new song. And this time, I was going to be the one to choose it.

I sat on my couch and teared up. My phone beside me buzzed, and I picked it up.

"Love you too <3," it said, in a text from Rob.

Of course he did. I am fucking awesome, after all.

THE END

To go back and see what happens if Naomi decides to go on tour, turn to page 303.

About an hour later, I was walking around Times Square with a mini–duffel bag full of a random assortment of anything from my closet that was even remotely stripper-ish. Rob didn't give me any store names, which made me uneasy—I would have liked to check their Yelp reviews. I mean, I'd never purchased stripper heels before, and I needed some reliable customer feedback to guide me through the process!

Without a clue as to what my destination was, I picked a random street to walk down. 44th Street, to be exact. I passed the tourist shops and the chain restaurants, and then a block later, there were several sex shops in a row. One of them had an array of smoking devices and dildos in the window, one had nothing but male mannequins wearing assless leather things, and one had multiple options of lingerie on headless minimannequins, along with pairs of high-heeled shoes displayed on towers of shoe boxes. That seemed to be the one for me! It was called "Sexy Store," or it just boldly announced that it was a sexy store on an awning.

I walked in, and it was in fact a sexy store. The inside was painted pink, with pink neon lighting everywhere. On first glance there were racks of feather boas, diamond-encrusted bikinis, walls of colorful lingerie in boxes, and a small but exciting selection of shoes showcased inside of a blinged-out display case.

There was a beautiful girl behind the register. She

was about my age, with long black hair and large, perky breasts. She was wearing a tight, knee-length leopard-skin dress, with gold accents that perfectly complemented her dark brown skin. She actually looked vaguely familiar, but I couldn't figure out where I knew her from.

I shopped through the selection of shoes. I had my eye on a pair of black stilettos, because they'd inevitably match with anything, but they were also the least exciting shoe in the display case. There was every shade of neon heel imaginable—orange, green, pink, yellow, and a striped rainbow one, but a neon rainbow with glitter all over it. None of these would match anything I'd brought with me, but truthfully, I wasn't all that excited about wearing anything I'd brought with me. I never was much of a neon person, but I was also ... never a stripper? So perhaps this change of career also called for a change in my usual color palette.

"Can I help you with anything?" said the girl behind the register. She paused and did a double take. "Naomi?" she said.

"Yeah," I said, turning from the rainbow platforms. "That's me! I'm sorry, you look super familiar . . . where do I know you from?" I said.

"We dated in college! I go by Natasha now." She shrugged her shoulders. That's why I recognized her! I had dated her when I was a freshman, before she transitioned. We'd always had amazing chemistry, but we'd broken up amicably before I left to study abroad, and we'd lost touch after she graduated.

"Oh my god! It's so good to see you again, I can't believe I ran into you."

"I know, what are the chances?"

I gestured to the display of colorful condoms and penis straws around the cash register. "How long have you been working here?" I asked.

"Working here? Ha! Honey, I own this place," she replied.

"Really?" I said. I was taken aback—not by the fact that she owned a sex store, but by the fact that someone who'd graduated just a couple of years before me owned their own business in Times Square. She'd been managing a store she owned while I had been steaming milk.

"Yeah! Well, for a while I worked as a hostess at a bar around the corner. I'd stop in here after work sometimes and check out the shoes and lingerie. One day I saw a "foreclosed" sign in the window, and I just felt like it was fate. I got a loan from my aunt, and here we are today!" she said.

"That's . . . incredible. It's a beautiful store—I mean, it definitely stands out from the rest of the ones on the block here. It drew me in, that's for sure," I said. She flipped her hair from one side to another. I found myself drawn to every move she made.

"Well, speaking of, and sorry for my rudeness, but what the hell *are* you doing here?" she laughed.

"Oh! Yeah . . . me. Well, talk about fate and stumbling on things . . . I got a job at Club 42 yesterday, and I need some clothes."

She did a double take. "Really? YOU?" Her mouth turned up into a half-smile.

"Yeah! Me! What's so weird about that?"

"Honey, you used to shower with your clothes on," she said.

"Hey, I took them off when I got in the shower," I replied, smiling at the memory.

"Touché."

"But yeah . . . I honestly do have no idea what I'm doing. So maybe you could help me pick something out?" I said, motioning to the expanse of outfits.

"I can do that! What did you need?" She walked around the counter and joined me on the other side.

"Well, I have some clothes, kind of? I mostly needed some shoes," I said.

"Lemme see what you have there." She grabbed my bag, opened it up, and just started to laugh. I had now officially been laughed at by a current significant other and an ex about my lack of stripper clothes, and I wasn't entirely sure how I felt about that.

"Alright," she said. "We're gonna just start over." She inspected me as if I were a model. "Let me help you out here. You've still got the same killer body, and just about anything would look good on you." She winked at me, and I couldn't help but notice that her lashes were long and bold and beautiful, and her eyes were a deep brown, and there was a brush of bronze eyeshadow across her eyelids. Truthfully, now that we were standing closer to each other, I couldn't stop staring at her, and while I knew she was only staring me up and down to figure out what version of stripper I should be, I liked to imagine she was also checking me out.

She walked behind the register and into a back room blocked with a velvet pink curtain. Moments later, she returned with a long neon yellow gown. Was gown the word? It was gown at the bottom, with a long flowy skirt, but the top was a bikini top, held to the bottom with a string of rhinestones. She also had a pair of clear stripper heels in her other hand.

"You still a size eight?" she said.

"Oh my god. Yes, how do you even remember that?"

"I remember a lot of things about you" she said, and she smiled.

I cocked my head when she handed the outfit to me. "Natasha, there's no way anything that's neon yellow will look good on me," I said.

"You're not wearing this to your wedding. You're wearing this inside of a dark strip club. You need to stand out on stage. Trust me. It's gonna look great on you," she said. "Just try it on!"

I swiveled side to side, wondering where to try such a thing on. "Where?"

"I don't have a fitting room built here yet, but you can go behind the register and put it on. Or, hey, I do own the store so . . ." Natasha went over to the front door and switched the sign in the window from "Open" to "Closed." Then she pulled down a black shade over the window. She shut the overhead lights off and turned on a few more of the neon lights in the store.

"Now, you can see what it looks like in the same lighting as the club!" she said. I stood there speechless, mesmerized by the thirty-seven different neon lights. "Come on, quickly, I can't keep the store closed for too long" she urged.

I turned around and stripped out of my sunflower-patterned summer dress and pointy flats. She looked me up and down.

"You never had an ass. Where did that ass come from?" she said.

"That's how you remember me? The girl who had no ass and a size eight foot?" I laughed.

"I always thought you looked like a hot supermodel. But supermodels have no ass. Now you're a supermodel *with* an ass. It's not fair," she said.

I tugged on the bikini top, trying to get it to fit. "I walked up a lot of stairs in my last apartment . . . and, oh, I've also been drinking a lot of beer." I laughed and finished slipping on the neon dress. Natasha tightened the strings on the back of my neck, and brought me in front of a mirror, standing behind me, with her hand momentarily around my waist.

"See? See how amazing you look!" she said. She had a point. The neon wasn't quite so harsh in this lighting, and the crystal connector from the top to the bottom of the gown sparkled in the dark. The heels gave me some sexy posture, and made the dress fall on me in a flattering way.

"I can't believe I'm buying something neon," I said.

"You Brooklyn hipsters think you're so different . . . but you all dress the fuckin' same! It's okay to step out of the thrift store every once in a while," she said.

"Okay, but I'm going to wear neon to the strip club, NOT to Skee-Ball." I laughed and turned toward her. "Thank you, Natasha," I said. We stood there facing each other, her dark, smooth skin illuminated by pink and blue lights. "Can you show me how this comes off?"

"It's designed to come off easily," she said. She unfastened the tie behind my neck, and the dress fell to the ground. A gust of air conditioning rushed through the vent right above us. My nipples grew erect, and goose bumps traveled down my body. "Sorry about that. It's always too hot or too cold in here," she said.

"My apartment's just like that too," I replied, my mind

still on the feeling of her hand brushing the nape of my neck. "So, what do I owe you?"

"You know what, this one's on me," she said. "Just promise to come back to buy your next outfit."

"You sure about that?" I said.

"Yes, I'm sure." She handed me my sunflower dress.

"Alright, I should get out of here," I said, trying not to sound reluctant.

"It was really, really good to see you Naomi," she said. I had to agree.

It's amazing how much difference my appropriately inappropriate clothing made. I walked into Club 42 with confidence. Tony showed me to the dressing room when I first arrived, and I sat in a room full of other naked women, who were speaking several different languages on their phones with their various sizes of giant breasts out, gluing lashes on their eyes, applying liner on their lips, and plastering thick layers of cover-up on their faces. When I threw my mini-duffel down and took out my collection of makeup and my new neon, no one batted an eye. I just seemed like I worked there. Also, when I walked through the door, I was *not* handed a flyer. The past twenty-four hours had changed my entire aura from a girl who spilled coffee to a girl who worked at a strip club.

Tony ambled through the dressing room with a clipboard, doing what appeared to be a head count of each girl there. The girls seemed as nonchalant about their nudity around Tony as he was. This entire establishment was set up with the intention to make people horny, but the dressing room was like a non-arousal zone, no matter how attractive anyone was.

"What's your stage name?" he asked me with a pen in hand. I'd forgotten about the fact that this type of work required a pseudonym. I wasn't entirely sure why it was necessary. If my parents, or anyone I'd prefer to keep this profession a secret from, came in here, the whole full nudity thing would definitely expose the fact that I am, in fact, me.

However, inventing a new name was also exciting. And as far as I could tell, this clipboard was not a legally binding document—I could pick a name today and then pick a different name tomorrow without any real consequences.

"Natasha!" I said, inspired by my neon dress.

"We already have a Natasha," he said. It was odd that he had enough respect for this Natasha to not let anyone else use her name, but also had no problem referring to her like an inanimate object.

"Nah, she don't work here anymore," said a woman with long brown hair, who was trimming her pubic hair over a small trash can.

"Oh. Sure then. Natasha it is." He wrote what was now my name on the clipboard. I felt 120 percent sexier, just calling myself that name. I wondered what Natasha would think if I told her about this. Would she be flattered? Would she find this creepy?

The day continued on, as days in strip clubs do. I slid my neon on and off. I went on stage, I danced to Top 40 hits I'd never much cared for and found myself liking them. I half-assed twerks, I spread my legs open for strangers. Some of them loved me, some of them didn't. I learned the art of giving a lap dance. On, off, dance, repeat. I made small talk with the other girls on the floor, and found that anyone in the club will be nice to you if you engage in conversation with them about how much the customers suck, and then give some kind of hope based on no facts at all that it should get busy later.

"Natasha coming to the stage next. Natasha, coming to the stage," The DJ said, while I was sipping on a bottle of root beer at the nonalcoholic bar. I walked to the stage, and a Cardi B song came on. It was "Press," which I thought was an odd selection because it's rather aggressive. It was funny to see all these businessmen nod along to the lyrics and tap their feet to the song that certainly they couldn't relate to. I wouldn't be surprised if some of the people here worked for the same media Cardi B was frustrated with in the song.

I shook my ass and felt the silk neon against my skin. The beat of this song made me dance with more determination, like a combination of protest march and dance. I slid the dress off, and the DJ asked for the "crowd"(about six guys and three women) to make it rain on me.

"Throw some dollar bills on stage if you want to see Natasha take more off!" he shouted. Don't tell anyone, but I was going to take the thong off at some point, regardless of how much money was thrown at me. I got on all fours, with my head facing the three customers on the right side of the stage, and my ass pointing toward another three on the left. I shifted my body and crawled around, and then turned the opposite direction, toward the other side of the stage—

"Natasha? Really?" I heard shouting in the direction of my ass. I spun around and saw Natasha (the original one) sitting near the stage with a big smile on her face. I crawled right up to her and pulled her toward me, putting my little breasts in her face, and all other people in the crowd near the stage clapped and hooed and hawed.

"Yes, that's my name!" I said. She threw dollar bills at me, and I slid off my neon thong, attempting to twerk to the beat of the chorus. Natasha clapped in approval. I tried to spread my attention around the stage, but I only wanted to dance for Natasha. No one seemed to mind. It would be safe to say that everyone here knew she was the most attractive customer. And I felt quite privileged knowing that this customer was here just to see me. At least, I thought she was.

I walked off the stage and I noticed her talking to Tony, who motioned me to come over to them. *What the hell could they be discussing?* I hoped there wasn't a rule here about how many Natashas could be inside the club at once.

"Hey . . . you," Tony said. He clearly didn't remember my name.

"Hey!" I replied, still smiling at Natasha, but trying to focus on Tony.

"This woman here wants to get one of our exclusive VIP suites with you."

"Oh?" I smiled, even though I had no idea what the exclusive VIP rooms were.

"Which type of room did you want?" Tony asked real Natasha. "We've got the shower show—that's fifteen minutes—or the champagne room—that's a half hour." I found it odd that something was called a champagne room, since there was no alcohol. Did this also mean that the shower show had no shower? I wasn't sure. But

I was about to find out. Natasha took out her credit card and handed it to Tony.

To see Naomi go with Natasha to the shower show room, turn to page 319.

To see Naomi go with Natasha to the champagne room, turn to page 325.

Tony led us through a door, which led to a hallway, which led to another door with a blinking neon sign on top of it that said "SHOWER SHOW." I wasn't sure if the blinking was because the sign wasn't plugged in properly or because it was meant to garner excitement about shower shows, but regardless, I was genuinely excited.

We were brought into an area with a shower stall enclosed by glass. Outside of the shower stall, there was a leather couch, a television, and some bottles of water, all lit with purple and blue lights. The whole thing was like the inside of a limousine, but with a shower inside of it.

Tony slid Natasha's credit card through a device, and when her card cleared, he said, "Have fun" and left the room. I had absolutely no idea what to do, but with the powers of my deductive logic, and the giant shower . . . I managed to figure out a place to start.

"You know it's my first day here?" I said to Natasha.

"Well, it's not mine." she laughed. I was noticing a pattern here. Apparently I had some sort of attraction to people who frequent strip clubs. I'm not sure exactly what that says about me, but this wasn't the time to delve into that. The image of Natasha sitting in a strip club in her short leopard dress, throwing dollar bills at women she had dressed in neon, was a hell of a lot sexier than Rob coming by in his unwashed pants, handing over whatever per-diem he got on tour, if he actually even tipped at all.

I followed my natural instincts and got inside the

shower. As soon as I stepped inside, loud R&B music started playing and the inside of the shower lit up. There was a bench and a hook in the corner of the shower—I assumed this was where I was supposed to put my clothes. I stripped off my dress for what felt like the four hundreth time that day, and for the four hundredth time, I greatly appreciated having the appropriate kind of stripper clothes.

Natasha comfortably sat on the leather couch just outside of the shower, with a smile on her face, waiting for the show. The shower had a removable showerhead and an array of sponges and soaps. I turned on the shower, and to its credit, it was the perfect warm temperature. This was a rarity in New York City. It would have been incredibly awkward if I'd had to do what I normally did at home, which was turn the water on and wait five minutes while freezing in the cold for the water to heat up. Come to think of it, this shower room was close to the size of my apartment. I should ask Tony if instead of fifteen-minute shows they offered fifteen-month leases.

I let the warm water drip down my body. I looked at Natasha through the glass door, and she stared right back at me. I swayed to a Post Malone song I wasn't very familiar with, and I have to admit, it was good shower music.

Natasha signaled me to come closer. I assumed the goal of the removable showerhead was to avoid getting your hair wet, but with this perfect water pressure and temperature, along with the thrill of the beautiful woman in front of me, I was becoming incredibly excited in all sorts of ways, and the threat of damp hair simply didn't scare me. I put the showerhead over my head and wet my hair. The water ran down my face. I was certainly testing the limits of my allegedly waterproof mascara.

Once I was doused and dripping with water, I took Natasha's cue and walked as close to her as I could—pressing my body against the glass of the shower. She stood up and touched the glass, putting her hands on my breasts, but for the glass between us. While I couldn't physically feel her at all, her touch created a sensation all through my body. I pressed myself harder against the glass, and it almost felt like I'd push right through it.

She got down on her knees and stuck her tongue out, touching the glass right near my pussy. I pushed my pussy up against the glass, and she moved her tongue up and down. She had a long tongue that was the perfect shade of pink. The steam of the shower caused a mist behind me, and my body made something similar to a snow angel against the glass. Natasha, on the other hand, was crystal clear on the other side of the glass, with her thick lips leaving traces of lipstick against the shower stall. The music was loud, so we spoke with our eyes and our body movements.

She sat back down on the couch and lifted her dress up. She reached inside of her black lace panties, rubbing the bulge underneath. "My girl cock," she said, smiling. She pulled down her dress from the top and revealed her round breasts. Watching her stroke her girl cock and her full breasts made me ache. The showerhead moved toward my pussy, as if a magnetic force had taken control of it.

I noticed on the nozzle there was a way to turn this robust water pressure up even higher, so I cranked it as far as I possibly could, and a sharp jet of water came blasting out. I spread my pussy open and sprayed it right against my clit. I watched Natasha stroking herself on the couch, and I pushed the water hard on my lips. She stood back up and put her hand against the glass, and I put my hand right up against hers. It was oddly romantic, like we were holding hands through glass, while we were both masturbating. It felt pure and filthy, clean and dirty.

I opened my legs wider and gyrated my pussy into the hard stream of warm water. I spread my lips, making a V with my fingers so the water could hit me in the right spot. Then I took a small squirt of soap and lathered it all over myself. The suds dripped down the sides of my pussy. This water was a million fingers and tongues, licking and flicking my clit in all the right spots. As I pushed my hips harder against the water, I could see Natasha's girl cock growing bigger. Her giant breasts hung just outside of her leopard dress, which was pulled right underneath them. Her long hair fell to the sides of her breasts, perfectly framing them.

I felt all the muscles in the erogenous zones in my outer pussy tighten up. It was amazing how strong an orgasm I could have without anything going inside me, but it was even more amazing that I could get one from . . . water.

I started to spasm, and my knees shook. I leaned forward against the glass with my left hand, the showerhead still in my right hand, so I wouldn't fall to the ground and hurt myself. This strong water pressure could potentially be dangerous in this slippery arena. Perhaps the reason why the water pressure was generally horrible throughout Brooklyn was for safety reasons, so none of us hipsters would crack our skulls while masturbating.

I stared right into Natasha's eyes. The glass fogged up, but I wiped the mist away with my fingers so I could

continue to watch her, as we both strived for completion. I wasn't sure how well she could hear me, but I
mouthed "I'm gonna cum" against the glass. She nodded,
her expression saying, "Oh yeah, I know you are." My
clit kept pulsating, again and again and again. I tried
to hold still, but I was shaking, my clit was so sensitive. Finally, after what felt like seven hundred orgasms,
my body relaxed. My pussy felt raw and sore, but in a
good way, like it had gotten a good workout. I moved
the showerhead up to my shoulders and let the water
massage me.

Natasha put her hand up against the glass, and her
eyes closed. I could see her thighs shaking, and her mouth
was open. I got down on my knees in the shower so I
was at the same level as her girl cock. I got as close to
the glass as I could, and then I saw her cum spurt out
onto the glass. I opened my mouth on the other side, as if
she was cumming in my mouth. Her cum dripped down
the clear glass, illuminated by the blue and purple lights.
The whole thing looked like some kind of stained glass
window, but . . . with cum.

At the end, we both laughed. After the orgasms were
out of our system, we could relax. Suddenly, a loud buzzer
noise went off, the music stopped, and the water turned
off. I supposed this was a sign that the fifteen minutes were
over. Natasha giggled, and she quickly found a blue spray
bottle behind the couch with paper towels. She wiped her
jizz off the glass. I towel dried myself on the other side,
and this moment of collecting ourselves reminded me of
the times we'd rushed and thrown our clothes back on
when we'd heard my dorm roommate jiggle the doorknob.

I was soaking wet. Tony came in, and Natasha was

back to being fully clothed next to a pristine, jizz-free shower glass wall.

"Natasha!" Tony yelled. Natasha jumped, startled. But Tony was looking at me. It took me a second in my cum-drunk state to remember that I was also Natasha.

"You're not supposed to get your hair wet! What's wrong with you?"

"Sorry Tony, I had no idea," I replied.

"Well, your shift is over anyways," he mumbled.

"I tipped her extra for the wet hair. It's like my thing," the original Natasha said.

"Oh . . . well . . . okay. Don't do that again."

I wasn't sure which Natasha he was talking to, but we both nodded and agreed to stop engaging in all wet hair activities. He led us out of the room, and we walked down the hallway behind him, giggling nonstop, just like we used to.

To go back and see Naomi go with Natasha to the champagne room, turn to page 325.

To continue with Naomi in this fantasy, turn to page 332.

"Follow me," Tony said. Tony didn't seem remotely impressed with the fact that this was my first day and I was already being taken into the presumably important VIP room. Perhaps somewhere on his clipboard there was a space for gold stars next to the strippers' names. There was an incentive program at Fix, and you got praised when you convinced anyone to add a flavor shot to their coffee . . . which I thought was actually disgusting. Whoever sold the most vanilla pumps got a free cronut. Another thing I thought was disgusting.

I was happy to have my first VIP room experience with someone I knew. I was also excited to get a little bit closer to Natasha, in a room that may or may not have champagne. Tony led us down a hallway, which led to another hallway, in which there was a row of doors. He unlocked the door of the room with the number three on it and let us in. It was a small, dark room, about the size of my bedroom, with a leopard couch and small table beside it with a bucket of ice. Inside of that ice was a bottle of "nonalcoholic brut," with a handful of champagne glasses, or nonalcoholic brut glasses, I guess.

"Alright, enjoy you two. See you in thirty, make sure you follow all the rules. I don't care if you're a hot chick or my 400-lb Uncle Joey in here, keep your hands to the side and keep your clothes on," Tony said to Natasha.

"Yes, of course," she replied. He shrugged his shoulders and walked out, closing the door behind him. Natasha and I were soon alone on the leopard couch, and I was nervous. I felt like we were on a first date. I remembered our actual first date, at the planetarium in the Natural History museum. The lighting in there was similar to the lighting in this room, now that I thought about it, only it wasn't quite as educational.

"Thanks for coming to see me—that was a really unexpected surprise," I said.

"Don't thank me, I wanted to come see you!" she replied.

"How much did this thing even cost?" I asked.

"About the price of five of those outfits you got today," she grinned.

"Well, I'll make sure to spend it all at your store, and we can just keep circling this money back and forth between us!" I replied. Genuinely, though, the thought of an economic system where cash flow goes from a strip club back to the store that sells stripper clothes, and then back to the strip club, was pretty humorous.

"Well, now that you have me all to yourself for the next thirty minutes, what would you like me to do?" I said, a coy look on my face.

"Well, have you given any lap dances yet?" she asked.

"Yes! A few of them. They're . . . kinda fun!" I said. I truly had found myself getting excited during some of the lap dances I did. There was just one layer of clothing between my naked body and the customers' clothed selves, and while I knew my job was technically to arouse the customers, I found myself getting quite aroused too. It was a unique way of practicing safe sex. If they had taught us how to give lap dances in our high school health class, perhaps we would have paid more attention.

"Well, I'd like to experience the very best lap dance you've ever given," she replied, batting her long eyelashes at me.

"Since I've only given about eight of them, and they were all only three minutes long, that should be easy." I paused. "And . . . well, none of them were as sexy as you . . . duh." I had a bad habit of using the word "duh" when I was nervous. It's a stupid word.

Natasha put her hands to her side, following Tony's instructions. I stood up and faced her, untying my neon dress from the back with one hand. It truly was miraculous how easily this thing could slip off. It made all the other clothing I'd ever bought seem so inefficient. To think of how much more I could have accomplished in life with the time I could have saved *not* buttoning and zipping tight-fitting jeans and blouses. I could have written a book. Or two!

I slid my thong off and put it on the table next to the "champagne." Then I straddled Natasha. Her leopard dress rose up and revealed her black lace panties. This was a hell of a lot sexier than the various pairs of pleated pants I'd been grinding on all day. I touched her breasts on top of her dress, and put my little breasts up against her face.

"I've always loved your perfect, perky breasts," she said. I took this opportunity to lift my little breast, stretch out my tongue, and lick my own nipple. Then I did the same to my other nipple, all while continuing to grind against her panties.

"Fuck!" she said. I could feel her starting to grow beneath me, and I was quite happy that my little breasts were able to inspire such a reaction. "My girl cock remembers you," she groaned.

I could feel her breath on my chest. I leaned into her, pushing myself into her body. I put my hands around the back of her neck and shimmied my body up and down. I pressed my pussy up against the bulge inside her panties, as we moaned heavily into one another's mouths.

Any small talk had stopped. We were both committed to this lap dance and deep into our dry hump. I shifted my positioning a little bit, and fuck. My moist pussy loosened up and just kinda spread itself open. Her covered girl cock now slid up and down between my pussy lips, right up against my clit. Such a thin, moist layer separating us from having hardcore sex, from her penetrating me, from her sliding up into me. The layer of separation turned us into wild dry-humping animals, grasping at whatever we could just to get closer to one another. I tightened my grip on the back of her neck, and she shifted her body forward so I could completely wrap my long legs around her. Up and down and up and down I rode her, without actually riding her. My clit was growing larger, pulsating. I breathed heavily, and when I kissed her neck, I could taste her vanilla-scented perfume on my tongue.

"You're making me so wet," I whispered.

"Oh yeah?" she replied.

"Oh . . . yeah," I said. I took my hand off her neck and put my finger on my own pussy. I swished it around like a cotton swab getting a sample, and I put the finger in her mouth. I just wanted her to taste me. I wanted my juices inside of her mouth, and I wanted her to see how turned on I was.

We locked eyes as she sucked the juices off my index finger. I really couldn't control myself. Did she have to keep her hands to herself? Did she really need to keep her panties on? I wanted her so badly. Our bodies were basically inside each other. I mean, wasn't the whole purpose of the VIP room so people could do more than they could do in the less important rooms?

I took her hands off the couch and put them on my breasts.

"Oh my god, what are you doing? You're gonna get us in trouble, lady," she said.

"I don't fucking care," I moaned.

I felt like a demon. "Can I?" I whispered, and Natasha nodded. I reached my hand down and pulled her girl cock out from underneath her panties. I grabbed the back of her head and kissed her lips, and it was like we were eating each other, we were kissing so hard.

I drew back long enough to ask, "Do you want to be inside me?"

"Yes," she breathed. I got up on her girl cock and it slid right inside my dripping wet pussy. It felt so right. I grinded back and forth on her, much like I had during the lap dance, but now her beautiful girl cock was actually in me, right where it was supposed to be.

"You dirty fucking girl," Natasha said. "Come on, dirty girl." Her girl cock hit my G-spot, and I started to tremble. My pussy quivered, and she shifted her position so she could fuck me harder and put pressure on the inside of my pussy. Then she told me to get on my feet on the couch and squat down on her, which I did. Holy fuck, that went so deep inside me. Everything was tensing up. I was shaking so hard, I wasn't sure I could take it anymore. But she held me in place and continued to fuck me. I wasn't quite sure what was happening. And then, a gush of liquid came out of my pussy. I was squirting.

"Yes, yes!" she said, which was good, because I was going to keep squirting whether she liked it or not.

And just then, the door opened. Both me and Natasha froze, but the liquid continued to drip out of me like I was some kind of leaky faucet.

"What the fuck is going on here?!" Tony said. "What the fuck did I say the rules were?" he screamed. I got off her lap, incredibly frustrated that I was interrupted mid-orgasm.

"It was me, Tony, I insisted on it. She didn't break the rules, I did," I said.

"Well you're a fucking liability. No turning tricks at this club. I'll have the feds all over here in a minute. Get out of here, I don't want to see you back."

"No, no, I wasn't turning tricks—see this is an ex-girlfriend of mine, and we were just reconnecting," I said.

"YOU WERE HAVING SEX WITH A CUSTOMER! BOTH OF YOU, GET THE FUCK OUT!"

I gathered up my things and slid my neon dress back on as quickly as I could. In this instance, its easy-on and easy-off capabilities really came in handy.

Tony escorted us out of the building like we were criminals. I was standing in the middle of Times Square with my neon dress and my clear heels, and it was quite strange in the broad daylight. Ironically, for the first time all day, I felt naked. I looked at Natasha.

"Girl, I'd apologize but this was your idea!" She laughed.

"I know. But it was worth it," I replied.

"Let's . . . get back to my store and finish what we started," she said, pulling me by the hand.

"Yes please," I said, nearly tripping after her in my heels.

"I'll have to put a tarp down to keep you from making a mess," she teased, kissing me on the cheek.

I had probably just set some kind of record, getting fired from two jobs in two days. My phone was still up in the dressing room at Club 42, and truthfully I was kind of relieved about that. I wasn't quite sure how to recap my first day at work to Rob . . . and I wasn't quite sure if I even needed to.

As we headed back to Natasha's shop to fuck each other's brains out, I saw so many other stripper stores. The chances that I'd stumbled into hers, of all the stores here, was a true sign of fate, and who was I to ignore such a beautiful destiny?

Natasha wasn't kidding. She had a tarp in the closet behind the register, and she unrolled it onto the floor. She pulled her leopard dress off, and then she pulled me down to the ground and slid into my pussy. She hit the spot right away, and the tarp immediately went to good use. Yes. Fuck. Again. Harder. Come on. Yes.

I had a handful of singles, fives, and twenties rubber-banded around a garter on my thigh, which could tide me over until I found another job. I wasn't too concerned about it. About five hundred orgasms from now, I'd figure out what to do next, but whatever it was, it definitely wouldn't be at Club 42, and it definitely would be with Natasha.

THE END

To go back and see Naomi go with Natasha to the shower show room, turn to page 319.

I was fresh and clean, having just showered with warm, hard water and orgasmed and whatnot. I truly felt like I'd come out of a spa. If only all the Brooklyn hipsters knew about the water pressure up here, there would be a pilgrimage for all the baristas and bartenders to the Midtown strip clubs. I was going to keep that water a secret. But, of course, the bigger secret here was Natasha.

I had a few texts from Rob on my phone asking how my day went. I knew we technically weren't in a relationship, after just a couple of dates, but that was a very relationship-y thing to ask. I couldn't stop thinking about Natasha, and I also had a strong yearning to report every detail about my day back to Rob. I was in my very own self-inflicted love triangle, without any proof whatsoever that either of the other two participants in the triangle had any love for me at all.

Natasha waited for me outside. I bumped into her as I exited the club with my ever-changing mini-duffel bag. What once held a sad ensemble of mismatched panties and burlesque outfits now held coordinating layers of neon, stiletto heels, and wads of cash. I wasn't entirely sure how much was in there, but it was certainly more than a week's salary plus tips at Fix. My hair was still wet, thrown up in a ponytail. It was hot outside, but a humid heat, trapping in the moisture of my hair.

"It was really good running into you today," Natasha

said, with a smirk on her face. "Would you . . . wanna get together later tonight?"

"I'd love to, but I have plans, kind of," I said. "Kind of" was truly the right way to sum up my plans, which were at best implied.

"Alright." she said, and she gave me a hug and a kiss on the cheek. It wasn't an innocent peck, like one you'd give to a family member, it was a heartfelt cheek kiss that said, "to be continued," and I sincerely believed that it would.

I sat on the subway, in the same rush hour traffic that all the nine-to-fivers sat in. With my wet hair and my duffel bag, I looked like someone who just came from a Crunch gym. Little did everyone know what kind of workout I'd actually had this afternoon.

I did return Rob's texts a few times and got no answer. I got off the train and decided to stop inside one of the bars around the corner from my apartment. I deserved an actual alcoholic beverage from an actual alcoholic bar. I stepped inside the small establishment and ordered a PBR. The unfriendly bartender chick with light purple dishwasher detergent colored hair put one in front of me and I paid seven dollars for the beer, and gave her a five-dollar tip on top of that. It was a rather generous percentage for putting a can in front of me, but I felt victorious, holding my first wad of stripper money. I sipped on the cold beer and felt sweat drip down my face. I texted Rob one more time, and his texts were green. A green iPhone text twenty-four hours after you sleep with someone for the first time is usually a glaringly obvious sign that whatever relationship you thought you had was over. If he cared about me at all, he'd find Wi-Fi.

I heard a loud laugh somewhere behind me at the bar. I was sitting in a dimly lit corner, where I wasn't really visible to the rest of the place. I turned around, and out of the corner of my eye, I saw Rob sitting at a table with another girl, who was holding his hand and laughing hysterically at whatever the hell he just said. Great. There was all the clarification I needed on the status of our non-relationship.

I snuck out of the bar. Rob and Miss Laughs-A-Lot were too engrossed in their own conversation to notice my getaway. In all honesty, I felt a mixture of sadness and relief. Just as I opened my apartment door, I received a text back from Rob stating "Gonna stay in tonight! I'm tired." with the sleepy face emoji. It was one thing for him to lie, but it was totally unfair to bring the emoji into it. The emoji deserved better than that. They were there for laughs and text flirting, not for lying.

I went to my bedroom and closed the door behind me. I threw my mini-duffel on the ground. I kept deleting the texts to Rob that I never sent, which varied from "oh sure you are" to "delete my number" to "okay talk to you tomorrow!" I swiped his name on my phone and deleted our entire romantic three-week history of text messages, and when my phone asked me if I was sure I wanted to delete this conversation, I clicked yes. That's my generation's equivalent of first-degree murder.

I took out the wads of cash in my duffel bag and began to count the singles, putting them in neat little piles of money. I let the last forty hours of my life sink in, from spilled coffee to sexy stripper. I looked at my collection of cash, took a deep breath, and felt . . . at peace.

I took my phone out, and my immediate thought was

to text Natasha. And while I truly did want to see her again, my fingers moved away from my contacts, and instead I cued up Spotify and put on Cardi B. I turned the phone volume up as high as it could go, got off my bed, put my arms on my dresser, and did what seemed like the most sensical thing to do right now, and that was . . . to bend my knees, stick my ass out, and twerk. I danced around and did all the stripper moves I'd learned in the eighty square inches of floor that I had. I couldn't stop smiling, and while I knew I looked absolutely ridiculous, I felt quite beautiful and comfortable in my own skin.

I sang along with Cardi. With a new career ahead of me, I was ready to make some moves.

For now, it was my turn to take the stage, and I wasn't going to stop twerking until I got to the end of this playlist, which contained all three Cardi B albums AND all their remixes. So it was going to be a while. This city had only begun to see the power of my neon, and whether it was on or off, I was going to keep on dancing.

THE END

To go back and choose another fantasy, turn to page 13.

Acknowledgments

I would like to thank my incredible husband, Aaron Thompson, aka Small Hands, for supporting me, loving me, and holding me as I completely lost my mind while writing this book. I would like to thank Shawn Alff for being such an amazing best friend muse/writing partner who sat with me drinking seven hundred cups of coffee throughout this process. Thank you Asa Akira–I couldn't have ever been an author without you. Thank you Cleis for believing in me and giving me a chance to express myself here, and letting me vomit in word form on three hundred plus pages in a row. Thank you to every single one of my fans and followers and supporters, and thank you to everyone who is reading these thank yous . . . because you got this book.

About the Author

JOANNA ANGEL is an award-winning adult film star, director, producer, best selling author, and entrepreneur. She was the owner and founder of the venerated adult studio BurningAngel Entertainment, which she started with just a few hundred dollars in her college dorm room, from 2002 to 2019. *Pacific Standard* magazine noted her as "one of the most powerful feminist icons in the adult industry." She's stormed mainstream media outlets with a mission to defy all stereotypes of sex workers by being a strong, educated, insightful, and powerful woman in adult film, with well over 100 awards and accolades for her efforts both in front of and behind the camera. She's been featured in the *New York Times, Forbes Magazine, LA Weekly*, and on Vice TV and CNBC, to name a few. She was inducted into AVN's Hall of Fame in 2016 and the XRCO Hall of Fame in 2017, and in 2012 was crowned a legendary "triple play" award by *NightMoves* magazine for her accolades as a director, performer, and exotic dancer.

Her first novel, *Night Shift*, was featured on *Cosmopolitan*'s list of "36 Legitimately Good Erotic Novels You Must Read," and was regarded by book clubs and reviewers across the nation as an honest, insightful, hilarious, and inclusive work of fiction. She was a featured author in *Best Women's Erotica of the Year, Vol. 5*, and a guest sex columnist for *Men's Health*. Angel broke barriers and paved her own way in the adult industry, and she's now doing the same in the world of erotic literature.